大学英语公共选修课教材

欧洲城市文化与文学

European Urban Culture and Literature

主编：程梅
编者：李静　薛红珠

南开大学出版社
天　津

图书在版编目(CIP)数据

欧洲城市文化与文学 / 程梅主编. —天津：南开大学出版社，2013.4
ISBN 978-7-310-04124-4

Ⅰ.①欧… Ⅱ.①程… Ⅲ.①城市文化—关系—欧洲文学—高等学校—教材 Ⅳ.①I500.6

中国版本图书馆 CIP 数据核字(2013)第 046495 号

版权所有　侵权必究

南开大学出版社出版发行
出版人：孙克强
地址：天津市南开区卫津路 94 号　邮政编码：300071
营销部电话：(022)23508339　23500755
营销部传真：(022)23508542　邮购部电话：(022)23502200

*

河北昌黎太阳红彩色印刷有限责任公司印刷
全国各地新华书店经销

*

2013 年 4 月第 1 版　　2013 年 4 月第 1 次印刷
210×148 毫米　32 开本　8 印张　228 千字
定价:20.00 元

如遇图书印装质量问题，请与本社营销部联系调换，电话:(022)23507125

前 言

欧洲的悠久历史将城市绘制成现代社会高度多元化的产物，柏林墙上的涂鸦、巴黎的路边咖啡馆、伦敦的博物馆、阿姆斯特丹的广场文化……这些城市和文化的发展为文学提供了开放的、社会的、多样的和多视角的研究空间和研究素材。"文化转型"加强了人们对都市的兴趣，为研究现代文化构成与发展带来了新的见解。文学中的城市既是想象构建的结果又是客观现实存在的城市原形的反映。从历史角度，欧洲城市的历史包含着封建制度的衰落、帝国主义和极权主义的兴起，城市的话语承载着历史的乐观和悲观，在生活的喧嚣中证明自己的存在。历史背景的不同造就了概念化城市的不同方式，使城市以不同形象呈现在公众面前和人们的想象中。

本书以文学作品和文化现象为研究目标，探索文学、文化与其相关学科的内在联系。具体从联合国确定的欧洲文化之都中选取十个历史厚重的欧洲城市——阿姆斯特丹、柏林、哥本哈根、都柏林、爱丁堡、伦敦、巴黎、布拉格、罗马和圣彼得堡，以城市为切入点，结合城市文化现象、文艺活动、城市风貌、特色建筑等艺术形式，以历史为背景，依靠城市阅读相关的文学作品，以文学为纽带，将城市和欧洲文化历史的不同方面聚在一起，从历史角度展示城市发展与文化的内在联系。所选的文学作品反映了近两个世纪以来的欧洲文学运动、思潮和流派。阅读这些作品，读者需要思考以下问题：文学中城市的表现形式如何影响作者和读者的城市概念化过程？文学中的城市主题能否、如何赋予城市新的文化内涵和历史意义？怎样利用这些文化内涵和历史意义？文学和城市的动态依存关系能否以及如何激发新的比较和理论化的模式？这些都是本书关注的重要问题。

　　本书将阅读范围划定为欧洲文学、文化，一方面，编者的欧洲留学经历使其对当地文化感触颇深，利于开展文学研究；另一方面，欧洲范围内丰富的文学文化内涵无法穷尽，编者在选择文本和视角时可以有多种选择、多种组合，这样的组合可以产生各种无法预料的变数，这种不确定性必然会形成新颖、独特的观点，使阅读变得有趣、神秘；再一方面，欧洲城市文化具备共性与特性兼而有之的特点，为阅读该文化提供了细致入微的比较空间，使阅读深入、全面，所选城市的历史和创新使阅读跨越时间距离，看到城市的文化发展前景。由于篇幅所限，本书不能涵盖所有欧洲主要城市，但编者希望这十个欧洲城市可以起到以点带面的作用，使读者加强对欧洲文学、文化的理解和认识。

　　本书所选素材包括散文、小说、日记、游记、回忆录等不同文学样式，具有典型性、历史性和现代性的特点。这些作品既有能够代表某一时期、反映某一城市风貌和社会现实的知名作家的名篇、名作，如乔伊斯的《都柏林人》、雨果的《巴黎圣母院》等，也有能够反映当代文化研究发展方向和思潮的当代文化学家如荷兰学者米克·巴尔（Mieke Bal）的文化分析篇章。这些作品虽然体裁不同、时代不同，反映不同的社会现实，但共同特点是它们都起到了确立城市文化身份的作用。有些作品虽然创作于一两个世纪以前，但是即便在科技发展日新月异的今天，这些作品对如何解读城市仍有深远的影响，城市也因为拥有了它们而增加了其历史性和文化性。这些文学文本虽不能涵盖一个城市的所有方面和全部历史，但是为管窥欧洲文化的历史、发展变化和现状提供了一个直观的窗口和全新的视角。

　　本书对海量文章进行了精挑细选，适合大学本科及以上水平的学生和英语爱好者阅读，希望通过阅读可以向读者展示欧洲文明、文化和文学。

Contents

Chapter 1   Amsterdam 1
    Surprising Amsterdam 2
    Amsterdam in Diary 8
Chapter 2   Berlin 25
    Cultural Berlin 26
    Historic Berlin 50
Chapter 3   Copenhagen 61
    Spotlight Copenhagen 62
    Copenhagen of Fairy Tales 67
Chapter 4   Dublin 74
    Dublin in History 75
    Dublin in Speech 79
    Literary Dublin 87
Chapter 5   Edinburgh 93
    Inspiring Edinburgh 94
    City of Literature—Edinburgh 100
Chapter 6   London 110
    London Today 111
    Memories of London 122
    London in Literature 130
Chapter 7   Paris 136
    Paris Today 137

Paris Impression 146
　　Paris in Literature 170
Chapter 8　Prague 176
　　Visiting Prague 177
　　Literary Prague 189
Chapter 9　Rome 218
　　Rome Today 219
　　Rome in Literature 227
Chapter 10　St. Petersburg 235
　　St. Petersburg Today 236
　　St. Petersburg in Literature 242
Bibliography 247

Chapter 1   Amsterdam

Amsterdam was a great surprise to me.
—James Weldon Johnson

Quotes Featuring Amsterdam

❧ I had always thought of Venice as the city of canals; it had never entered my mind that I should find similar conditions in a Dutch town.
—James Weldon Johnson

❧ We want to legalize marijuana. But we can't sell it in cafes like in Amsterdam because we'd get all the unemployed Germans coming here.
—J. X. Dolezal

❧ In Amsterdam the water is the mistress and the land the vassal. Throughout the city there are as many canals and drawbridges as bracelets on a Gypsy's bronzed arms.
—Felix Marti-Ibanez

Key Words
Culture, nightlife, architecture, museums, and Anne Frank's diary.

Questions
1. What surprises you most after reading "Surprising Amsterdam"?
2. Do you know some other amazing facts about Amsterdam or the Netherlands?
3. How do you understand the statement "Paper has more patience than people" in Anne Frank's diary?

Surprising Amsterdam   惊人的阿姆斯特丹

Amsterdam is a city of many sides. People are familiar with its rich history, beautiful canals, and many museums. The article offers a general picture of Amsterdam, which helps its reader to discover the secrets of Amsterdam. The amazing aspect lies in Dutch people's liberal attitude towards drugs, sex, gay marriage and euthanasia.

Surprising Amsterdam

Current Dutch Culture[①]
The Netherlands is a culturally very diverse country, with inhabitants from all over the globe. Especially in the large cities: Amsterdam for instance has people from 170+ nationalities living there.

The original inhabitants are (in)famous for being straightforward,

---
① 选自 http://www.tripadvisor.com/Travel-g188553-s202/The-Netherlands:Culture.html。

very direct and speaking their minds, which foreigners sometimes might see as rude. But don't worry! It's (usually) not meant that way! One of the other main characteristics of Dutch people is that they're very down-to-earth. Show-offs and people who brag about how much money they're worth are usually put to their place. There's a Dutch saying (Doe maar gewoon, dan doe je al gek genoeg!) which would literally translate into something like: "Just act normal, then you're acting crazy enough as it is!"

The Dutch are very open to other cultures; something that reflects on the cuisine① as well. Traditionally, a standard evening meal would consist of potatoes, vegetables and a piece of meat, but foreign products and ingredients are more and more added to the daily cooking.

As it being such an open and internationally orientated country, almost everyone can make him- or herself understandable in English and/or another language, besides Dutch. That doesn't mean that the residents won't appreciate it when you, as a foreign traveler, try to speak Dutch. You'll probably find though that people tend to rapidly switch to English, since they feel that to be easier and faster.

When meeting a Dutch person, it's very common to shake hands or when you know someone better, to give that person three "kisses" on the cheeks. A big no-no is to ask someone how much money he or she makes in a year! Asking that would be considered VERY rude and would end up in getting a snappy② answer like "none of your business."

The Netherlands is also well known for its liberal attitude towards specific subjects, such as gay rights or marriage, euthanasia, soft drugs, freedom of speech, abortion etc. That doesn't mean that locals can't get extremely upset sometimes when it comes to "drug tourism." Smoking a

---

① 美食。
② 聪明的，生动的。

joint[①] in public is not recommended and could give you a lot of angry faces. Locals in Amsterdam for instance love tourists, but can't stand people who only go there to get stoned[②] and/or drunk. As in all liberal societies, there are two sides of the medal. Yes, you are allowed to do and say a lot but you also have to get along and compromise and be diplomatic to keep the peace.

Amsterdam: What It's Like[③]

As I stepped out of a KLM[④] jet, on my very first trip to Amsterdam, I expected to see a rather sleepy city, populated by plump[⑤], red-cheeked people who spent their time strolling along quaint[⑥] canals.

What a surprise I had in store!

⊙ On my first afternoon there, I passed restaurant after restaurant where dark-skinned, turbaned[⑦] waiters were serving exotic dishes of the East Indies to residents and tourists alike.

⊙ I walked through a massive amusement area—the famous "Rembrandtplein"—where literally scores of cafes and cabarets[⑧] were offering the kind of entertainment you expect to find only in Paris—but available here for one-third the price!

⊙ I sat at sidewalk cafes in the student section where bearded existentialists were excitedly holding forth on the world's problems and philosophies.

⊙ I saw the shops of chic couturiers[⑨] standing side-by-side with

---

① 含有麻醉剂的香烟。
② 在软毒品支配下的，吸食大麻后身不由己的。
③ 选自 *Surprising Amsterdam*, by Arthur Frommer, 1966, New York: The Frommer/Pasmantier Publishing Corporation。
④ 荷兰皇家航空，即 Royal Dutch Airlines。
⑤ 丰满的。
⑥ 诱人的，古怪的。
⑦ 戴头巾的，戴小帽的。
⑧ 餐馆中的歌舞表演。
⑨ 裁缝店，女装店。

open-air herring① stands, at which lovely Dutch girls, in modern bouffant hairdos, were dipping chunks of raw fish into bowls of chopped-up onions and chomping away!

⊙ I sipped cocktails in a cafe on the 13th floor of a futuristic skyscraper overlooking the port of Amsterdam, and then descended in an elevator to an area, several square miles in size, where scarcely a building had changed since the 17th and 18th Centuries!

Amsterdam—as you've undoubtedly grasped from the above exposition—is a city of fantastic surprises, a place crammed with sights and activities that seem to bear not the slightest resemblance to the picture of tulips, cheese, and wooden shoes that most visitors expect to find.

That's not to say, of course, that the famed quaintness of Amsterdam doesn't still exist. There will be times when you round a corner to come upon one of the city's 50 canals, and to view one of its 500 bridges, and as you gaze upon the vista② of quiet waters that flow between an unbroken line of trees and gabled old mansions, you will catch your breath at the sheer beauty of it all. And indeed, the massive central section of Amsterdam, whose architecture has been maintained unaltered for centuries, has been called "the largest open-air museum in the world."

But the predominant impression of Amsterdam is that of an active, throbbing, cosmopolitan city. In that regard, it mirrors the prosperity and progress of Western Europe—to such an extent that if I were asked to describe Amsterdam in a single phrase, I'd say that it has become a microcosm of everything that modern-day Europe represents. It is, of course, one of the chief trading ports on the continent, and all of the ships and trains and planes that every day pour into Amsterdam, in staggering numbers, make it a true crossroads city—a Europe in miniature—and therefore an unbelievably exciting place.

---

① 鲱鱼。
② 远景。

惊人的阿姆斯特丹

当代荷兰文化

荷兰是个文化多样的国家，居民来自世界各地。尤其在大城市，比如阿姆斯特丹，有一百七十多个民族的居民生活在那里。

荷兰本地人以简单、率真、直接表达自己的想法而著名（或者说，以此而声名狼藉），有时在外国人看来这有些粗鲁。但是，别担心！（通常）不会那样！荷兰人另一重要特点是他们非常朴实。喜欢炫耀和吹嘘自己身价之人通常哪来哪去。荷兰语中有句谚语，字面翻译类似为："像普通人那样做事，那么你就会表现得足够疯狂！"

荷兰人对其他文化很开放，这也反映在美食方面。荷兰传统的晚餐包括土豆、蔬菜和少量的肉，但是，现在荷兰人的日常烹饪中越来越多地加入了外国产品和原料。

因为荷兰是个开放、面向世界的国家，所以，除了荷兰语，如果说英语和/或另一种语言，几乎每个人在这里都可以找到能听懂自己语言的听众。如果你是外国游客想尝试说荷兰语，当地居民还是会很高兴的。但是，你可能会发现，人们往往会迅速切换到英语，因为他们觉得这样交流更方便、更快捷。

遇到荷兰人时，通常可以握手，或者熟人之间可以亲吻对方的面颊三下。一定不要问别人的年收入！这将被视为非常没有礼貌，而且对方立马会像这样回答："这不关你的事。"

荷兰还以其对一些特定事情的开放态度而出名，例如同性恋权利或同性婚姻、安乐死、软毒品、言论自由、堕胎等。但这并不是说如果你此行的目的是"毒品旅游"，当地人会对此欣然接受。不建议你在公共场所吸食大麻烟卷，那样，许多人会很生气地看着你。比如，阿姆斯特丹当地人喜欢游客，但是不能容忍那些到这里来只为吸毒和/或喝酒之人。正如在所有开放社会一样，事物存在两方面。是的，你可以做许多事情，说许多话，但是，你还必须与他人和睦相处，必要时作出妥协,有礼有度,实现和平。

感受阿姆斯特丹

走出荷航飞机,第一次来到阿姆斯特丹,我想自己应该会看到一个相当懒散的城市,那里,身材丰满、面颊红润的人们悠闲地沿着古色古香的运河漫步。

而等待我的却是莫大的惊喜!

⊙ 在阿姆斯特丹的第一天下午,我走过一家家餐厅。那里,肤色黝黑、包着头巾的服务员正在为当地居民和外地游客端上一些充满异国情调的东印度群岛菜肴。

⊙ 我走过一处大型的休闲娱乐区——著名的"伦勃朗广场"。那里,多家咖啡厅和夜总会提供只能在巴黎才能享受到的娱乐形式,但价钱只有巴黎的三分之一。

Rembrandtplein　伦勃朗广场

⊙ 我坐在路边咖啡馆的学生区,那里,胡子拉碴的存在主义者们滔滔不绝地大谈世界问题和哲学。

⊙ 我看到优雅的女装店与露天鲱鱼摊并排而立;鲱鱼摊前,留着现代蓬松发型的可爱荷兰女孩将大块的生鲱鱼蘸着碗里的碎洋葱放进嘴里,大快朵颐。

⊙ 我在一座俯瞰阿姆斯特丹港的未来派摩天大厦十三楼咖啡厅喝着鸡尾酒,然后,乘电梯下来,来到一处方圆几平方英里大小的区域;那里,自十七、十八世纪以来,几乎没有一座建筑发生任何改变。

毫无疑问,正如你已经从上面的叙述中了解的那样,阿姆斯特丹是座令人惊喜的梦幻城市,是个充满美丽风景和精彩活动的地方,这些风景和活动完全不同于大多数游客希望看到的郁金香图片、奶酪和木鞋。

当然,这并不是说阿姆斯特丹名震四方的古朴风雅不复存在了。有时,你转过拐角,一下子来到城市五十条运河其中一条的面前,看到五百座桥中的一座,当你凝视着流经连排绿树和山墙环绕的老式豪宅的平静水域,你会屏住呼吸享受所有这一切的纯粹美。确实,阿姆斯特丹城市中心的大片区域,其建筑结构几个世纪以来不曾改变,被誉为"世界上最大的露天博物馆"。

但是,对阿姆斯特丹最主要的印象是它是座活跃、跳动的国际化城市。这从一方面反映了西欧的繁荣和进步——如此繁荣和进步以至于如果让我用一个短语描述阿姆斯特丹,我会说,它已经成为现代欧洲所代表的一切的缩影。当然,阿姆斯特丹还是欧洲大陆最重要的贸易港口之一,每天,船舶、火车和飞机涌入阿姆斯特丹,阿姆斯特丹以惊人的数字使自己成为真正的枢纽城市——小欧洲,因此,成为令人震惊、令人兴奋的地方。

Amsterdam in Diary 日记中的阿姆斯特丹

In her diary, Anne Frank set her family relationship, boyfriends, worries, hopes and dreams for the future against fears of being discovered. She thought a lot about life, and recorded her thoughts in her diary.

The Diary of a Young Girl[①]

◎ Anne Frank

SATURDAY, JUNE 20, 1942

Writing in a diary is a really strange experience for someone like me. Not only because I've never written anything before, but also because it seems to me that later on neither I nor anyone else will be interested in the musings[②] of a thirteen-year-old schoolgirl. Oh well, it doesn't matter. I feel like writing, and I have an even greater need to get all kinds of things off my chest.

"Paper has more patience than people." I thought of this saying on one of those days when I was feeling a little depressed and was sitting at home with my chin in my hands, bored and listless[③], wondering whether to stay in or go out. I finally stayed where I was, brooding[④]. Yes, paper does have more patience, and since I'm not planning to let anyone else read this stiff-backed[⑤] notebook grandly referred to as a "diary," unless I should ever find a real friend, it probably won't make a bit of difference.

Now I'm back to the point that prompted me to keep a diary in the first place: I don't have a friend.

Let me put it more clearly, since no one will believe that a thirteen-year-old girl is completely alone in the world. And I'm not. I have loving parents and a sixteen-year-old sister, and there are about thirty people I

---

① 选自 *The Diary of a Young Girl: The Definitive Edition*, edited by Otto H. Frank and Mirjam Pressler, translated by Susan Massotty, New York: Bantam Books, 1997。
② 沉思，冥想。
③ 无精打采的，倦怠的。
④ 沉思。
⑤ 硬皮的。

can call friends. I have a throng① of admirers who can't keep their adoring② eyes off me and who sometimes have to resort to using a broken pocket mirror to try and catch a glimpse of me in the classroom. I have a family, loving aunts and a good home. No, on the surface I seem to have everything, except my one true friend. All I think about when I'm with friends is having a good time. I can't bring myself to talk about anything but ordinary everyday things. We don't seem to be able to get any closer, and that's the problem. Maybe it's my fault that we don't confide in each other. In any case, that's just how things are, and unfortunately they're not liable to change. This is why I've started the diary.

To enhance the image of this long-awaited friend in my imagination, I don't want to jot down③ the facts in this diary the way most people would do, but I want the diary to be my friend, and I'm going to call this friend Kitty.

Since no one would understand a word of my stories to Kitty if I were to plunge right in, I'd better provide a brief sketch of my life, much as I dislike doing so.

My father, the most adorable father I've ever seen, didn't marry my mother until he was thirty-six and she was twenty-five. My sister Margot was born in Frankfurt am Main in Germany in 1926. I was born on June 12, 1929. I lived in Frankfurt until I was four. Because we're Jewish, my father immigrated to Holland in 1933, when he became the Managing Director of the Dutch Opekta Company, which manufactures products used in making jam. My mother, Edith Hollander Frank, went with him to Holland in September, while Margot and I were sent to Aachen to stay with our grandmother. Margot went to Holland in December, and I

---

① 群。
② 爱慕。
③ jot down: 草草记下。

followed in February, when I was plunked down① on the table as a birthday present for Margot. I started right away at the Montessori nursery school. I stayed there until I was six, at which time I started first grade. In sixth grade my teacher was Mrs. Kuperus, the principal. At the end of the year we were both in tears as we said a heartbreaking farewell, because I'd been accepted at the Jewish Lyceum, where Margot also went to school.

Our lives were not without anxiety, since our relatives in Germany were suffering under Hitler's anti-Jewish laws. After the pogroms② in 1938 my two uncles (my mother's brothers) fled Germany, finding safe refuge③ in North America. My elderly grandmother came to live with us. She was seventy-three years old at the time.

After May 1940 the good times were few and far between: first there was the war, then the capitulation④ and then the arrival of the Germans, which is when the trouble started for the Jews. Our freedom was severely restricted by a series of anti-Jewish decrees⑤: Jews were required to wear a yellow star; Jews were required to turn in their bicycles; Jews were forbidden to use street-cars; Jews were forbidden to ride in cars, even their own; Jews were required to do their shopping between 3 and 5 P.M.; Jews were required to frequent⑥ only Jewish-owned barbershops and beauty parlors; Jews were forbidden to be out on the streets between 8 P.M. and 6 A.M.; Jews were forbidden to attend theaters, movies or any other forms of entertainment; Jews were forbidden to use swimming pools, tennis courts, hockey fields or any other athletic fields; Jews were forbidden to go rowing; Jews were forbidden to take part in any athletic activity in public; Jews were forbidden to sit in their gardens or those of their friends

---

① plunked down: 突然落下。
② 大屠杀。
③ 避难。
④ 投降。
⑤ 法令。
⑥ 光顾。

after 8 P.M.; Jews were forbidden to visit Christians in their homes; Jews were required to attend Jewish schools, etc. You couldn't do this and you couldn't do that, but life went on. Jacque always said to me, "I don't dare do anything anymore, 'cause I'm afraid it's not allowed."

In the summer of 1941 Grandma got sick and had to have an operation, so my birthday passed with little celebration. In the summer of 1940 we didn't do much for my birthday either, since the fighting had just ended in Holland. Grandma died in January 1942. No one knows how often I think of her and still love her. This birthday celebration in 1942 was intended to make up for the others, and Grandma's candle was lit along with the rest.

The four of us are still doing well, and that brings me to the present date of June 20, 1942, and the solemn dedication of my diary.

MONDAY, JULY 26, 1943

Dear Kitty,

Yesterday was a very tumultuous[①] day, and we're still all wound up[②]. Actually, you may wonder if there's ever a day that passes without some kind of excitement.

The first warning siren[③] went off in the morning while we were at breakfast, but we paid no attention, because it only meant that the planes were crossing the coast. I had a terrible headache, so I lay down for an hour after breakfast and then went to the office at around two.

At two-thirty Margot had finished her office work and was just gathering her things together when the sirens began wailing[④] again. So she and I trooped[⑤] back upstairs. None too soon, it seems, for less than

---

① 混乱的。
② wound up: 兴奋, 紧张。
③ 警报。
④ 呼啸。
⑤ 成群而行。

five minutes later the guns were booming so loudly that we went and stood in the hall. The house shook and the bombs kept falling. I was clutching my "escape bag," more because I wanted to have something to hold on to than because I wanted to run away. I know we can't leave here, but if we had to, being seen on the streets would be just as dangerous as getting caught in an air raid①. After half an hour the drone② of engines faded and the house began to hum③ with activity again. Peter emerged from his lookout post in the front attic, Dussel remained in the front office, Mrs. van D. felt safest in the private office, Mr. van Daan had been watching from the loft④, and those of us on the landing spread out to watch the columns of smoke rising from the harbor. Before long the smell of fire was everywhere, and outside it looked as if the city were enveloped in a thick fog.

  A big fire like that is not a pleasant sight, but fortunately for us it was all over, and we went back to our various chores. Just as we were starting dinner: another air-raid alarm. The food was good, but I lost my appetite the moment I heard the siren. Nothing happened, however, and forty-five minutes later the all clear was sounded. After the dishes had been washed: another air-raid warning, gunfire and swarms⑤ of planes. "Oh, gosh, twice in one day," we thought, "that's twice in one day," we thought, "that's twice too many." Little good that did us, because once again the bombs rained down, this time on the others of the city. According to British reports, Schiphol Airport⑥ was bombed. The planes dived and climbed, the air was abuzz with the drone of engines. It was very scary, and the whole time I kept thinking, "Here it comes, this is it."

---

① 袭击。
② 嗡嗡声。
③ 发出嗡嗡声。
④ 阁楼。
⑤ 群。
⑥ Schiphol Airport: 史基辅机场，荷兰最大的机场。

I can assure you that when I went to bed at nine, my legs were still shaking. At the stroke of midnight I woke up again: more planes! Dussel was undressing, but I took no notice and leapt up, wide awake, at the sound of the first shot. I stayed in Father's bed until one, in my own bed until one-thirty, and was back in Father's bed at two. But the planes kept on coming. At last they stopped firing and I was able to go back "home" again. I finally fell asleep at half past two.

Seven o'clock. I awoke with a start and sat up in bed. Mr. van Daan was with Father. My first thought was: burglars. "Everything," I heard Mr. van Daan say, and I thought everything had been stolen. But no, this time it was wonderful news, the best we've had in months, maybe even since the war began. Mussolini has resigned and the King of Italy has taken over the government.

We jumped for joy. After the awful events of yesterday, finally something good happens and brings us ... hope! Hope for an end to the war, hope for peace.

Mr. Kugler dropped by and told us that the Fokker aircraft factory had been hit hard. Meanwhile, there was another air-raid alarm this morning, with planes flying over, and another warning siren. I've had it up to here with alarms. I've hardly slept, and the last thing I want to do is work. But now the suspense[①] about Italy and the hope that the war will be over by the end of the year are keeping us awake.

Yours, Anne

WEDNESDAY, MAY 3, 1944

Dearest Kitty,

First the weekly news! We're having a vacation from politics. There's nothing, and I mean absolutely nothing, to report. I'm also

---

① 悬念。

gradually starting to believe that the invasion will come. After all, they can't let the Russians do all the dirty work; actually, the Russians aren't doing anything at the moment either.

Mr. Kleiman comes to the office every morning now. He got a new set of springs for Peter's divan[①], so Peter will have to get to work reupholstering[②] it. Not surprisingly, he isn't at all in the mood. Mr. Kleiman also brought some flea powder for the cats.

Have I told you that our Boche has disappeared? We haven't seen hide nor hair of her since last Thursday. She's probably already in cat heaven, while some animal lover has turned her into a tasty dish. Perhaps some girl who can afford it will be wearing a cap made of Boche's fur. Peter is heartbroken.

For the last two weeks we've been eating lunch at eleven-thirty on Saturdays; in the mornings we have to make do with a cup of hot cereal. Starting tomorrow it'll be like this every day; that saves us a meal. Vegetables are still very hard to come by. This afternoon we had rotten boiled lettuce. Ordinary lettuce, spinach and boiled lettuce, that's all there is. Add to that rotten potatoes, and you have a meal fit for a king!

I hadn't had my period[③] for more than two months, but it finally started last Sunday. Despite the mess and bother, I'm glad it hasn't deserted me.

As you can no doubt imagine, we often say in despair, "What's the point of the war? Why, oh, why can't people live together peacefully? Why all this destruction?"

The question is understandable, but up to now no one has come up with a satisfactory answer. Why is England manufacturing bigger and

---

① 沙发床。
② 重新装潢。
③ 月经。

better airplanes and bombs and at the same time churning out① new houses for reconstruction? Why are millions spent on the war each day, while not a penny is available for medical science, artists or the poor? Why do people have to starve when mountains of food are rotting away in other parts of the world? Oh, why are people so crazy?

I don't believe the war is simply the work of politicians and capitalists. Oh no, the common man is every bit as guilty; otherwise, people and nations would have re-belled long ago! There's a destructive urge in people, the urge to rage, murder and kill. And until all of humanity, without exception, undergoes a metamorphosis②, wars will continue to be waged, and everything that has been carefully built up, cultivated and grown will be cut down and destroyed, only to start allover again!

I've often been down in the dumps③, but never desperate. I look upon our life in hiding as an interesting adventure, full of danger and romance, and every privation as an amusing addition to my diary. I've made up my mind to lead a different life from other girls, and not to become an ordinary housewife later on. What I'm experiencing here is a good beginning to an interesting life, and that's the reason—the only reason—why I have to laugh at the humorous side of the most dangerous moments.

I'm young and have many hidden qualities; I'm young and strong and living through a big adventure; I'm right in the middle of it and can't spend all day complaining because it's impossible to have any fun! I'm blessed with many things: happiness, a cheerful disposition④ and strength. Every day I feel myself maturing, I feel liberation drawing near, I feel the beauty of nature and the goodness of the people around me. Every day I

---

① churning out: 粗制滥造出。
② 变形。
③ 脏乱的地方。
④ 性格。

think what a fascinating and amusing adventure this is! With all that, why should I despair?

　　Yours, Anne M. Frank

安妮日记

◎ 安妮·弗兰克

Anne's Notebook　安妮日记本

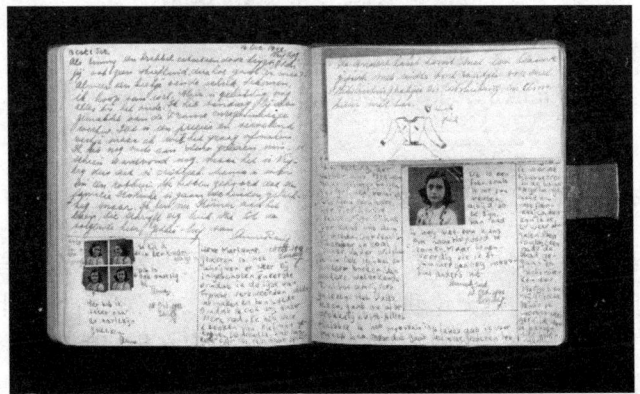

Inside Anne's Notebook　安妮日记本里面

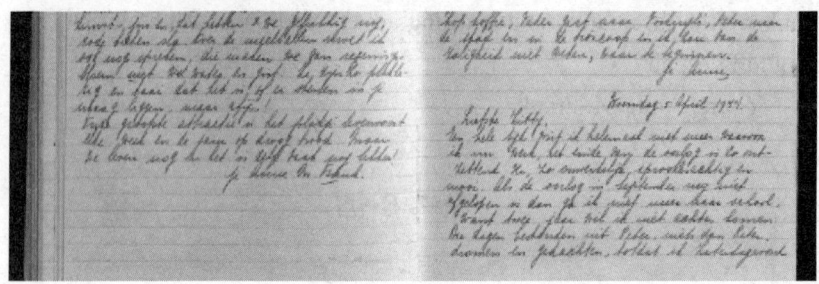

A Page of Anne's Diary　安妮日记其中一页

Anne Frank's House in Amsterdam　阿姆斯特丹的安妮故居

1942 年 6 月 20 日，星期六

写日记对我来说真是个很奇怪的经历，不只是因为我从来没写过这种东西，更因为我觉得无论我或者别人长大后，都不会对一个十三岁小女生的苦思冥想感兴趣吧。好吧，不管了，现在想写就写吧，现在的我更需要一吐为快。

这两天，我觉得有点郁闷的时候想到一句话："纸比人更有耐性。"

我双手托腮，倍感无聊又无精打采，心里纠结着是要待在屋里还是出去。最后还是哪儿也没去，陷入了沉思。的确，纸是比人更有耐性，既然我没打算让任何人看这本俗称"日记"的硬壳笔记本，除非能够找到一个真正的朋友，否则的话，叫什么名字没多大区别。

现在，我要谈一谈是什么原因促使我写日记的：主要因为我没有朋友。

让我说得更明白点儿吧，没有人会相信一个十三岁的女孩儿在这个世界上是完全无依无靠的，而我的确也不是。我有爱我的父母，一个十六岁的姐姐，也有那么三十个左右能称为"朋友"的人。我还有一群追求者，他们的爱慕眼光始终无法从我身上移开，有时候还得靠一只小破镜子才能看一眼我在教室里的样子。我还有慈爱的婶婶和一个温暖的家。哦，表面上看起来我拥有一切，当然除了一位真正的朋友。我能想到的和朋友们在一起的时间都是快乐的。我不想让自己诉说那些每天都会发生的平凡琐事。问题是，我们似乎无法彼此靠近，这也许是我的问题，因为我们不能相互信任。不管怎么说，事情就是这样了，很不幸的是，情况也不会有什么改变。这就是为什么我开始写日记的原因。

为了提升心目中期盼已久的朋友形象，我并不想像大多数人那样事无巨细地在日记里描述事实，而是希望日记能够成为我的朋友，我给她起名叫凯蒂。

如果我直接进入主题，根本没有人会明白我对凯蒂说的是什么。所以尽管我不喜欢这样，但还是最好简单介绍一下我的生活吧。

我的爸爸，是我见过最可爱的爸爸，直到三十六岁时才娶了我妈妈，妈妈当时二十五岁。我姐姐玛格特1926年出生在德国美因河畔的法兰克福，我是1929年6月12日出生的，四岁前一直生活在法兰克福。因为我们是犹太人，爸爸在1933年移民到了荷兰。当时，他是荷兰欧佩克达公司的执行经理，这个公司生产果酱制造设备。妈妈名叫伊迪丝·霍兰德·弗兰克，当年9月跟爸爸一起移民到了荷兰，而当时我和姐姐被送到了亚琛的外婆家。玛格特12月去了荷兰，紧接着转年2月，我被当作玛格特的生日礼物也被带到了荷兰。后来我就读蒙特梭利幼儿园,在那里一直读到六岁,之后上了小学一年级。六年级时我的老师是科普卢斯夫人,她也是校长。六年级结束的时候,和科普卢斯夫人道别时我们都流下了伤心的眼泪,因为我被犹太公立中学录取了,玛格特也在那里读中学。

我们的生活并不是无忧无虑的,因为在德国的亲戚仍然饱受希特勒反犹太教法律的迫害。1938年对犹太人大屠杀后,我的两个舅舅逃离了德国,去北美避难。我年迈的外婆来到荷兰与我们一起生活,当时她已经七十三岁了。

1940年5月以后,几乎就没有什么好日子了。首先是第二次世界大战打响了,紧接着是停火协议,之后德国人就来了。对于犹太人来说,这意味着麻烦开始了。我们的自由受到了反犹太法令的极大限制:犹太人必须要佩戴黄色的星星作为标志;犹太人必须上缴自己的自行车;犹太人禁止乘坐公共汽车;犹太人禁止乘坐小汽车,即使是自己的车也不行;犹太人只能在下午三点至五点之间买东西;犹太人只能在犹太人经营的理发店和美容院理发或美容;犹太人在晚八点到早六点之间禁止上街;犹太人禁止进入戏院、电影院以及任何其他娱乐场所;犹太人禁止使用游泳池、网球场、曲棍球场以及其他任何运动场地;犹太人禁止划船;犹太人禁止在公共场合参与任何体育运动;犹太人禁止在晚八点以后出现在自己或朋友的花园中;犹太人禁止到基督教徒家里拜访;犹太人必须就读犹太学校,等等。你这个也不能做,那个也不能做,但是生活还得继续。雅克经常跟我说:"我什么都不敢做了,因为怕违反了禁令。"

1941年夏天,外婆生病必须要做手术,因此我的生日也没怎么庆祝。1940年夏天荷兰战争刚刚结束,因此那一年我的生日也没怎么庆祝。1942年1月,外婆去世了,没有人知道我时常想念她,仍然深爱着她。1942年的生日打算弥补前两年没有庆祝的遗憾,在众多生日蜡烛中有一支是专门为悼念外婆而点燃的。

我们一家四口还好,今天已经是1942年6月20日了,我认真写我的日记。

1943年7月26日，星期一

亲爱的凯蒂：

　　昨天是混乱的一天，现在我们仍然心有余悸。实际上，你可能会纳闷，我们是否会有一天能安心度过。

　　吃早饭时，响起了第一次警报，但是我们并没在意，因为这只是意味着飞机飞越海岸线。当时，我头疼得厉害，所以早饭后躺了一小时，然后，下午两点去了办公室。

　　两点半，玛格特完成了办公室的工作，正在收拾东西，这时，警报再次响起。于是，我们两个返回楼上。不一会儿，也就不到五分钟的样子，外面枪炮声大作，于是，我们跑出房间，站在过道里。房子在摇晃，炮弹不断落下。我紧紧抱着"逃生包"，更多的是因为我想手里抓点什么，而不是因为我真的想逃走。我知道我们不能走，如果非走不可，在街上被人看见会跟受困于空袭中一样危险。半小时后，飞机引擎的嗡嗡声渐渐消失，房子里的人们又开始活动起来。彼得从前面阁楼的瞭望台下来，杜塞尔还待在前面的办公室里，范·丹太太感觉自己的私人办公室最安全，范·丹先生一直在阁楼上观望，平台上的我们散开，观看港口升起的股股烟雾。不久，空气中弥漫着硝烟的味道，一眼望去，整座城市似乎笼罩在浓雾中。

　　像那样的大火不是什么好景象，但是好在对我们来说这些都过去了，我们各自忙着自己的事情。正要吃晚饭时，警报再度响起。虽然晚饭很丰盛，但我一听到警报声立刻没有了胃口。然而，什么事情也没发生。四十五分钟后，警报解除。洗完碗后，空袭警报声、炮火声、一队队飞机轰鸣声再次响起，我们想："哦，天哪！一天两次！那是一天两次呀！太多了。"这么想无济于事，炮弹再次雨点般落下，这次遭殃的是城市中的另一些人。据英国报道，史基辅机场遭到了轰炸。飞机俯冲、上升，轰鸣声响彻天空。真可怕，我一直在想，"飞机来了，炸弹来了。"

　　向你保证，九点钟上床睡觉时，我双腿还在颤抖。午夜钟声敲响时，我又醒了，听到了更多的飞机轰鸣声！杜塞尔在脱衣服，但我没注意，听到第一声枪炮声，我立刻跳了起来，完全清醒了。我在父亲的床上待到一点钟，在我自己床上待到一点半，两点钟又回到父亲的床上。但是，不断有飞机飞来，最后，终于停火了，我又回到了自己的"窝"，直到两点半我才睡着。

　　七点钟，我突然醒来，坐在床上。范·丹先生正和我父亲在一起。我的第一反应是：有贼！我听到范·丹先生说"所有的东西"，我以为所有的东西都被偷了。但事情不是这样，这次是好消息，几个月以来最好的消息，或许甚至是开战以来最好的消息：墨索里尼辞职，意大利国王接管了政府。

　　我们高兴得跳了起来。昨天经历了那些恐怖时刻，今天终于迎来了好消息，带给我们……希望！希望战争结束，希望和平到来。

　　库格勒先生顺路来访，告诉我们弗克尔飞机制造厂惨遭重创。而且，今天早上又响起了空袭警报，飞机在天上盘旋，警报再次响起。我被警报声吓坏了，晚上无法入睡，白天不想工作。但是现在意大利的局势发展以及年底前停战的希望令我们兴奋不已。

　　安妮

1944年5月3日，星期三

最亲爱的凯蒂：

　　首先是一周的消息！我们正在远离政治，休假。没有什么，我是说绝对没有任何事情可以向你报告。我现在也开始相信反攻就要开始了。毕竟，他们不能让俄国人清理一切；实际上，俄国人此刻也是按兵不动。

　　现在库雷曼先生每天上午又来上班了。他给彼得的沙发床带来了一组新弹簧，所以彼得还得忙着安装弹簧。可以理解，彼得没有一点心情做这种差事。库雷曼先生还给猫咪们拿来些除跳蚤粉。

　　我跟你讲过布彻不见了吗？从上周四以来，我们既不见她藏在哪，也不见她一根毛发。她或许已经上了猫的天堂，不知哪个肉食者正美美地享受一顿大餐哩。也说不定哪个富有的小姑娘正戴着用布彻皮毛制成的帽子呢。彼得伤心极了。

　　两周以来，我们一直是周六十一点半吃午饭；早上用一杯热麦片粥对付一下。从明天开始将每天如此，这样可以省下一餐。蔬菜仍然很难弄到，今天下午我们吃的是水煮烂莴苣。就是普通的莴苣，菠菜和水煮莴苣，就这些。这些就着烂土豆吃，真可以算是美味佳肴。

我已经两个多月没来月经了，但是上周日终于来了。尽管很忙乱、很麻烦，可我还是很高兴。

你一定可以想象，我们经常满怀绝望地问："战争有什么意义？人们为什么不能和平相处？这一切破坏到底是为了什么？"

问这些问题是可以理解的，但目前为止没有人拿得出完满的答案。为什么英国人的飞机愈造愈大，愈造愈精，同时又一直弄出一大堆需要重建的新房子？为什么每天花几百万打仗，却拿不出一分钱用于医学研究、资助艺术家或救济穷人？为什么有些人挨饿，而世界其他地方却有堆积如山的食物在腐烂？哦，人类为什么这么疯狂？

我不相信战争只是政客和资本家搞出来的，芸芸众生的罪过和他们一样大；不然，许多人民和民族早就起来反叛了！人心里有一股毁灭的冲动，发怒、杀人的冲动。除非所有人无一例外都经过一场蜕变，否则还会有战争，苦心建设、培养和种植起来的一切都会被砍倒、摧毁，然后又从头来过！

我经常心情沮丧，可是从不绝望。我将我们躲藏在这里的生活看成一场有趣的探险，充满危险和浪漫，并且将艰辛匮乏当成丰富日记的材料。我已下定决心要走和其他女孩子不一样的人生，不想以后变成一个平凡的家庭主妇。我在这里的经历是一段有趣人生的好开头。碰到最危险的时刻，我都必须往它们幽默的一面看，并且笑一笑，理由——唯一的理由——就在这里。

我年轻，有许多尚未发现的特质；我年轻又坚强，正在进行一场大探险；我正在探险过程之中，不能因为没有什么好玩的事而只顾整天唉声叹气！我很有福分：幸福、乐观的性格，以及力量。每天我都感觉自己在成熟，感觉解放正在临近，感觉大自然的美好和周围人的善良。每天我都想，这是一场多么迷人有趣的探险！有此种种，我为什么绝望？

安妮敬上

Who Is Anne Frank?

☞ Born in Frankfurt-am-Main, Germany, in 1929, and died in 1945, shortly (about two weeks) before liberation by British troops.

☞ A Jewish girl whose family was forced to move to Amsterdam in 1933 to escape German persecution.

☞ Anne had a passion for writing, and kept up her diary throughout the hiding in Amsterdam.

☞ Anne and her sister were eventually transferred to the Bergen-Belsen concentration camp, and both died of typhus (伤寒) there.

☞ The diary was published after the war and became an immediate success.

☞ The story of Anne's life was made into a Hollywood film in 1959.

Chapter 2   Berlin

Paris is always Paris and Berlin is never Berlin!
—Jack Lang

Quotes Featuring Berlin

✎ Whoever controls Berlin controls Germany and whoever controls Germany controls Europe.
—Vladimir Lenin and Karl Marx

✎ Berlin is a city condemned forever to becoming and never to being.
—Karl Scheffler

✎ Berlin is the newest city I have come across. Even Chicago would appear old and gray in comparison.
—Mark Twain

✎ Berlin combines the culture of New York, the traffic system of Tokyo, the nature of Seattle, and the historical treasures of, well, Berlin.
—Hiroshi Motomu

Key Words
Berlin Wall, graffiti, minority cultures, and street scenes.

Questions
1. What do you think is the most representative of a culture? Or, in other words, what makes a city different from another?
2. Where can you find graffiti? What do you think the function of it?
3. Is graffiti a form of art? If it is, in what ways is it artistic?

Cultural Berlin 文化柏林

"Glub" is an Arabic word which means "kernels," "hearts," or "seeds." The author, a native European, picks up a foreign word glub *and the foreign habit of seeds-eating from a European city and takes it as a subject matter in her cultural analysis.*

Food, Form, and Visibility: *Glub* and the Aesthetics of Everyday Life[①]

© Mieke Bal

Making Visibility: Filmmaking as Analysis

… The question I began to ask was, how the "look" of the cities has become more aesthetically more pleasing—livelier, more "colorful" if you like—in recent years. This aesthetic can also be phrased as "interesting," provided this word means genuine interest, or phrased as "engaging," as in

---

① 选自"Food, Form, and Visibility: *Glub* and the Aesthetics of Everyday Life" in *Postcolonial Studies*, Vol. 8, No. 1, 2005。

making us interested, in opposition to dis-interestedness. The absence of scholarship① on this aspect is a bit unnerving②. However, when you think of it, it makes sense: a city's "look" is hard to pin down, let alone document and analyze. This recognition brought me to consider a different form of analysis, a mode that would ... "perform" the analysis "not *about* but *with*" the people concerned. The closest I was able to come was through the medium of film. Film is a tool for making visible that which is there for everyone to see but which remains unseen because it does not have a form that stands out. It lends itself to an attempt to grasp without smothering③ the emergent phenomena whereby the city absorbs the vitality of novelty④.

This is why I have recently embarked⑤ on filmmaking as a way of exploring the way things look—as distinct form, say, explaining why they look that way. I got together with a filmmaker, Shahram Entekhabi, who is, according to current parlance⑥, also a migrant, originating from Iran and living in Berlin. As a tool for research, the film we made, *GLUB* (*Hearts*), is not an *object* of analysis but an *instantiation*⑦ of that activity. It became the central element of a video installation that I would like to briefly describe. The idea was Entekhabi's. During a vacation to Turkey, he realized that there might be a connection between two seemingly unconnected phenomena. The first pertaining to the present, is that the art world in Berlin—always a slightly stiff, bourgeois⑧ city—has become much more lively during the last decade, while most people inhabiting and

---

① 学术，学术成就。
② 令人不安的。
③ 使窒息，抑制。
④ 新颖。
⑤ 开始。
⑥ 说法。
⑦ 实体化。
⑧ 中产阶级的。

animating[①] the Berlin art world are foreigners. The second, emerging from his "constellation[②] of memories," is that the streets in some neighborhoods in the city are more "dirty," which makes them more likable, even aesthetically pleasing.

While having seen it in Berlin and long before that, in Iran, but without having really noticed it, it was in Turkey that Entekhabi recognized the middle-eastern habit of eating seeds—sunflower, pumpkin, and other kinds of seeds, on the street. Seeds—the eating of them, the shells, the shops and stalls, the people cracking the shells and spitting them out: you see it and you don't, hidden as it is in ordinariness. It is a phenomenon that embodies the invisibility that comes with both the hyper[③]-visibility of pervasive presence, and the formlessness of what is situated between countability and mass. Utterly material, seeds are countable items but their countability does not matter. Instead, what characterizes seeds or *glub* is their massive presence. This cultural habit determines the way the street looks, not only because the shells are dropped, but also because eating is a communal activity, which makes the interaction between people look different—less in-different. Entekhabi speculated[④] that it is this aspect, a "symptom" of migration that only becomes visible once you notice it, that has made Berlin so much more lively, both as an urban place and indirectly as an art world. In terms of my attempt to articulate an aesthetics of the everyday, the Berlin art world and *glub* become each other's metaphor[⑤]. As soon as he mentioned this to me, we had a project. Both of us began to associate around the idea of seeds, and to collect visual memories.

---

① 赋予生命，使有活力。
② 群集，荟萃。
③ 高度的。
④ 推测。
⑤ 比喻，暗喻。

Glub, the Arabic word for hearts, is used for these edible[①] roasted and salted seeds, a low-cost appetizer[②] or snack. Beginning with the many meanings of the seeds—traditionally eaten in many non-European societies but mostly associated with the Arabic world—we took this hyper-visible phenomenon of the near-invisible because formless transformation of parts of the inner cities, due to seed-eating, as a point of departure for a stroll[③] through the urban center. From there, the film explores the many meanings and connotations[④] of seeds, and the implementation[⑤] of a "migratory aesthetics" in the Berlin urban landscape and attendant[⑥] art scene. Inhabiting the world of seeds, enveloped[⑦] by the smell of seeds being roasted, the inhabitant of the contemporary city is imperceptibly[⑧] encouraged to be more communicative, to shed haste, and to mitigate[⑨] the hitherto strict separation of home and the outside world.

Immigrant neighborhoods have more seed shells on the streets than the more self-enclosed, bourgeois neighborhoods. As a result, they attract more birds, particularly pigeons. Feeding the pigeons is a widespread tourist activity. Along these lines, seeds connect long-term displacement[⑩] through migration with short-term outings of tourism. *Birds* transport seeds, and now *people* do, transporting a cultural habit from elsewhere to Western Europe. While the art world partly shifted from the Western neighborhoods to the former East-Berlin *Bezirke*[⑪], Kreuzberg[⑫] is the

---

① 食用的。
② 开胃食品。
③ 散步。
④ 含义。
⑤ 实行。
⑥ 伴随的。
⑦ 包围。
⑧ 不知不觉地。
⑨ 缓和。
⑩ 移位。
⑪ 区。
⑫ 柏林的克罗伊茨贝格区，原本是东德时代的工业区，现在越来越成为艺术社区。

most noticeable area enlivened by immigrants and their restaurants, and it has, indeed, become fashionable, or "hot."

Both galleries and seed shops have established themselves in Kreuzberg. Like part of Berlin after the *Wende*[①], seeds contain the potential to grow, to flourish, to evolve, change and reproduce. Both in bodily postures[②] that come with the eating of seeds, and in the connotations attached to seeds, there is a slight gender aspect to this habit as well. The concept of seed has perhaps different connotations for men than for women, although that difference comes from a mis-conception of seed in human reproduction. But that seeds remind people of their own potential to grow and multiply is obvious.

Seeds are also food. Eaten between meals, almost permanently, they are a form of non-food. This function of seeds as unofficial food connects seeds to invisibility and formlessness, but its constant consumption, which produces cracking sounds, smells of roasting, and waste that changes the feel of the street and the sound of walking, makes it at the same time hyper-visible. Seeds are less related to religion as an inevitably fixed connotation of the idea of migration, than to the unemployment in the homelands. This condition, granting little money and much time, both explains and justifies migration. As one immigrant from Tunisia, Tarek Mehdi, explains in the film:

> you know our people
> have little work, so they have lots of spare time
> so they buy *glub*, eat it, to pass
> the time … it becomes like a tradition
> people eat it with the family spend the evening
> with the whole family sometimes

---

① 改造。
② 姿势。

it's very nice

Together with the acknowledgement that this eating is something like an "invented tradition," this statement derives positive enjoyment from a situation of unemployment and boredom. There is no need to idealize the situation this man describes, or to deny that this situation is rooted in the colonialism[①] behind postcoloniality, in order to still see the cultural resilience[②] expressed in these few words. In addition to clearly enjoying eating *glub*, the speaker also draws social value from the bonding that results.

…

But the link between seeds and religion is not entirely absent either—which is important in view of the cultural status of religion, its function in group-life, particularly in Arabic culture. While not subject to food laws, *glub* is related to the intricacies[③] of pleasure, wealth, and the obligations of charity. In a section significantly titled "Ibn Sudun's Sweet Nothings" of his study of food in classical Arabic literature, Geert Jan van Gelder quotes a mock doxology[④] from medieval literature, where God is praised for the creation of the particular economy of *glub*:

> He made sellers subservient to swallowers, those who sit in their shops and those who are ambulant[⑤]. He made the kernels of pistachio[⑥] nuts, having been cracked, whole.

Here, as in other cases, van Gelder mentions that the relationship between

---

① 殖民主义。
② 弹性。
③ 错综复杂。
④ 颂歌。
⑤ 能走动的，流动的。
⑥ 开心果。

glub and its users is both *metaphorical*—the sellers as well as the swallowers thrive and grow like seeds—and *metonymical*[①]—the economy is sustained. And, to make the analogy[②] between this classical tradition and the Berlin art world even more specific, let me add that van Gelder illustrates how in Arabic literature, eating and writing—eating and describing, or in other words, eating and cultural production—are each other's metaphor.

With these and many other associations in mind, then, we took the video camera and started to explore Berlin, especially Kreuzberg and especially the art world. The crossing of seed eating and art, two hitherto[③] unconnected domains, yielded a great number of unexpected connections. The formlessness of the large quantities of seeds, for example, yielded sometimes to quite beautiful forms, sometimes to the need to focus on the faces, and the mouths of the people eating them—or, for that matter, talking about that eating habit. As the film progressed, we also became aware of the close connection between the invisibility and as well as hyper-visibility of seeds, and ... formlessness, with its critical thrust.

...

If we now bring together the three elements of the aesthetic of seed eating—reciprocal[④] recognition, a constellation of visual memories underlying our visual habitus[⑤], and this militant[⑥] performative use of formlessness—we can begin to see what kind of aesthetic we are looking for, or, more suitably, *performing*. All this time, mind you, we are talking about an eating habit, about a tiny snack that is as addictive as any, that produces thirst, communication, and waste. Nothing special, nothing

---

① 换喻的，转喻的。
② 类比。
③ 到目前为止。
④ 相互的。
⑤ 习惯。
⑥ 好战的，激进的。

spectacular, and, most importantly, nothing that gives rise to ethnic restaurants as a form of tourism.

Instead, this migrant eating habit comes to develop many different cultural elements, or memories, according to where a person grew up. For example, Maryam Mameghanian-Prenzlow from Iran associates *glub* eating with polite manners, when she stated,

> we don't have for instance autobiographies
> many autobiographies because ...
> it's not polite to speak, to tell
> who I am, what I do
> it's very communicative also because
> you can't talk while eating seeds

Here, the shift, without transition, from a rule of polite behavior to a function of the seeds fulfil in a culture of restraint, is perhaps more telling than elaborate[①] analyses of food laws, however insightful[②] they may be. From this short but twofold statement, we not only learn something essential about Iranian literature, but we are also offered an explanation of *glub* that complements the earlier one. For here, there is no question of unemployment and poverty to explain the habit. Nor is there, again, any mention of religion. What matters most, perhaps, in this statement is the tight bond it established between cultural values, eating, and literature.

An Aesthetic of Everyday Life?

Whereas the two immigrants we have heard so far both associated seed eating with memories of their homeland, some others we interviewed brought up the appeal of this habit on the urban westerner. Dawoud

---

① 详细的。
② 深刻的。

Changizi, an Iranian merchant who manages a fancy seeds and nuts shop in Kreuzberg, spoke about his customers in the following way, which resonates[①] with both Mehdi's and Mameghanian-Prenzlow's explanations:

> what are they? [his customers]
> Muslims as well as Germans
> they are ... how to say this ...
> between two cultures
> they discovered how we get on, enjoying
> sitting together, chatting, and eating seeds
> they got the hang of it, that feeling ...
> and so they buy 200-300 grams and
> sit all night long in front of the TV eating seeds
>
> ...

Thus *glub*, the tiny hearts of seeds that are at the heart of cultural habits, in all their diversity, stand for ... those "things that quicken the heart." Changizi, interpreting his customers, also interprets a culture of "post-colonial food." This culture is not based on the quick fix of the urban tourist enjoying the foodscape enriched by ethnic restaurants. Instead, it is a mixed culture in a more profound sense, simply but effectively expressed in the shopkeeper's statement. This scene may take on different specifics for each participant, but this malleability[②] is precisely the contribution of *glub* to an aesthetic of the host city.

The connections facilitated by *glub* eating can be based, for example, on a desire to get a taste of the Tunisian[③] excess time, and used by the

---
① 共鸣。
② 易适应性,可塑性。
③ 突尼斯(人)的。

western urbanite to unhasten her life. Or such a connection can be based on the recognition of restraint[①] as a form of politeness, rekindling[②] manners that contemporary life has made less relevant but no less desirable. Or it can evoke specific memories, like the one told by yet another participant in the film whose narrative[③] impulse was triggered by the handful of *glub* we proffered[④]:

> I was a very young boy
> walking in the street of Dar Es-salaam[⑤] …
> I had a handful of these seeds
> and on the way to this tree there was
> an enclosed space
> I remember there was a plank missing
> in the fence
> and I peeped through this fence
> and I saw a swimming pool with
> a couple of white women
> that was my first proper encounter with
> a white person
> but I was so scared because I'd
> never seen a white person
> that I tripped[⑥] over backwards
> spilling all those seeds … (Shaheen Merali)

The narrative impulse we witness here, sprung up with amazing frequency

---

① 克制。
② 重新点燃。
③ 叙述的。
④ 提供。
⑤ 达累斯萨拉姆（坦桑尼亚共和国首都）。
⑥ 轻快地走，轻快地跳舞。

whenever we mentioned, showed, or offered *glub* during the project. The multiple stories composed the "manifold[①] story" …, and perform something between a person and a cultural voice— importantly, those two cannot be distinguished. As Dolphijn phrases it, this story is an instance of "[v]oices that should not be reduced to the people that produced them, but that create an altogether different space." The memory Merali evokes is simultaneously utterly personal and significantly cultural, belonging to this single boy who was part of a group of Indian immigres[②] in West-Africa.

To substantiate[③] my claim that film can provide an instance of cultural analysis—to solicit[④] debate and replace, say, a lecture—a "scholarly" or academic attitude of looking is required. In a pedagogical[⑤] setting, for example when presenting *GLUB* to students, the film can only work performatively when its viewers co-perform it. To this effect, I tend to propose students to look at it, actively, in two ways. First, I ask them to consider the associations I have mentioned, and think about other possible motives that they think contribute to the look of any city they are interested in. Hence, the question: "Have you seen this seed-eating habit in Paris, Rome, or Sydney," can be supplemented[⑥] with the question: "What else have you noticed that makes this city different from, say, the classical capital you know, or thought you knew?"

Second, by way of connecting this aesthetic question to a more political one, I request that students consider the shift the film is trying to perform, from an obsession[⑦] with mosques[⑧] and violence, to a careful

---

① 多方面的，多层次的。
② 移民。
③ 使具体化，证实。
④ 提起。
⑤ 教学的。
⑥ 补充。
⑦ 着迷。
⑧ 清真寺，伊斯兰教寺院。

consideration and enjoyment of the specific aesthetic aspects of migration, such as the "look" and "feel" of Western European cities. For our film, this is the connection between seed eating and art—from one domain of fertility[①] to another, each being a metaphor of the other to the benefit of both. For example, the film, as the few quotations from it already intimate[②], is full of what we ended up calling "wisdom slogans," uttered by the characters in relation to their situation of not-being-at-home. One example from the end of the film suffices[③] to demonstrate the genre[④]:

> my idea of life is to stand in the street
> to be ready for what comes along
> instead of preparing for what I think might come along
> (Jimmie Durham)

Students may pick up on these stories, or the cityscapes[⑤] in which practically everyone appears to be eating seeds, and which suggest new ideas to them. Moreover, students come up with different associations themselves, ideas that also contribute to a shift in thinking about what we might call the "cultural politics" of migration. Offering audience some *glub*—enticing[⑥] them to produce, hear, and be sensitized to the sound that predominates in the film—encourages students to come up with their own stories, which are shared by the members of the group during the subsequent discussion period.

As I already suggested, an integral part of the phenomenon analyzed—and another tool for analysis that supplements scholarship—is

---

① 肥沃，多产。
② 暗示，宣布。
③ 足够，满足。
④ 类型，样式。
⑤ 城市风光照片或绘画。
⑥ 诱惑。

the exuberant[1] storytelling that occurred during filming. The non-theme, non-substance, and non-concept of seeds clearly compelled everyone we spoke to—from people in the street, shoppers and shopkeepers, to artists, curators[2], or computer programmers to practically burst out in storytelling as soon as they gathered that seed eating was the subject of the film. This linguistic generosity suggested that an extended video installation made sense.

 This installation, then, became the second part of the project. We assembled those stories that were too long or otherwise not suitable for the (30 minutes-only) film, and we put these on one of two sound tracks. The other track registers the sound of cracking and eating the seeds, looking into the camera, against an even white background. The sound of that eating, produced by these individuals making eye contact with the visitor of the installation, reinforces, echoes, and responds to the sound of seed eating in the film and in the gallery where visitors are offered unlimited supplies of seeds to eat during their visit. This sound installation creates an eerie[3] uncertainty about levels of reality.

...

 Through a performative exploration of the sense-based aesthetic of the everyday in the urban environment, this project engages the relationship between (non)food and the social process of seed eating in the public sphere ... I was interested to see whether readers, viewers or students, instead of staying inconsolable[4] after the demise[5] of an ethnic purity that never existed, are able to be "grudgingly[6] amused" by the current look of the world's capital cities ... For Shahram Entekhabi, there

---

① 丰富的。
② 管理者。
③ 可怕的，怪异的。
④ 无法安慰的，极为伤心的。
⑤ 死亡，终止。
⑥ 勉强地，不情愿地。

were artistic goals to be met. As we talked the project through, however, the difference between academic and artistic ambitions didn't amount to much. Both practices are analytic inquiries. Both articulate what is not yet articulated. And in the process of doing so, both struggle to give form to the ideas, phenomena, and images struggling to receive perpetual or intellectual form. That, too, we grudgingly acknowledged, amused us.

食物、形式和可见性：瓜子与日常生活之美学

◎ 米克·巴尔

Seed Eaters 吃瓜子的众人

可见性：电影制作作为分析工具

……我想问的问题是，近些年，城市风貌如何从美学角度变得更令人心旷神怡——如果你喜欢这样说，如何变得更有生气、更丰富多彩。这种美感也可以叫做"有趣"，因为"有趣"意思是真正令人感兴趣，或者也可以称作"吸引人"，因为可以激起我们的兴趣，而不是让我们失去兴趣。令人不安的是，学术界缺乏这方面的研究。然而，想一想，缺乏研究有它的道理：很难准确概括一座城市的外貌，更别说论证或者分析这座城市了。认识到这一点，我考虑是否可以使用一种不同的分析形式，这种形式可以说是"行为"分析……这种分析不是关于某些有关人员的，而是与这些有关人员一起共同分析。我能做到的最可行的方式是通过电影这种媒体。电影是一种工具，它展示了那些每个人都看到的、但却没有人注意的事物，因为这些事物缺乏突出的表现形式；电影试图去了解而不是抑制自然发生的现象，正是从这些现象中城市汲取了活力和新奇。

这就是最近为什么我开始将电影制作作为探索事物外观的一种方法——比如说，作为一种解释为什么事物看上去如此的独特方式。我与一位电影制作人尚莱姆·因特卡比合作，根据当前的说法，他也是移民，祖籍伊朗，现在住在柏林。我们将电影作为研究工具，制作影片《瓜子》，《瓜子》不是分析的对象，而是分析的实例表现。我将简短叙述《瓜子》成为录制影像核心元素的过程。想法是因特卡比提出的。一次在土耳其度假时，他意识到两种表面上看起来没有任何联系的现象之间或许存在某种关联：第一种现象是与现实相关的柏林艺术世界，柏林这个总是显得有点刻板的中产阶级城市，最近十年却变得比以往更有活力了，因为大多数生活在柏林、赋予柏林艺术世界生机的居民是外国人；第二种现象出自因特卡比的众多记忆片段，据他回忆，柏林一些社区的街道显得更"脏"，而这却使得这些街区更招人喜欢，甚至从美学角度看更令人心悦。

因特卡比在柏林见过的这种现象，好久之前在伊朗也看到过，但没有真正注意到，而在土耳其他才真正留意中东人这种在街上吃瓜子的习惯——葵花籽、南瓜籽和其他各种瓜子。瓜子——吃瓜子，瓜子壳、瓜子店、瓜子摊，人们嗑瓜子，然后吐出瓜子皮：你看见又没看见这些现象，它们隐藏起来，正如日常事物一样显现出来。这种现象既体现了无处不在的超可见性形式，又体现了介于屈指可数和数量众多之间无形的不可见性形式。瓜子完全是物质的、可数的东西，但是它的可数性却无关紧要，而瓜子的特点又是它的大量存在。吃瓜子这种文化习惯决定了街道的外貌，不仅因为那些扔在地上的瓜子壳，而且还因为吃瓜子的群体行为使人与人之间的交流方式显得不同——显得不那么冷漠。因特卡比推测认为，正是这种特别留意才识别出来的移民"特征"，使既作为地理意义上的城市又间接作为艺术世界的柏林变得那么富有生气。至于我想表达城市日常生活美感的愿望，可以说柏林艺术世界和瓜子彼此互相比喻。因特卡比一跟我提起这些想法，我们就着手实施一个项目。我们两个人都开始围绕瓜子展开联想，搜集视觉记忆素材。

  glub 是阿拉伯语的"瓜子"，指那些食用的炒熟的咸瓜子，一种低成本的开胃小吃。从传统上来说，吃瓜子是许多非欧洲国家的社会现象，这些国家大多与阿拉伯世界相关。我们从瓜子的多种意义开始；因为城市中心许多地方由于吃瓜子而悄然发生无形的变化，我们将这一超乎可见而又近乎不可见的现象作为出发点，散步穿越中心城区。从城市中心开始，影片探讨了瓜子的许多意义和内涵，在柏林城区和艺术场景之间实现"迁移美学"。居住在瓜子世界里，被炒瓜子的味道包围着，这座当代城市的居民潜移默化受此影响，变得更喜欢交流了，他们放慢速度，冲淡了瓜子流行以前家与家外世界的严格区别。

  移民社区的街道上散落着比更为自我封闭的中产阶级社区更多的瓜子壳。因此，这些社区吸引了更多的鸟，特别是鸽子。喂鸽子是分布广泛的旅游活动。这样一来，瓜子连接了因迁移导致的长期位移与外出旅游造成的短期位移。鸟传播瓜子、种子，而现在人类将一种文化习惯从他处传播到西欧。当柏林的艺术世界部分地从西欧社区转移到前东德地区，克罗伊茨贝格区成为最引人注目的区域，因为有了众多移民和他们经营的饭馆，克罗伊茨贝格区显得生机勃勃。确实，克罗伊茨贝格区已经变得非常时尚了，或者说"火爆"了。

Seed Eaters in Berlin　柏林街头吃瓜子的人

Chapter 2　Berlin

　　在克罗伊茨贝格区，既分布着艺术馆，也散落着瓜子店。像改造后的柏林部分地区一样，瓜子（即种子）具有生长、繁荣、进化、改变和繁殖的潜力。无论人们吃瓜子时的身体姿势，还是赋予瓜子（或种子）生命力的含义，这个习惯还稍稍带有一点性别意义。种子的概念对于男女或许有不同的含义，这种不同来自不同性别对种子在人类繁殖中的不同理解。但是，显而易见，种子让人们想起他们自己生长、繁殖的能力。

　　瓜子也是食物；而人们在两餐之间吃瓜子，瓜子几乎永远是一种非食物形式。瓜子作为非正式食物的作用，与它的不可见性和无形性相联系，但是人们常常消费瓜子，发出嗑瓜子的声音，散发出炒瓜子的味道，吐出瓜子皮，这一切改变了街道的感觉和走在上面的声音，这些现象同时又太容易看到。作为迁移概念毋庸质疑的固定含义，相比较与宗教的联系，瓜子与移民前在故乡的失业更加相关。失业这种情况没给人们带来钱，却给了他们大量时间，这既解释了移民的原因，又说明了移民的合理性。来自突尼斯的移民塔瑞克·梅迪在影片中解释说：

> 你知道我们这些人
> 没什么事情做，就有了许多闲工夫，
> 于是买瓜子吃，打发时间……
> 这成为一种传统
> 与家人一起吃瓜子
> 晚上有时全家人一起度过
> 感觉非常好

　　认可吃瓜子有些类似于一种"发明创造出的传统"，同理，梅迪的讲述源自乐观享受失业与无聊的状况。没有必要为了还想看到这些话语表达的文化活力，而将梅迪描述的情况理想化，也没有必要否认这种状况的根源在于后殖民背后的殖民主义。除了明显地享受吃瓜子，梅迪还从吃瓜子产生的关联中得出社会价值。

……

但是，瓜子与宗教的联系并不是完全不存在——鉴于宗教的文化地位，特别是阿拉伯文化中宗教在群体生活中的作用，这一点非常重要。虽然没有受到食物法则的制约，但是瓜子与乐趣、财富和慈善机构义务等错综复杂的事物相关。在研究古典阿拉伯文学中的食物时，吉尔特·詹恩·范·戈尔德用了醒目的标题《伊本·苏丹的香甜小吃》，他引用了一段中世纪文学中的类似颂歌，赞扬上帝创造了独特的瓜子经济：

> 上帝使商贩对消费瓜子的人很客气，那些顾客坐在店铺里吃着瓜子，或者在街上四处走来走去吃着瓜子。上帝创造了开心果，可以整个地嗑开。

这里，与其他情况一样，范·戈尔德提到瓜子和瓜子消费者之间既是比喻关系——卖瓜子的商贩和消费者像种子一样繁荣、增长，又是换喻关系——经济持续发展。此外，为了使吃瓜子的古典传统与柏林艺术世界之间的类比更具体，我补充认为，范·戈尔德说明了在阿拉伯文化中饮食与写作——饮食与描写，或者换个说法，饮食与文化产出——彼此如何互为比喻。

头脑中有了这些和其他许多联想，接下来，我们开始拿着摄像机考察柏林，重点拍摄克罗伊茨贝格区和那里的艺术世界。吃瓜子和艺术这两个到目前为止完全不相干的领域，它们的相遇产生出许多无法预料的联系。例如，大量瓜子的无形有时让位于美丽的形式，有时让位于聚焦面孔的需要，有时让位于人们吃瓜子或者为了吃瓜子而谈论吃瓜子时的口形。随着影片的进行，我们逐渐明白了瓜子的不可见性、超可见性和有着巨大推动力的无形性的密切关系。

……

如果我们现在将吃瓜子的三个美学因素——互相认可、人们视觉习惯中隐含的众多视觉记忆，以及这种无形的激进行为形式——放在一起，可以开始看到我们在寻求哪种美，或者更恰当地说，我们在展现哪种美。需要提醒的一点是,我们谈论的始终都是关于一种饮食习惯,关于一种微不足道的、与其他小吃一样容易使人上瘾的小吃,这种小吃会使人口渴,会促进交流,会制造垃圾。没有什么特别之处,没有什么惊人之处,然而,最重要的是,正是这种普通的东西成就了作为一项旅游内容、具有民族特色的餐饮行业。

然而,这种移民饮食习惯根据个人成长环境逐渐发展成为多种不同的文化因素或者文化记忆。例如,来自伊朗的玛丽彦·梅姆翰尼安-普伦孜洛将瓜子与礼貌的行为举止联系起来,她这样说:

> 比如,我们没有自传
> 没有太多的自传,因为……
> 我是谁、我是做什么的
> 将这些说出来、讲出来,是不礼貌的
> 吃瓜子便于交流还因为
> 你吃瓜子时无法讲话

这里,在内敛文化中,从礼貌行为规则到瓜子作用中间没有任何过渡的转换,但这或许比无论多么深刻、尖锐、详细地分析食物法则更能说明问题。从这简短的但包含双层含义的话语中,我们不仅学到了有关伊朗文化的基本知识,而且还补充了前面对于瓜子的理解。这里,没有失业、贫困问题解释这个习惯;与前面一样,也没有提及任何宗教问题。或许这些话语中最重要的是文化价值、饮食和文化之间的紧密联系。

日常生活之美?

到目前为止,我们听到的那两位移民都把吃瓜子与自己家乡的记忆联系起来,而我们采访的其他一些人谈及了这个习惯对西方城市人的吸引力。达乌德·常逸梓是一位伊朗商人,在克罗伊茨贝格区经营着一家别致的坚果店,他谈到顾客时的情景令人回想起梅迪和梅姆翰尼安-普伦孜洛的叙述。他这样说:

他们(顾客们)是谁?
穆斯林和德国人
他们……怎么说呢……
介于两种文化之间
他们发现我们如何适应新的文化,享受地
坐在一起,聊天、嗑瓜子
他们领会到其中的独特意义,那种感觉……
于是,他们买上200~300克
然后整晚坐在电视机前吃瓜子

……

　　于是,种子的芯——瓜子——成为文化习惯的核心,以各种表现形式出现,代表了……那些"使心跳加速的事物"。常逸梓解读他的顾客,同时也在解释一种"后殖民饮食"文化。这种文化的基础不是城市旅游者享受当地少数民族特色浓郁的小吃的权宜之道,而是更深意义上的文化融合,坚果店店主的谈话简单而有效地表达了这一点。这一场景针对每位文化参与者可能表现出各不相同的细节,但是,这种易适应性恰恰是瓜子对移民城市某种美感的贡献。

　　例如,吃瓜子激发的种种联系,可以基于西方城市居民希望放慢生活脚步、享受突尼斯式富余时间的尝试。或者,这种联系可以基于认可内敛是一种礼貌,这种礼貌形式重新恢复了一些现代生活使其变得不那么必要、但事实上并不是真的不需要了的行为举止。或者,这种联系能激发某些特定的记忆,就像影片中的另一位被采访者所言,我们给他一把瓜子激起了他的表达冲动:

我是个年轻的男孩子
走在达累斯萨拉姆的街道上
手里抓着一把这样的瓜子
通向这棵树的路上
有一处封闭空间

我记得护墙中间
少了一块木板
于是我向护墙里窥视
看到了一个游泳池
还有几个白人妇女
那是我第一次真正遇见
白人
但是我非常害怕，因为
我从未见过白人
轻快地跳着舞
瓜子全洒了……（沙赫恩·梅拉里）

拍摄期间，无论什么时候我们提起、拿出或者提供些瓜子，我们看到的叙述冲动都会以惊人的频率出现。多个故事构成了一个多方面的故事……完成了个人声音与某种文化声音之间的转换——重要的是，个人与文化二者无法区分。正如杜尔菲因所说，这个故事是"不应该将声音归于那些发出声音的人，而是应该创造一种完全不同的空间"的事例。梅拉里回想起的记忆是个人的，同时很明显这个记忆完全又是文化的，即这个记忆属于这个在西非构成印度移民群体一分子的男孩。

为了证明我提出的电影能够提供文化分析例证的观点（或者为了激发讨论，以代替讲座），需要具备"学者的"或学术的观察态度。比如，在教学环境中，给学生放映影片《瓜子》时，只有观众共同参与影片才能发挥作用。为了达到这个效果，我建议学生从两方面积极地看待影片。首先，我让学生们思考我提到过的一些联系，思考其他可能有助于促成某个他们感兴趣城市的风貌的动力。因此，"你在巴黎、罗马或者悉尼是否见过这种吃瓜子的习惯"，这个问题之外应该补充问另一个问题："你还注意到别的什么事物，使这个城市区别于你知道的或者你认为自己知道的某个古都？"

其次，通过将这个美学问题与更政治化的问题联系起来，我要求学生思考影片想要完成的目的，即从关注清真寺和暴力，到认真考虑和欣赏移民特有美学现象之间的转换，例如西欧城市的外貌、感觉。对于我们的影片，这是吃瓜子与艺术的联系——从一个领域的活力到另一个领域的繁荣，彼此互为比喻、彼此双赢。例如，正如影片中一些人的叙述所暗示的，影片充满了人物有关他们身处异乡环境的描述话语，最后我们将这种话语叫做"至理名言"。影片结尾处的一个事例足以证明这种表现形式：

> 我的生活理念是站在街上
> 随时应对将要发生的事
> 而不是应对我认为要发生的事（吉米·杜伦）

学生们可以利用这些故事，或者几乎每个人都在吃瓜子的城市照片，这些素材可以激发他们产生新的想法。此外，学生们产生的不同联想和观点也会有助于思考我们称之为迁移"文化政治"的转换。给观众们一些瓜子，以吸引他们思考、倾听或者使他们对影片中持续不断的嗑瓜子声感到敏感；随后的讨论环节，鼓励学生讲出自己的故事，与小组其他同学分享。

正如我已暗示的，影片中出现大量的讲故事片段，这些片段构成了分析吃瓜子这一现象不可缺少的组成部分，也是补充学术分析的另一种工具。很明显，瓜子的缺乏主题、缺乏实质、缺乏概念促使与我们交谈的每个人——从街上的路人、店主、店员，到艺术家、管理者或者电脑程序员——当他们猜出吃瓜子是影片的主题时，几乎全部爆发出讲故事的冲动。这种语言的慷慨暗示着有必要继续加工拍摄的影像素材。

那么，接下来的制作成为此项目的第二部分。我们搜集的那些故事，或者因为篇幅太长，或者因为其他原因不适合这部短短三十分钟的影片，我们把这些故事放进了两个声道中的其中一个。另一个声道录制了人们朝着白色平面背景，看着摄像机嗑瓜子、吃瓜子的声音。他们发出的吃瓜子声音、拍摄影片时他们与旁观者的眼神交流，强化、回应、重复了影片人物吃瓜子的声音以及艺术馆里游客参观时可以无限量吃瓜子的声音。这种声音设置产生了现实情况中意想不到的不确定性。

……

通过行为探寻这种城市环境中以感性为基础的日常美感,这个项目讨论了(非)食物与公共领域吃瓜子的社会过程……我对此非常有兴趣:读者、观众或者学生是否感到当前世界大都市的面貌勉强还算有趣,而不是在从未存在过的种族纯洁终止后仍感到伤心沮丧……对于尚莱姆·因特卡比来说,需要实现一些艺术目标。然而,当我们从头至尾探讨这个项目时,学术和艺术目标之间的分歧显得无足轻重了。这两方面的实践活动都是分析性调查,二者都诉说了尚未诉说的事情;在此过程中,二者都努力将一些想法、现象以及形象等赋予具体表现形式,努力获得永久的或理智的形式。这也是我们所认可的,我们为此感到快乐。

Who Is Mieke Bal?

☞ Born in 1946.
☞ Dutch cultural theorist and critic, and video artist.
☞ Professor of theory of literature in Amsterdam Univ.
☞ Founding director of the Amsterdam School for Cultural Analysis (ASCA).
☞ Theoretical fields of interest: cultural analysis, critical semiotics, feminist theory, and relations between verbal and visual arts.

> ☞ Analytical fields of interest: contemporary literature, Hebrew Bible, and Rembrandt, etc.
> ☞ Most influential works: *Narratology, Acts of Memory, Double Exposures, Looking in,* and *Travelling Concepts in the Humanities.*

Historic Berlin 历史柏林

The greatest graffiti project, the Berlin Wall, serves as an open museum of arts and history. This form of showing and exposing has triggered scholars to think about its function of telling, acting, and performing.

Killing Kool: The Graffiti Museum[①]

◎ Sonja Neef

The Write/Right Side of the Wall

The politics of a fixed distinction between an inner and an outer side, or a left and a right side, or a Western and an Eastern side, effected highly dramatic repercussions[②] in the case of the Berlin Wall. No other wall offered such an ideal painting surface, and it became a concrete canvas[③] of the biggest graffiti project ever.

13 August 1961. The German Democratic Republic (GDR) started building what it called its *"antifaschistischer Schutzwall"* ("antifascist protective wall"), walling in West Berlin over a length of 164 km and

---

① 选自"Killing Kool: The Graffiti Museum" in *Art History*, Vol. 30, Issue 3, June 2007. Kool, 即英文 cool。
② 反响，后果。
③ concrete canvas: 混凝土的油画布。

turning it into an island on the mainland of "real socialism." Initially consisting of barbed wire① and brick walls, the Wall was continuously modernized and strengthened. ...

The Wall of the fourth generation rang in the hour of the graffitists, all the more so because the panels were now interweaving② seamlessly③ like an endless canvas, which the GDR had even whitened. To whiten the western side of the Wall, a cage needed to be built for the painters, who were surveyed by armed border guards. Through this brightening up, the government aimed at making people from both sides used to, and thus indifferent to, the Wall, counting on ... that "nothing is so invisible as a monument."

For the monument of the Wall, however, its whiteness did make a difference, ... because it became the almost not perceptible④ element that turned the invisible visible. Graffitists played with the invisibility by integrating the wall's materiality, including its political order, into their art works. Or—following Mieke Bal's proposition—to "make the otherwise mute object speak back."

And the Wall spoke back. Frequently used motifs⑤ included breaks, holes, doors, windows, or zips opening the illusion of a *mis en abime*⑥ into another world. The graffito below was made by Iranian painter Yadiga Azizy in Berlin Kreuzberg between Legien- and Leuschnerdamm in 1988. As a *trompe l'oeil*⑦ it restored the torn view on a church of which the tower had been disconnected from the nave⑧. The illusionist⑨ logic of the

---

① barbed wire: 带刺铁丝网。
② 交织。
③ 无缝隙地。
④ 可察觉到的，可见的。
⑤ 母题。
⑥ *mis en abime*: 法语词，意为"图像中的图像"。
⑦ *trompe l'oeil*: 三维的逼真绘画技巧。
⑧ （教堂的）中殿。
⑨ 错觉的。

view disempowered the Wall as a separating force, and, paradoxically enough, it did so by using the Wall as it medium. The graffito created a sutureless[①] "place" disrespecting the material architectonic frame, which it transgressed, or to pick up Baudrillard[②]'s terminology[③], "superimposed[④]" or "erogenized[⑤]." The graffito turned the Wall into an area of transit rather than of separation, at least symbolically.

Border-Crossings

For Michel de Certeau[⑥], such formation, displacement, or crossing of a boundary, is a discursive act, a speech act performed by a first person authorized to stipulate[⑦] or constitute the border. De Certeau discusses the performative dimension of the border by the example of a rite[⑧] that, in ancient Rome, was performed by priests called *fetiales* prior to any contact with a foreign people … As the *fetiales* prepared the occupation of the foreign land by first taking possession of it symbolically, the Wall's graffiti, I contend, performed a symbolic conquest of the space of the border. In 1982 artists around the world were invited to participate in a graffiti competition "*Uberwindung der Mauer durch Bemalung der Mauer*" ("Overcoming the Wall by Painting the Wall"), sponsored by the Haus am Checkpoint Charlie[⑨]. Christophe Bouchet and Thierry Noir painted the bright and fanciful *Red Dope on Rabbits* on Bethaniendamm/Adalberstrabe in 1985. Nora Aurienne made arrows and snakes seemingly flung against the Wall; and, most famously, in October 1986 Keith Haring created a

---

① 无缝合的。
② 鲍德里亚，法国哲学家、现代社会思想大师。
③ 术语。
④ 叠加。
⑤ 刺激。
⑥ Michel de Certeau: 米歇尔·德·塞杜，法国耶稣会信徒、学者。
⑦ 规定。
⑧ 仪式。
⑨ the Haus am Checkpoint Charlie: 柏林墙博物馆。

panoramic[①] mural[②] chaining his famous figures over a length of 100 m in the Zimmerstrabe next to Checkpoint Charlie. These graffiti projects all enacted the Wall's possibilities for being transgressed, and, in doing so, they turned it from an identifiable, stable and fixed "place" into what Michel de Certeau has called a "space" that is marked by movement rather than by stability, a concept that Marc Auge further developed into the idea of the "non-place." In turning the Wall from an ugly architectonic monster into a gigantic global art work of an immeasurable economic value, the art competition aimed at transforming its owner from a financially broke totalitarian[③] regime into an art collector and dealer. Selling the art works, however, would imply breaking down the Wall.

And so it happened.

However, the bargain was not struck by the authoritative first person that had built the Wall as a bulwark[④] against freedom of travel, trade and expression of opinions. Rather, when the Wall came down, murals were broken out of it by souvenir hunters and other "Wall peckers," and the best pieces were offered up for sale. Even today, visitors to the Haus am Checkpoint Charlie can pick up a 5 g piece of inner German history for 20 euros. Only a few parts of the former Wall were conserved to become the official Wall memorial: namely, a section near the Berlin Parliament carrying a giant fleeing figure by Jonathan Borofsky, and another one along the Bernauer Strasse in Wedding. In retrospect, it seems that it was precisely this economic drive which made the Wall come down. The symbolic forecast of a successful transgression by means of graffiti art works became true in the first place in that economic sense of a free and globalized market economy.

---

① 全景的。
② 壁画。
③ 极权主义的。
④ 堡垒。

Such issues of ownership, along with matters of preservation, according to Mieke Bal, belong to the central interests of the museum that, as an official institution, holds the first-person position of a true "value factory." At a time when the power legitimizing any civil, military, political or trade action across the border was exclusively reserved for the officials of the GDR, the graffiti symbolically superimposing West onto East shocked the basis of this first-person authority. Its discursive utterances (Do not cross! Stay East! Stay West!) were now answered by those otherwise mute subjects to whom they were directed or who, at least, witnessed them passively. In this shift of speech act positions, the Wall did not just expose graffiti, but it also put on display its specific mode of showing; to echo Bal once more, the double exposure of a subject showing an object and, in doing so, staging an exposure of the self.

The Wall, I conclude, has always been a "double exposure" in this sense. Whereas the GDR intended it to be invisible and mute, it was, at least from the outside (the Western side), resplendent[①] and jarring[②]. And when its symbolic forecast was fulfilled, it destroyed its own colourful archival memory store and became invisible. It disappeared, but not without leaving a trace, taking the shape of new discourses and new "museum's talks" on the dialectic split of the double exposures of "in/visibilities." Thus regarded the museum can no longer claim to function only as a constative[③]. Its discourse also functions as a performative because it performs the subject, tagging or spraying in the same process that generates the graffiti's addressees as travelers, or, to echo Marc Auge[④], "commuters between places." In this double take, the museum *does* graffiti as a writing on the wall which has "force" *because* it

---

① 华丽的。
② 突出的。
③ 述愿的，表述的。
④ **Marc Auge:** 马克·奥格，法国人类学家。

has "meaning."

酷杀：涂鸦博物馆

◎ 索尼娅·尼夫

View from the West Berlin Side of Graffiti Art on the Wall in 1986
1986 年柏林墙西面的涂鸦艺术

柏林墙的书写

区分里外、左右、东西的政治在柏林墙事件中造成了巨大反响。没有任何其他一堵墙能像柏林墙一样提供如此理想的画面，柏林墙成为有史以来最大涂鸦工程的混凝土画布。

1961 年 8 月 13 日，德意志民主共和国开始修建被称为"反法西斯保护墙"的柏林墙，在西柏林用围墙围起了长达 164 公里的区域，将西柏林变成"真正社会主义"本土上的一座岛屿。起初，这座墙用砖砌起，上面用铁丝网拦着，后来不断加固、不断将其现代化……

第四代柏林墙响起了涂鸦者的声音，这种情况越发如此，因为一幅幅涂鸦画密密地交织在一起，像一张无边的画布一样，民主德国甚至粉刷了这张画布。为了粉刷柏林墙的西面，需要为被边境武装卫兵监视的粉刷工们修建一座笼子。政府希望通过粉刷柏林墙可以使两边人民习惯乃至无视这堵墙,因为"没有任何东西可以像纪念碑一样令人熟视无睹"。

然而,对于这座纪念碑式的柏林墙,它的焕然一新确实产生了不同……因为它不知不觉间将看不见的东西变得看得见了。涂鸦者通过将墙体的实际存在(包括它的政治秩序)与艺术品相结合,玩味着事物的不可见性。或者,按照米克·巴尔的说法,使"(否则)保持沉默的物体作出了回答"。

Mis en abime in Berlin Wedding, Bernauer Strasse
位于柏林维丁区伯诺尔街的"图像中的图像"

柏林墙回答了。经常使用的母题包括裂缝、孔洞、门、窗户,或者拉链状开口,这些图案可以产生打开另一世界的图像中图像的错觉。下图是 1988 年伊朗画家亚迪加·阿泽孜在柏林克罗伊茨贝格区的列金路和鲁斯克纳路之间所作的涂鸦作品。这幅画运用三维逼真绘画技巧,复原了一座顶部与中殿断开的残缺教堂的景象。这一景象的错觉逻辑没有使柏林墙作为一种分隔力量发挥作用,相反,它矛盾地将分隔墙体作为一种连接媒介。这幅涂鸦忽略了墙体的建筑框架,创造了一处无缝的"地方",它穿越了这处地方,或者用鲍亚的术语,它"叠加"或者"突出"了这处地方。涂鸦至少象征性地将柏林墙变成转换区域而不是分隔区域。

Yadiga Azizy, Mural in Berlin Kreuzberg between Legien-and Leuschnerdamm
亚迪加·阿泽孜在柏林克罗伊茨贝格区的列金路和鲁斯克纳路之间的涂鸦作品

跨越边境

对米歇尔·德·塞杜来说，这样的构成、置换或跨越边境是一种话语行为，是允许有权如此的主体规定或组织边境所执行的言语行为。德·塞杜用古罗马牧师与任何外国人接触之前所进行的礼仪为例，讨论边境的行为范围……当牧师准备占领外国土地时，首先象征性拥有这块土地，这里我主张，柏林墙的涂鸦象征性地征服了边境空间。1982年，世界各地的艺术家应邀参加由柏林墙博物馆主办的"描绘柏林墙，征服柏林墙"涂鸦大赛。1985年，在贝塔尼恩路/阿达尔贝特街，克里斯托弗·布彻特和蒂里·诺伊尔创作了色彩明亮、别出心裁的《红兔子》；诺拉·艾德丽安绘制了好像要扑向柏林墙的箭头和蛇；更著名的是，1986年10月，基思·哈林在季默街紧挨着柏林墙博物馆创作了一幅长达一百多米的一连串人形全景壁画。这些涂鸦工程都确立了跨越柏林墙的可能性，于是，这些作品将柏林墙从可识别的、稳定的、固定的"地点"，变成了米歇尔·德·塞杜所称的、以运动而不是以稳定为特征的"空间"，迈克·安基将"空间"概念进一步发展成"非地点"想法。涂鸦比赛将柏林墙从一个丑陋的建筑怪物变成经济价值无法衡量的全球巨大艺术品,它的目的在于将其主人从一个经济上破产的极权政权变为艺术品的收集者和交易者。然而,出售这些艺术品将意味着摧毁柏林墙。

Red Dope on Rabbits 《红兔子》

Berlin Zimmerstrasse 柏林季默街涂鸦

而事情真的发生了。

然而,买卖柏林墙的主体不是修建柏林墙作为阻止旅游、贸易和言论自由的堡垒的有权如此的主体;柏林墙倒了,纪念品搜寻者和其他"柏林墙淘宝者"从中淘出许多壁画,出价拍卖其中一些优秀作品。即便今天,参观柏林墙博物馆的游客花二十欧元就能淘到一块五克重的德国国内历史片断。只有少数保留下来的前柏林墙墙体片断成为官方的纪念墙:即靠近柏林议会处,由乔纳森·博罗夫斯基创作的《奔放的人》的那一段,还有在维丁区沿着伯诺尔大街的另外一段。回想起来,似乎正是因为经济利益的驱动才使柏林墙倒下了。用涂鸦艺术作品实现成功跨越的象征性预示首先因为自由的全球化市场经济意识而变成现实。

Running Man 《奔跑的人》

Dismantled Pieces of the Berlin Wall, Bernauer Strasse, Wedding
维丁区伯诺尔街被拆散的柏林墙

根据米克·巴尔的理论，柏林墙的归属和保护问题属于博物馆感兴趣的中心问题，博物馆作为官方机构，占有真正"价值工厂"主体的位置。当时，只有民主德国的官员才有权将跨越边境的任何民事、军事、政治或贸易行为合法化，涂鸦象征性地将西方强加于东方，动摇了这种主体的权威地位。那些涂鸦话语所针对的或者至少被动地见证的这种主体权利回答了涂鸦的话语声（严禁超越！待在东边！待在西边！）。如果不是因为涂鸦，这些主体将一直是沉默无语的。这种话语行为的位置转换中，柏林墙不仅展示了涂鸦，还展示了涂鸦独特的表达方式；再次引用巴尔的话，对主体的双重展示不仅展示了某个物体，而且这样一来，还展示了自己。

总而言之，在这个意义上，柏林墙一直进行着"双重展示"。当民主德国打算让柏林墙不显眼、不讲话时，柏林墙至少从外部（西边）表现出华丽与壮观。当涂鸦完成了象征性预示，它毁灭了自己五颜六色的档案记忆存储，变得不显眼了。涂鸦消失了，但它在辩证划分"看见/看不见"的双重展示中并非没有留下任何痕迹，并非没有采用新的话语形式或新的"博物馆话语"形式。于是，博物馆无法再主张自己能够作为一种既定的因素运行。博物馆的话语也可以作为一种行为方式发挥作用，因为博物馆以将涂鸦的观众变为旅行者的同样程序执行了主体的标记或者喷涂；或者用马克·奥格的说法，涂鸦"往返于两地之间"。在这种双重任务中，博物馆将涂鸦作为墙面书写，这种书写因为其丰富意义而具有力量。

Chapter 3   Copenhagen

Copenhagen is like a fine, dry martini.
—Steve

Quotes Featuring Copenhagen

🍃 If Copenhagen were a person, that person would be generous, beautiful, elderly, but with a flair.

—Connie Nielsen

🍃 So the old Copenhagen interpretation needs to be generalized, needs to be replaced by something that can be used for the whole universe, and can be used also in cases where there is plenty of individuality and history.

—Murray Gell-Mann

🍃 Being born in a duck yard does not matter, if only you are hatched from a swan's egg.

—Hans Christian Andersen

Key Words

Fairy tales, spires, and landmarks.

Questions

1. Copenhagen is a city of fairy tales. How do stories or literary writings influence your impression of a city?
2. Do you know any fairy tales written by Hans Christian Andersen?
3. Can you name some English words or phrases that come from Andersen's stories? Try to explain these words or phrases.

Spotlight Copenhagen   迷人的哥本哈根

The word "spotlight" means strong light directed on to a particular place or person. No doubt, this place or person will become the center of attention. The following article tells how Copenhagen attracts people's attention.

Spotlight on Copenhagen[①]

Are you too old for fairy tales? If you think so, Copenhagen is sure to change your mind.

　　See the city first from the water. In the harbor sits Denmark's best-known landmark: the Little Mermaid[②]. Remember her? She left the world of the Sea People in search of a human soul in one of Hans Christian Andersen's beloved fantasies. From the harbor you can get a feel

---

① 选自 http://www.ebigear.com/news-124-30737.html。
② the Little Mermaid: 小美人鱼铜像，根据安徒生童话《海的女儿》铸塑而成。

for the attractive "city of green spires①." At twilight or in cloudy weather, the copper-covered spires of old castles and churches lend the city a dream-like atmosphere. You'll think you've stepped into a watercolor painting.

Copenhagen is a city on a human scale. You don't have to hurry to walk the city's center in less than an hour. Exploring it will take much longer. But that's easy. Copenhagen was the first city to declare a street for pedestrians only. The city has less traffic noise and pollution than any other European capital.

Stroll away from the harbor along the riverbanks, you'll see the modest Amalienborg Palace first. Completed in the mid-18th century, it still houses the royal family. The Danish Royal Guard is on duty. At noon, you'll watch the changing of the guard. The guards are not just for show, however. Danes will always remember their heroism on April 9, 1940. When the Nazis invaded Denmark, the guards aimed their guns and fired. Soldiers fell on both sides. The guards would all have been killed if the king hadn't ordered them to surrender.

Churches and castles are almost all that remain of the original city. Copenhagen became the capital of Denmark in 1445. During the late 16th century, trade grew, and so did the city. But fires in 1728 and 1795 destroyed the old wooden structures. Much of what we see today dates from the 19th and early 20th centuries.

See one of the spires up close—really close—at the 17th-century Church of Our Savior. Brave souls may climb the 150 stairs winding outside the spire to its top. If you're afraid of heights, or if it's a windy day, you can forget the climb. But then you'll miss the magnificent view.

Once the earth is under your feet again (you'll enjoy the feeling), cross the nearest bridge to Castle Island. The curious yet majestic-looking

---

① 尖塔。

spire ahead tops the oldest stock exchange in Europe, built in 1619. Its spire is formed from the entwined tails of three dragons. They represent Denmark, Sweden and Norway.

Keep going, to the Christiansborg Palace. The town of Copenhagen began here. Stop and visit the medieval castle. Parliament and the Royal Reception Chambers are open, too. Then continue to Nyhavn, a narrow waterway dug by soldiers in 1673. You'll understand why Hans Christian Andersen made this charming waterway his home. A specially-built mirror outside his apartment window allowed him to peek unseen at the world outside.

Nyhavn is peaceful, an ideal place for lingering and people-watching. You'll usually see them dressed casually, though they are among Europe's rich people. Danes are taught not to stand out in a crowd. But they do know how to party, especially during holidays.

To see them having fun, and to have some fun yourself, cross Andersens Boulevard and enter Tivoli Gardens. You won't be alone. More than five million people a year come here. They come to dance, dine, take in outdoor and indoor concerts, see ballets and laugh at the comedy. One tip: Bring a lot of money. About 20 restaurants are among the city's most expensive. Even without money, you can still enjoy the proud old trees, the colored night lights and the beautiful gardens. You might feel as if you are in a fairy tale.

美不胜收的哥本哈根

你是否已经老得不想听童话了？如果你是这么认为的话，哥本哈根一定能够改变你的想法。

要看这座城市，先从水看起。丹麦最有名的标志性建筑——小小美人鱼就坐落在港口处。记得她吗？在汉斯·克里斯蒂安·安徒生的一个童话里，她离开了海底世界，想变成一个真正的人。安徒生的许多幻想故事都很受欢迎哩。从这个港口你可以领略到这座迷人的"绿色塔尖之城"的魅力。黎明时分或天气阴霾的时候，旧堡垒和教堂的镀铜塔尖给这个城市蒙上了梦一般的气氛。你会以为自己步入了一幅水彩画中。

The Little Mermaid　小美人鱼铜像

　　哥本哈根是一个很人性化的城市。你不需要在一小时内匆匆地将市中心走完。考察这个城市要花上更长的时间。但那也是件很轻松的事。哥本哈根是第一个划出步行街的城市。比起欧洲其他国家的首都，这个城市的交通噪音和污染少了许多。

　　自港口沿着河岸漫步，最先映入眼帘的是风格朴实的阿玛利安堡皇宫。阿玛利安堡皇宫于十八世纪中期完工，皇室家族至今居住于此。皇家卫队仍在这里执行任务。中午可以观赏卫兵换岗的仪式。但是，这些卫兵绝不仅仅是装装样子而已。丹麦人永远记得他们在1940年4月9日的英勇事迹。当时纳粹分子入侵丹麦，这些卫兵举枪瞄准并且开火。双方都有士兵阵亡。如果国王不叫他们投降的话，这些卫兵可能全都战死沙场了。

Amalienborg Palace　阿玛利安堡皇宫

教堂与古堡大概是古城遗留下来的唯一的东西。哥本哈根于1445年成为丹麦的首都。十六世纪末，贸易发展带动了城市的发展。但是，城中的旧式木建筑在1728年和1795年的两场大火中毁于一旦。今天我们所看到的大部分建筑都是在十九世纪和二十世纪初建造的。

仔细看其中一个塔尖——真正靠近地看——这座建于十七世纪的"我们的救世主"教堂。勇敢的人可能会爬上那在尖塔外蜿蜒而上直通塔顶的一百五十层阶梯。如果你有恐高症，或者当天风很大，那就免了吧。不过，你会因此错过那壮观的景色。

当你再次稳稳地踏在土地上（你会喜欢这种感觉的），你可以通过最近的桥到城堡岛。前方有个1619年建造的欧洲最古老的证券交易中心，上面的塔尖奇特而又宏伟。塔尖由三只龙尾缠绕而成，分别代表丹麦、瑞典和挪威。

继续往前，走到基斯汀堡。哥本哈根源自此处。停下来游览这个中世纪的古堡。议院和皇家接待室也同样开放，然后继续往尼哈芬走去，它是1673年由士兵挖成的狭窄水道。你会明白为什么汉斯·克里斯蒂安·安徒生把这个迷人的水道当成自己的家。通过公寓窗外的一面特制的镜子，他能够看到外面的世界而又不被人发现。

尼哈芬是个宁静的地方，它也是个逗留和观看行人的理想处所。虽然这里的居民是欧洲最有钱的人，但是你通常都会看到他们穿得很随意。丹麦人所受的教育是在人群中不要显得鹤立鸡群。但是他们却很喜爱聚会,特别是在假日的时候。

要看丹麦人嬉乐,要想自己找到乐趣,你可以走过安徒生大道,进入提弗利花园,在这儿你是不会寂寞的。每年有超过五百万的人来此旅游。他们来这里跳舞、就餐、欣赏户外和室内音乐会,看芭蕾舞表演,观看喜剧,开怀大笑。给你一个建议:多带钱。二十家左右的餐厅是本城里最昂贵的。即使没有钱,你仍可以欣赏那些傲人的老树、五光十色的彩灯,以及美丽的花园。你可能会以为自己置身于童话故事当中呢。

Copenhagen of Fairy Tales 童话哥本哈根

Hans Christian Andersen wrote fairy tales with Copenhagen as the background. No doubt, the city is now in fairy tales, by fairy tales, and of fairy tales. The following tale tells that, sometimes, an incorrectly relayed message will become more erroneous in its circulation.

"It's Quite True!"[①]

◎ Hans Christian Andersen

"That is a terrible affair!" said a Hen; and she said it in a quarter of the town where the occurrence had not happened. "That is a terrible affair in the poultry-house. I cannot sleep alone tonight! It is quite fortunate that there are many of us on the roost[②] together!" And she told a tale at which

---

① 选自安徒生著,纪飞编译:《安徒生童话全集》(*Andersen's Fairy Tales Collection*),北京:清华大学出版社,2006年。
② 栖木,鸡棚。

the feathers of the other birds stood on end, and the cock's comb fell down flat. It's quite true!

But we will begin at the beginning; and that was in a poultry-house in another part of the town. The sun went down, and the fowls[①] jumped up on their perch[②] to roost. There was a Hen, with white feathers and short legs, who laid her right number of eggs, and was a respectable hen in every way; as she flew up on to the roost she pecked herself with her beak[③], and a little feather fell out.

"There it goes!" said she; "the more I peck myself the handsomer I grow!" And she said it quite merrily, for she was a joker among the hens, though, as I have said, she was very respectable; and then she went to sleep.

It was dark all around; hen sat by hen, but the one that sat next to the merry Hen did not sleep: she heard and she didn't hear, as one should do in this world if one wishes to live in quiet; but she could not refrain from telling it to her next neighbour.

"Did you hear what was said here just now? I name no names; but here is a hen who wants to peck her feathers out to look well. If I were a cock I should despise her."

And just above the Hens sat the Owl, with her husband and her little owlets; the family had sharp ears, and they all heard every word that the neighbouring Hen had spoken, and they rolled their eyes, and the Mother-Owl clapped her wings and said,

"Don't listen to it! But I suppose you heard what was said there? I heard it with my own ears, and one must hear much before one's ears fall off. There is one among the fowls who has so completely forgotten what is becoming conduct in a hen that she pulls out all her feathers, and then lets

---

① 家禽，鸡。
② 栖木。
③ 喙。

the cock see her."

"*Prenez garde aux enfants*[①]," said the Father-Owl. "That's not fit for the children to hear."

"Hoo! hoo! to-whoo!" they both hooted in front of the neighbour's dovecot to the doves within. "Have you heard it? Have you heard it? Hoo! hoo! there's a hen who has pulled out all her feathers for the sake of the cock. She'll die with cold, if she's not dead already."

"Coo! doo! Where, where?" cried the Pigeons.

"In the neighbour's poultry-yard. I've as good as seen it myself. It's hardly proper to repeat the story, but it's quite true!"

"Believe it! believe every single word of it!" cooed the Pigeons, and they cooed down into their own poultry-yard. "There's a hen, and some say that there are two of them, that they have plucked[②] out all their feathers, that they may not look like the rest, and that they may attract the cock's attention. That's a bold game, for one may catch cold and die of a fever, and they are both dead."

"Wake up! wake up!" crowed the Cock, and he flew up on to the fence; his eyes were still very heavy with sleep, but yet he crowed. "Three hens have died of an unfortunate attachment to a cock. They have plucked out all their feathers. That's a terrible story. I won't keep it to myself; let it travel farther."

"Let it travel farther!" piped the Bats; and the fowls clucked and the cocks crowed, "Let it go farther! let it go farther!" And so the story travelled from poultry-yard to poultry-yard, and at last came back to the place from which it had gone forth. "Five fowls," it was told, "have plucked out all their feathers to who which of them had become thinnest out of love to the cock; and then they have pecked each other and fallen

---

① *Prenez garde aux enfants*: 法语，意思是"提防孩子们听到"。在欧洲人眼中，猫头鹰是一种很聪明的鸟儿，是鸟类中的所谓"上流社会人士"，故此讲法文。

② 拔掉。

down dead, to the shame and disgrace of their families, and to the great loss of the proprietor①."

And the Hen who had lost the little loose feather, of course did not know her own story again; and as she was a very respectable Hen, she said.

"I despise those fowls; but there are many of that sort. One ought not to hush up such a thing, and I shall do what I can that the story may get into the papers, and then it will be spread over all the country, and that will serve those fowls right, and their families too."

It was put into the newspaper: it was printed; and it's quite true—that one little feather may swell till it becomes five fowls.

"完全是真的！"②

◎ 汉斯·克里斯蒂安·安徒生

"那真是一件可怕的事情！"母鸡说。她讲这话的地方不是城里发生这个故事的那个区域。"那是鸡屋里的一件可怕的事情！我今夜不敢一个人睡觉了！真是幸运，我们今晚大伙儿都栖在一根木头上！"于是她讲了一个故事，弄得别的母鸡羽毛根根竖起，而公鸡的冠却垂下来了。这完全是真的！

不过我们还是从头开始吧。事情是发生在城里另一区的鸡屋里面。太阳落下了，所有的母鸡都飞上了栖木。有一只母鸡，羽毛很白，腿很短，她总是按规定的数目下蛋。在各方面说起来，她是一只很有身份的母鸡。当她飞到栖木上去的时候，她用嘴啄了自己几下，弄得有一根小羽毛落下来了。

"事情就是这样！"她说，"我越把自己啄得厉害，我就越漂亮！"她说这话的神情是很快乐的，因为她是母鸡中一个心情愉快的人物，

---

① 业主，所有人。
② 出自 http://www.tianyabook.com/antusheng/antu26.html。

虽然我刚才说过她是一只很有身份的鸡。不久她就睡着了。

周围一片漆黑。母鸡跟母鸡站在一边，不过离这只母鸡最近的那只母鸡却睡不着。她在静听——一只耳朵进，一只耳朵出；一个人要想在世界上安静地活下去，就非得如此做不可。不过她禁不住要把她所听到的事情告诉她的邻居：

"你听到过刚才的话吗？我不愿意把名字指出来。不过有一只母鸡，她为了要好看，啄掉自己的羽毛。假如我是公鸡的话，我才真要瞧不起她呢。"

在这些母鸡的上面住着一只猫头鹰和她的丈夫以及孩子。她这一家人的耳朵都很尖：邻居刚才所讲的话，他们都听见了。他们翻翻眼睛，于是猫头鹰妈妈就拍拍翅膀说：

"不要听那类的话！不过我想你们都听到了刚才的话吧？我是亲耳听到过的；你得听了很多才能记住。有一只母鸡完全忘记了母鸡所应当有的礼貌：她甚至把她的羽毛都啄掉了，好让公鸡把她看个仔细。"

"提防孩子们听到，"猫头鹰爸爸说。"这不是孩子们可以听的话。"

"我还是要把这话告诉对面的猫头鹰！她是一个很正派的猫头鹰，值得来往！"于是猫头鹰妈妈就飞走了。

"呼！呼！呜——呼！"他们俩都喊起来，而喊声就被下边鸽子笼里面的鸽子听见了。"你们听到过那样的话没有？呼！呼！有一只母鸡，她把她的羽毛都啄掉了，想讨好公鸡！她一定会冻死的——如果她现在还没有死的话。呜——呼！"

"在什么地方？在什么地方？"鸽子咕咕地叫着。

"在对面的那个屋子里！我几乎可说是亲眼看见的。把它讲出来真不像话，不过那完全是真的！"

"真的！真的！每个字都是真的！"所有的鸽子说，同时向下边的养鸡场咕咕地叫："有一只母鸡，也有人说是两只，她们都把所有的羽毛都啄掉，为的是要与众不同，借此引起公鸡的注意。这是一种冒险的玩意儿，因为这样她们就容易伤风，结果一定会发高热死掉。她们两位现在都死了。"

"醒来呀！醒来呀！"公鸡大叫着，同时向围墙上飞去。他的眼睛仍然带着睡意，不过他仍然在大叫。"三只母鸡因为与一只公鸡在爱情上发生不幸，全都死去了。她们把她们的羽毛啄得精光。这是一件很丑的事情。我不愿意把它关在心里；让大家都知道它吧！"

"让大家都知道它吧！"蝙蝠说。于是母鸡叫，公鸡啼。"让大家都知道它吧！让大家都知道它吧！"于是这个故事就从这个鸡屋传到那个鸡屋，最后又传回它原来所传出的那个地方去。

这故事变成："五只母鸡把她们的羽毛都啄得精光，为的是要比较出她们之中谁因为被那只公鸡抛弃而变得最消瘦。后来她们相互啄得流血，弄得五只鸡全都死掉。这使得她们的家庭蒙受了羞辱，她们的主人蒙受了极大的损失。"

那只落掉了一根羽毛的母鸡当然不知道这个故事就是她自己的故事。因为她是一只很有身份的母鸡，所以她就说：

"我瞧不起那些母鸡；不过像这类的贼东西有的是！我们不应该把这类事儿掩藏起来。我尽我的力量使这故事在报纸上发表，让全国都知道。那些母鸡活该倒霉！她们的家庭也活该倒霉！"

这故事终于在报纸上被刊登出来了。这完全是真的：一根小小的羽毛可以变成五只母鸡。

Who Is Hans Christian Andersen?

☞　1805–1875.

☞　Danish author, fairy tale writer, and poet, noted for his children's stories.

☞　Major stories: "The Steadfast Tin Soldier," "The Snow Queen," "The Little

Mermaid," "Thumbelina," "The Little Match Girl," and "The Ugly Duckling."
- ☞ His poetry and stories were translated into more than 150 languages.
- ☞ His stories inspired motion pictures, plays, ballets, and animated films.
- ☞ "The Emperor's New Clothes" and "The Ugly Duckling" passed into the English language as well-known expressions.
- ☞ April 2, Andersen's birthday, is celebrated as Int'l Children's Book Day.

Chapter 4   Dublin

When I die Dublin will be written in my heart.
—James Joyce

Quotes Featuring Dublin

- I was happy in Dublin because it is very cosmopolitan.

—Rick Savage

- If you're a writer in Dublin and you write a snatch of dialogue, everyone thinks you lifted it from Joyce. The whole idea that he owns language as it is spoken in Dublin is a nonsense. He didn't invent the Dublin accent. It's as if you're encroaching on his area or it's a given that he's on your shoulder. It gets on my nerves.

—Roddy Doyle

- I go off into Dublin and two days later I'm spotted walking by the Liffey with a whole bunch of new friends.

—Ron Wo

Key Words
History, tourism, city life, and literature.

Questions
1. Dublin is a city of history. How is a city's history represented by its culture, literature and architecture?
2. According to Naoise O'Muiri's speech "People Make Cities Great and Different," what is characteristic of Dublin?
3. How does a city influence its writers or vice versa?

Dublin in History 历史都柏林

The history of Dublin is presented as a burden. However, this burden also exerts a force that makes the city rich in literature.

The Burden of History[①]

◎ John Tomedi

Through an intolerable heap of historical ironies, Dublin, the capital of Ireland, came to produce some of the greatest literature in the English language. Its history is labyrinthine[②]: Dublin has seen immigrations, invasions, and emigrations; it has suffered shifts in politics, in religion; it has had times of extraordinary wealth and times of poverty; it has viewed

---

① 选自 *Bloom's Literary Place—Dublin*, by John Tomedi, with Introduction by Harold Bloom, Philadelphia: Chelsea House Publishers, 2005。
② 迷宫似的，曲折的。

itself with self-deprecation and chauvinism①; it has been a center for nationalism and internationalism. Perhaps it has endured as much as any old town, but few cities have maintained the degree of creative intellect—and imparted such a sense of place—to project that storied history into its literature.

There is something extraordinary in this. All cities, to a certain degree, become cultural centers, drawing talented and creative individuals from the surrounding countryside. But until relatively recent times, Dublin has had little affinity to the rest of the Irish population. It never spoke Irish; its population was of English colonists and their Anglo-Irish children, who too often cared little for (or sought to be rid of) the culture of the country's Gaelic②-speaking, Catholic population. Considering this, it is not so surprising that Dublin's literature has always been in English. Even the fact that Dublin's is a markedly different literary tradition from that of the rest of English literature can be explained in post-colonial terms. More intriguing is the fact that Dublin has offered up some of the greatest authors in the English language. By what magic had this city, a small, provincial capital for much of its history, come to engender the satires③ of Swift, the speeches of Burke, the plays of Sheridan and Synge and O'Casey, the lyrics④ of Moore, the essays of Davis, the narratives of Carleton and Stephens and O'Brien and Joyce, and the poetry of Mangan and Yeats? Something in the water, perhaps?

Around the turn of the twentieth century, William Butler Yeats became the center of a literary movement in Dublin that looked to the ancient Irish past and the folklore of the Irish peasantry⑤ for inspiration.

---

① 沙文主义。
② 盖尔语。
③ 讽刺作品。
④ 抒情诗。
⑤ 农民阶级。

Offshoots of this movement, despite an earlier infatuation[①] with bucolic[②] Ireland, found Irish character in urban Dublin. The Irish literary revival became one of the most productive periods in the history of literature, and in the course of the movement the rest of the world discovered what the Irish peasants had long known: that the people of Ireland are natural storytellers. Through the twists and turns of Dublin's story, somewhere between the Irish capacity for wit, humor, and narrative, the Dublin's struggle to identify what sort of culture it was, a unique and impressive literary tradition emerged.

Jonathan Swift was the first of the great men of letters to take up the plight of the Irish. But while Swift himself was seminal[③] to the culture that grew out of the city, it was Dublin that made Swift, not the other way around. And it was the warring confluence of kings and cultures that made Dublin.

历史重负[④]

穿越历史的重重烟云,爱尔兰首都都柏林创造了英语语言文学史上最为光辉的一部分。都柏林有着错综复杂的历史:异族入侵、国民外迁、移民迁入,它都经历过;政治变换、宗教更替,它都遭受过;国富民强、一穷二白,它都遇到过;自我贬低、沙文主义,它都主张过;民族主义、国际主义,它都曾经是中心。也许,古老的城市都曾经承受过很多,但是很少有哪个城市像都柏林一样保有如此高的创造性才智和如此浓厚的乡土情结,进而化历史为文学。

这里有一点特别值得关注。所有的城市,在某种程度上都是一个

---

① 迷恋。
② 田园风味的。
③ 深远的。
④ 出自白玉杰、豆红丽译:《都柏林文学地图》,上海:上海交通大学出版社,2011年。

文化中心，吸引着周边乡村的有识之士。但是，都柏林不一样，直到近年来，都柏林对其余爱尔兰民众一直没有什么吸引力。在都柏林，其人民则为英国殖民者及其盎格鲁裔子孙，他们不关注（甚至试图脱离）这个国家讲盖尔语的天主教人民的文化。鉴于此，都柏林文学作品一直都是用英语写成的。不仅如此，都柏林的文学传统与其余英语国家的文学传统的显著差异也可以从后殖民主义的角度加以阐释。更让人好奇的是：都柏林涌现了一批最为伟大的英语作家。究竟是什么魔力使得这个历史上的省会小城孕育出斯威夫特的辛辣讽刺，伯克的精彩演说，谢立丹、辛格、奥卡西等人的伟大剧作，穆尔的美妙诗歌，戴维斯的精美散文，卡尔顿、斯蒂芬斯、奥布赖恩、乔伊斯等人的传神叙事以及曼根和叶芝的唯美诗歌？难道真的是水土养人吗？

二十世纪之初，叶芝成为都柏林文学运动的核心人物，该运动向古爱尔兰历史和爱尔兰民间传说寻求灵感。作为该运动的衍生物，爱尔兰文学一改以往对田园生活的迷恋，转而在都柏林都市里寻求爱尔兰角色。爱尔兰文艺复兴成为文学史上最为多产的阶段之一，与此同时，在文学运动过程中，外界也终于发现了一直以来爱尔兰广大农民所熟知的一点：爱尔兰人都是天生的故事家。在都柏林迂回曲折的历史中，在爱尔兰人天赋的智慧、幽默和叙述才能中，在都柏林寻找自身文化认同的奋斗中，一种独一无二、令人印象深刻的文学传统也应运而生。

乔纳森·斯威夫特是爱尔兰文学史上的开路先锋。尽管斯威夫特本人对都柏林文化有着重大影响，但是都柏林造就了斯威夫特，而非斯威夫特造就了都柏林；造就都柏林的是国王之间与文化之间的冲突与汇合。

> **Who Is Harold Bloom?**
>
> ☞ Born in 1930.
> ☞ American literary critic and Sterling Professor of Humanities at Yale Univ.
> ☞ He received his PhD in 1955 at Yale and won the John Addison Porter Prize the following year.
> ☞ He teaches two classes at Yale: one on the plays of Shakespeare, the other on poetry from Geoffrey Chaucer to Hart Crane.
> ☞ He has published more than 20 books of literary criticism, several books discussing religion, and one novel, and edited hundreds of anthologies since 1959.
> ☞ His books were translated into more than 40 languages.
> ☞ He was honored as "probably the most celebrated literary critic in the United States," and "America's best-known man of letters."

Dublin in Speech 演说都柏林

At the Summit of the World Cities Tourism Federation, Dublin's Lord Mayor Naoise O'Muiri delivered a speech in which he addressed the uniqueness of the city.

People Make Cities Great and Different[1]

◎ Naoise O'Muiri

We live in a global village. Travel anywhere and you will find global

---

① 选自都柏林市长纳欧伊斯·欧·缪瑞在 2012 年 9 月 15 日 "世界旅游城市联合会" 成立大会上的发言，http://www.bjta.gov.cn/wngzzt/sjcslhkkms/xsfk_xsfk/352955.htm。

brands and hotel rooms that are the same in any city in the world. These similarities can be comforting to the international traveler but we travel to experience difference and to learn from other places and cultures. So we need to ensure that each of our cities offers something unique that attracts people for business, pleasure and education.

What we value most in my city of Dublin is the fusion of people, ideas and places. Put these three things together and you create the unique characteristics that make each city different. We need to understand and nurture the uniqueness of each of our cities for this is what gives us the competitive edge[①] in an increasingly similar world.

The greatest asset any city can have is its people, the greatest resource is its history and culture and the greatest driver is its creativity and innovation. I would like therefore to speak about the uniqueness of my city of Dublin. It is a small city by world standards, just 1.8 million people, but it is a city of big ideas and creative energy. Its size is part of its charm as you can walk the city easily and you are always close to the green countryside, the mountains and the sea. From the city centre in a mere 20 minutes you can travel to the green countryside or the sandy beaches along the sea. Dublin is a unique place, a city founded on a river where the River Liffey flows into the Irish Sea, with mountains to the South, and rich farmland to the West and the North. It is the gateway to Ireland. It is an historic city, founded by Viking[②] traders from Norway and Denmark, and a city that has been shaped by many cultural influences.

It is that historical and current interaction of different cultures in Dublin that has made us a global city. We are also shaped by our extensive trading relationships with every corner of the world. Our history of colonial occupation has also played a key role in the shaping of Dublin. Because of centuries of emigration and exile you will find people of Irish

---

① 优势。
② 北欧海盗，斯堪的纳维亚人。

origin in almost every nation on the earth. They have helped shaped the politics, the education systems, the business life, and the culture of countries as diverse as Chile, Japan, France, South Africa, Russia, the United States, Britain and Australia. Dublin has always through its people and the Irish love of poetry, song and literature been at the centre of the world.

Dublin is today a modern European city located on an island that is the bridge between mainland Europe and North America. We may be on an island but we are very much at the centre of what today remains the largest trading highway in the world between North America and Europe. While we have our own ancient language of Irish which is still spoken today, everyone speaks English and this is important in our economic and cultural positioning. Dublin is an easy place to visit, to live in and to study.

The major developments at Dublin Airport have made Dublin one of the most modern airports in Europe and one of the best for passenger and cargo travel. Today we also hold the unique distinction of being the only airport in Europe where you can leave for the United States and clear all United States Custom and Immigration procedures before you depart. This means the flights from Dublin land in America as domestic arrivals.

Dublin is a city open for visitors, open for investment and open for business. Did you know that Dublin attracts more international investment than any other European country? It has established a reputation for being a place of innovation, invention and creative business. Today Dublin is the European centre of global digital and technology research and business product development. Companies like IBM have chosen Dublin for their Global Smart City Centre. Companies like Intel have made Dublin the heart of their innovation labs throughout Europe. Financial companies like Citibank have placed their innovation centre in Dublin. Google and Facebook have developed their European Headquarters in Dublin. Why is this so?

Dublin and Ireland are recognised internationally as having a smart, well educated and technologically competent population. Dublin attracts because of its cultural life, its friendly people, its history and its green environment. It is a city that attracts many young people from every country in the world who come to work and study. Today you will hear over 140 languages spoken in its streets.

Dublin has a reputation as one of the best places in the world to do business. Dublin attracts people. The Irish are seen as one of the friendliest people on the planet and you will always be welcome in Dublin. We are interested in what others think and the opinions that they have. In fact today at this event I am pleased to show that we do wish to know what your opinion is of Dublin and to share with you our city. For the first time we have expanded our citizen survey beyond Dublin and we are asking people attending this Summit and visiting our stand at the expo[①] to participate in our Beijing Survey designed to find out what you know and think about Ireland. The web address for the survey and information on Dublin is www.dublin.ie/beijing and through this web address we will also encourage Irish People to visit Beijing.

International investors know that they will be able to recruit talent in Dublin. They know that Dublin is a European global centre of connection because of its people. Here they will find people from most cultures and language groups. This helps them to do global business from Dublin. Dublin is also one of the most competitive European destinations in terms of the cost of accommodation and of living.

People are Dublin's greatest asset and people like Dublin. In fact we have discovered that people who visit Dublin fall in love with the city. We were particularly proud in the last year to welcome world leaders such as the Chinese Vice President Xi Jinping and Barack Obama the President of

---

① 博览会。

the United States. One interesting fact that many may not know is that Barack Obama is of Irish descent, his great grandfather having emigrated to America from Ireland.

So Dublin is a good place to visit and invest in. It is a uniquely Irish city with a cosmopolitan[①] feel because of its strong global connections. It is a global centre for business, for education and for travel. We are delighted to be here at the launch of the World Cities Tourism Federation[②] because through this body we can promote Dublin as a destination. Cities need to work together to encourage their citizens to visit other citizens, learn about other cultures, broaden their own knowledge and explore co-operation in business. The World Cities Tourism Federation can provide us its members with a way of doing just that.

I congratulate our hosts and our sister city of Beijing on this imaginative and timely initiative. Cities are already our future, they are the drivers of our economies, the places of education and innovation, the space which shapes music, literature and cultural expression and the focal points of population growth on the planet. They are the gateways to our rural areas and rich countryside. They are the connecting points on our planet through which global transport, trade and commerce flow. So it is only right that today through the World Cities Tourism Federation we should promote tourism and collaborate in promoting to our citizens the idea of travel and cultural exchange between the member cities of the WCTF.

---

① 世界性的。
② World Cities Tourism Federation: 世界旅游城市联合会。2012 年 9 月 15 日在北京召开成立大会，是世界上首个以城市为主体的旅游组织，也是首个总部落户中国的国际性旅游组织。

人民令城市伟大、不同

◎ 纳欧伊斯·欧·缪瑞

我们生活在地球村。无论走到哪儿,在世界任何一个城市,都可以找到相同的全球品牌和旅馆房间。这些共性令国际游客很舒服,但是,我们旅游的目的是去感受不同,去了解其他地方和文化。因此,我们需要确保每座城市能够提供独特的东西,吸引人们因商业、娱乐、教育目的而光临。

在我们都柏林市,我们最珍视的是人民、思想和地理的融合。将这三方面综合起来,就会形成使得每个城市与众不同的独特之处。我们需要理解和培养每个城市的独特之处,正是如此,才能在日益同化的世界中赢得竞争优势。

每座城市拥有的最大财富是它的人民,最大的资源是它的历史和文化,最大的动力是它的创造力和创新性。因此,我想谈谈我们都柏林的独特之处。按照世界标准,这是个小城市,人口只有一百八十万,但是这是座拥有伟大思想和创新力量的城市。城市不大,这就是它的魅力所在,因为你可以很容易步行走遍全市,总可以近距离接触绿色的乡村、群山和大海。从市中心只需二十分钟就可以到达郁郁葱葱的乡村或沙滩海岸。都柏林是个与众不同的地方,这座城市依河而建,在此,利菲河流入爱尔兰海,南部群山环绕,西部和北部耕地富饶。都柏林是通往爱尔兰的门户,是座由来自挪威和丹麦的北欧商人建立的历史名城,一座受到多种文化影响而形成的城市。

River Liffey 利菲河

　　历史和现代不同文化的交流已经使都柏林成为一座国际城市。都柏林还受到与世界各地广泛贸易往来的影响。殖民占领的历史也在塑造都柏林的过程中起到重要作用。因为多个世纪的移民和流放，几乎在世界上任何一个国家都可以找到爱尔兰人后裔。这些人参与到了许多国家的政治、教育体系、商业生活和文化中，如智利、日本、法国、南非、俄罗斯、美国、英国和澳大利亚。都柏林总是因自己的人民及其对诗歌、歌曲和文学的爱尔兰式热爱而成为世界的中心。

　　今天的都柏林是座位于岛屿上的现代化欧洲城市，是连接欧洲大陆和北美的桥梁。虽然身处岛屿，但是都柏林是当今世界最重要的贸易通道北美和欧洲往来路线的中心。虽然我们今天还在使用古老的爱尔兰语，但是，这里每个人都会说英语，这对我们的经济和文化定位非常重要。都柏林是个适合观光、居住和学习的好地方。

　　都柏林机场的建设发展使其成为欧洲最现代的机场之一，也是最好的客运和货运机场之一。如今，它还是去美国无需报关和移民手续的欧洲唯一机场。这意味着从都柏林到美国的飞行就像在国内旅行一样方便。

　　都柏林是适合旅游、投资和经商的开放城市。你知道吗，都柏林比其他任何欧洲国家都吸引了更多的国际投资。都柏林作为创造、发明和新兴产业之地声名远扬。今天，都柏林是全球电子技术研究和商业产品开发的欧洲中心。一些公司如 IBM 已经选择都柏林作为自己的全球智能城市中心。一些公司如因特尔已将都柏林作为自己在全欧洲的创新实验室中心。像花旗银行这样的金融公司已将自己的开发中心放在都柏林。谷歌和 Facebook 已在都柏林发展了自己的欧洲总部。这是为什么？

都柏林和爱尔兰拥有国际公认的智慧、受过良好教育和技术能力强的人口。都柏林因其丰富的文化生活、友好的人民、悠久历史和绿色环境而充满吸引力。这座城市吸引了世界各国的许多年轻人前来学习、工作。今天你可以在都柏林的街道上听到一百四十多种语言。

都柏林令人向往，它拥有世界上开展业务最佳地点之一的口碑。爱尔兰人是地球上最友好的人民之一，在都柏林你总会受到热烈欢迎。我们有兴趣知道别人的想法和观点。事实上，在今天这个特别的时刻，我很高兴地表示：我们确实非常希望了解你们对都柏林的看法，希望与你们一起分享我们的城市。我们第一次将市民调查扩展到都柏林以外的地方，请求参加此次峰会和参观世博会展位的人们参加我们的北京调查，这次调查的设计目的是为了了解你们对爱尔兰知道些什么，你们如何看待爱尔兰。此次调查及都柏林的相关信息请登陆网址 www.dublin.ie/beijing，我们还将通过这个网站鼓励爱尔兰人参观北京。

国际投资商知道他们能够在都柏林招募到人才。他们知道都柏林因为它的人民而成为欧洲全球联系中心。在这里，他们可以找到来自大多数文化和语言群体的人才。这有助于他们立足都柏林在全球开展贸易。就住房费用和生活费用而言，都柏林也是欧洲最具竞争力的地方。

人民是都柏林最大的财富，人们喜欢都柏林。事实上，我们已经发现，来都柏林旅游的人们会爱上这座城市。尤为荣幸的是，去年都柏林迎来了世界领导人，如中国副主席习近平和美国总统贝拉克·奥巴马。有个许多人可能都不知道的事实，即奥巴马是爱尔兰后裔，他的曾祖父从爱尔兰移民去了美国。

因此，都柏林是旅游和投资的好地方。因为与全球紧密相连，这个独特的爱尔兰城市有着国际大都市的感觉。它是全球商业、教育和旅游中心。我们很高兴在这里参加世界旅游城市联合会的成立大会，因为通过这个机构，我们可以促进都柏林成为旅游目的地。城市需要联合起来鼓励自己的居民访问其他城市的居民，了解其他文化，扩展自己的知识，并且开发商业领域的合作。世界旅游城市联合会可以为我们这样的成员提供实现这些目标的方式。

对主办方和姐妹城市北京充满想象力和适时的倡议，我表示祝贺。城市是我们的未来，是经济的驱动力，是教育和创新的场所，是表达音乐、文学和文化形式的空间，也是地球人口增长的焦点。城市是通往边远农村和富庶乡村的门户；在我们的星球上，城市连接全球交通、贸易和商业流向。因此，今天，我们通过世界旅游城市联合会促进旅游业，联合起来促进成员城市间公民旅游和文化交流。

Literary Dublin　文学都柏林

The final story "The Dead" in Dubliners *is about the living and the dead. The story sets its readers into thinking: who is the really dead in the story?*

The Dead[①]

◎ James Joyce

She[②] was fast asleep.

　　Gabriel, leaning on his elbow, looked for a few moments unresentfully on her tangled hair and half-open mouth, listening to her deep-drawn breath. So she had had that romance in her life: a man had died for her sake. It hardly pained him now to think how poor a part he,

---

① 选自 *Dubliners*, The Project Gutenberg Etext, 2001。
② 指 Gabriel 的妻子 Gretta。

her husband, had played in her life. He watched her while she slept, as though he and she had never lived together as man and wife. His curious eyes rested long upon her face and on her hair, as he thought of what she must have been then, in that time of her first girlish beauty, a strange, friendly pity for her entered his soul. He did not like to say even to himself that her face was no longer beautiful, but he knew that it was no longer the face for which Michael Furey had braved death.

Perhaps she had not told him all the story. His eyes moved to the chair over which she had thrown some of her clothes. A petticoat string dangled to the floor. One boot stood upright, its limp upper fallen down: the fellow of it lay upon its side. He wondered at his riot of emotions of an hour before. From what had it proceeded? From his aunt's supper, from his own foolish speech, from the wine and dancing, the merry-making when saying good-night in the hall, the pleasure of the walk along the river in the snow. Poor Aunt Julia! She, too, would soon be a shade with the shade of Patrick Morkan and his horse. He had caught that haggard[①] look upon her face for a moment when she was singing *Arrayed for the Bridal*. Soon, perhaps, he would be sitting in that same drawing-room, dressed in black, his silk hat on his knees. The blinds would be drawn down and Aunt Kate would be sitting beside him, crying and blowing her nose and telling him how Julia had died. He would cast about in his mind for some words that might console her, and would find only lame and useless ones. Yes, yes: that would happen very soon.

The air of the room chilled his shoulders. He stretched himself cautiously along under the sheets and lay down beside his wife. One by one, they were all becoming shades. Better pass boldly into that other world, in the full glory of some passion, than fade and wither dismally[②] with age. He thought of how she who lay beside him had locked in her

---

① 憔悴的。
② 阴暗地。

heart for so many years that image of her lover's eyes when he had told her that he did not wish to live.

Generous tears filled Gabriel's eyes. He had never felt like that himself towards any woman, but he knew that such a feeling must be love. The tears gathered more thickly in his eyes and in the partial darkness he imagined he saw the form of a young man standing under a dripping tree. Other forms were near. His soul had approached that region where dwell the vast hosts of the dead. He was conscious of, but could not apprehend[①], their wayward and flickering existence. His own identity was fading out into a grey impalpable[②] world: the solid world itself, which these dead had one time reared and lived in, was dissolving and dwindling.

A few light taps upon the pane made him turn to the window. It had begun to snow again. He watched sleepily the flakes, silver and dark, falling obliquely[③] against the lamplight. The time had come for him to set out on his journey westward. Yes, the newspapers were right: snow was general all over Ireland. It was falling on every part of the dark central plain, on the treeless hills, falling softly upon the Bog of Allen and, farther westward, softly falling into the dark mutinous[④] Shannon waves. It was falling, too, upon every part of the lonely churchyard on the hill where Michael Furey lay buried. It lay thickly drifted on the crooked crosses and headstones, on the spears of the little gate, on the barren thorns. His soul swooned[⑤] slowly as he heard the snow falling faintly through the universe and faintly falling like the descent of their last end, upon all the living and the dead.

---

① 理解。
② 难掌握的。
③ 倾斜地。
④ 反抗的。
⑤ 昏厥。

死者[1]

◎ 詹姆斯·乔伊斯

她睡熟了。

  加布里埃尔斜靠在臂肘上，心平气和地对她乱蓬蓬的头发和半开半闭的嘴唇望了一会儿，倾听着她深沉的呼吸。这么说，在她一生中曾有过那段恋爱史。一个人曾经为她而死去。此刻想起他，她的丈夫，在她一生中扮演了一个多么可怜的角色，他几乎不太觉得痛苦了。她安睡着。他在一旁观望，仿佛他和她从没像夫妻那样一块生活过。他好奇的眼光长久地停留在她的面庞上，她的头发上。他想着，在她有着最初少女美好的那个时候，她该是什么模样，这时，一种奇异的、友爱的、对她的怜悯进入他的心灵。甚至对自己，他也不想说她的面孔如今已不再漂亮了，然而他知道，这张面孔已不再是那张迈克尔·富里不惜为之而死的面孔。

  也许她没把事情全告诉他。他的眼光移向那把椅子，那上面她撂了几件衣服。衬裙上的一条带子垂在地板上，一只靴子直立着，柔软的鞋帮已经塌下去了，另一只躺在它的旁边。他奇怪自己在一小时前怎么会那样感情激荡。是什么引起的？是他姨妈家的晚餐，是他那篇愚蠢的讲演，是酒和跳舞，在过道里告别时的说笑，沿着河在雪地里走时的快乐心情，是这些引起的。可怜的朱莉娅姨妈！她自己不久后也要变成跟帕特里克·莫坎的幽灵和他的马在一道的幽灵了。当她唱着《打扮新娘子》的时候，他在刹那间从她面孔上发现了那种形容枯槁的样子，不久以后，也许他会坐在那同一间客厅里，穿了丧服，绸帽子放在膝盖上。百叶窗关着，凯特姨妈坐在他身边，哭着，擤着鼻涕，告诉他朱莉娅是怎么死的。他搜索枯肠，想找出一些可以安慰她的话，但却只找到一些笨拙的、用不上的话。是的，是的，这不要多

---

[1] 出自 http://blog.sina.com.cn/s/blog_5d7adaa60100gc6q.html。

久就会发生了。

　　屋里的空气让他感到了两肩的寒冷。他轻轻钻进被子,在他妻子身边躺下。一个一个地,他们都会成为幽灵。最好是趁着某种热情旺盛之际果敢地走向那世界,而不是随着年华的凋谢而凄清地枯萎灭亡。他不由想到在他身边躺着的她,这么多年来是怎样在心中珍藏着她情人对她说不想再活时的那双眼睛的形象。

　　大量的泪水涌进了加布里埃尔的眼睛。他从不曾对任何女人有过这样的情感,但他知道这就是爱。他眼中的泪水积聚得更满了。在半明半暗的微光中,他想象着一个年轻人在一棵滴着水珠的树下的身影。另外的一些身影也在走近。他的灵魂已挨近了那住着众多死者的领域。他已经意识到,却没能理解他们变幻万千、若隐若现的存在。他自身正消逝着去向一个灰色的无法捉摸的世界:这坚固的世界,这些死者曾一度养育、生活的世界,它正在溶解,化为乌有。

　　玻璃上传来的几声轻响吸引着他把脸转向窗户,雪又降了下来。他睡意朦胧地望着雪花,银色的、暗淡的雪花,斜斜地迎着灯光飘落。是该他动身到西方去旅行的时候了,是啊,报上说得好:整个爱尔兰全在下雪。它在阴郁的中部平原的每一片土地上落着,在光秃秃的山丘上落着,轻轻地落入艾伦沼泽,再向下,又轻轻地落在黑森森的、奔腾激荡的香农河的浪涛中。它也落在安葬着迈克尔·富里的孤独的教堂墓地的山坡上那每一片泥土中。它纷纷扬扬,厚厚地覆盖在歪斜的十字架和墓石上,落在一扇又一扇小墓门的尖顶上,落在荒凉的荆棘丛中。他的灵魂慢慢地睡去,当他听着雪花穿越宇宙在飘扬,轻轻地,微微地,如同他们的最后结局那样,飘落在所有生者和死者身上。

Who Is James Joyce?

☞ 1882–1941. He was born to a middle class family.

☞ Irish novelist and poet, one of the most influential writers in the modernist avant-garde of the early 20th century.

☞ Best-known works: *Ulysses* (1922), the short-story collection *Dubliners* (1914), and the novels *A Portrait of the Artist as a Young Man* (1916) and *Finnegans Wake* (1939).

☞ In his early twenties he emigrated permanently to continental Europe, living in Trieste, Paris and Zurich.

☞ His fictional universe does not extend beyond Dublin, and is populated largely by characters who closely resemble family members, enemies and friends from his time there.

☞ "For myself, I always write about Dublin, because if I can get to the heart of Dublin I can get to the heart of all the cities of the world. In the particular is contained the universal."

Chapter 5   Edinburgh

Edinburgh society ... a highbrow literature celebrity society.
—Irvine Welsh

Quotes Featuring Edinburgh

❧ I had never imagined that any city in these islands could be at once so beautiful and fantastic.
—J.B. Priestley

❧ I've found mine an enormous benefit in Edinburgh. It handles speed bumps and potholes very well and they're less likely to damage the car. The roads being as they are, everyone should get a four-wheel drive. Even if the roads improved, there's still no reason why people shouldn't use 4×4s in Edinburgh. They take up no more road space and most run on diesel, so they're more economical. I really can't see a problem.
—Bruce Young

❧ If you like name brand, you know Edinburgh is the place to go, they've got plenty of them.
—Tiffany Anderso

Key Words
Castles, festivals, literature, and great writers.

Questions
1. What inspires you most after reading "Edinburgh: Inspiring Capital"?
2. Do you think your city is inspiring? Why or why not?
3. Do you know any detective stories written by Arthur Conan Doyle? How do you like them?

Inspiring Edinburgh 令人鼓舞的爱丁堡

Edinburgh, the capital of Scotland, is inspiring in many ways. It inspires people to come to visit it and enjoy many experiences here, to stay and live here.

Edinburgh: Inspiring Capital[①]

Edinburgh, Scotland's capital, has been inspiring citizens and visitors alike for centuries. Today this beautiful city forms the backdrop to innovation in business, the arts, science and academia.

Every year around five million people visit the Edinburgh region to enjoy a wealth of experiences—from nightlife to culture to outdoor activities. Many fall in love with the city and return to live or to invest in its future, drawn by the quality of life, strong economy and unique atmosphere.

---

① 选自 *Edinburgh: Inspiring Capital*, VIP%20Brochure%20PDF%20final。

Edinburgh is a vibrant city framed by a stunning[①] landscape and world famous architecture. East, West and Midlothian each add their distinctive character to the city region—from the stunning coastline of North Berwick to the striking Pentland Hills.

The World Heritage Site at the heart of the city combines the medieval Old Town, the Georgian New Town and award winning modern architecture.

Inspiring Impression

Edinburgh makes a great first impression—then gets better. Its spectacular skyline of castle and crag[②], classical columns and spires is the backdrop to a cultural programme that lasts all year. Edinburgh is simply one of Europe's great capitals.

Edinburgh is definitely a city to stroll around. Edinburgh Castle, prominent in so many city views, is on everyone's list. The Royal Mile comes next, the spine of Old Edinburgh, this historic street links the castle with the Palace of Holyrood House. Nearby Victoria Street leads down to the Grassmarket, from where the full height of the castle can be appreciated.

The atmosphere of the other Edinburgh—the elegant 18th century New Town—can be sampled from Charlotte Square, but further explored by heading north and downhill into the residential streets with their distinctive cobbles, private gardens and symmetrical facades.

Back in the city centre, the shopping choice is wide, the entertainment and nightlife by way of pubs and restaurants sophisticated and varied—try the George Street, Rose Street area—a good antidote[③] if you've gone into "cultural overload."

---

① 惊人的。
② 悬崖。
③ 解药。

Leith, Edinburgh's port, with its river frontage and old warehouses, has a quite different character and a great selection of excellent restaurants.

Inspired to Visit

Edinburgh's festivals are world famous. Every summer the city's population doubles for the International Festival, Fringe[①] and a host of other festivals celebrating film, literature, television and jazz. During the summer the city streets buzz with music and performers from around the world.

In winter, with its bright, crisp days and long, haunting nights, Edinburgh takes on a magical quality. Christmas is a special time for shoppers and revelers. The city's streets sparkle with the glow from half a million Christmas lights, creating a truly magical experience. The Edinburgh Wheel, ice rink[②] and continental street markets add to the festive atmosphere. The climax of Edinburgh's Winter Festivals is the celebrated Hogmanay street party in Princes Street, when thousands gather to enjoy music and fireworks and join in arguably the world's best New Year celebrations.

But the Inspiring Capital is about much more than festivals. Year round the city attracts tourists drawn by its beauty, wealth of galleries and museums and the warm welcome of its people. The city centre is both beautiful and compact, and the sights of the Old and New Towns can easily be covered on foot. The bus service is excellent and cheap and includes the airport shuttle, which runs 24 hours a day.

The region surrounding Edinburgh is also rich in both culture and natural beauty. The city is framed in a stunning array of coast and countryside. Scotland is, of course, famous for its golf and there are a

---

① 艺术节。
② 溜冰场。

number of world famous courses within a short distance of Edinburgh, including Muirfield which hosted the Open Championship in 2002. The John Muir Way in East Lothian offers a wealth of natural beauty for walkers and birdwatchers.

Belhaven Bay in Dunbar is a magnet for surfers. The Pentland Hills attract walkers and climbers.

Inspired to Live

Edinburgh offers residents all the facilities of a major international capital in a compact and friendly city. Residents enjoy national galleries and museums, shops ranging from major chains to exclusive boutiques[①] and a range of world cuisine in the city's restaurants and bars.

Edinburgh's waterfront is being regenerated to offer a new vision of city living. This innovative development will offer a high quality site for housing, business, education and leisure, combining the buzz of urban living with a stunning waterside and parkland setting.

Many people choose to live in or near the centre, in traditional stone "tenements" (apartment blocks) or Georgian townhouses. The surrounding areas offer something for every taste, from studio flats to family homes with gardens. Edinburgh is rich in green space. It has the volcanic wildscape of Holyrood Park at its heart, as well as beautiful parks at The Meadows, Princes Street Gardens and Inverleith. The Royal Botanic Garden is world renowned for its scientific work, but to its many visitors it is a place of relaxation and beauty. There is easy access to the coast and countryside of the Lothians. The combination of nightlife, employment, green space and good schools makes it appealing to students, young professionals and families.

---

① （女士）时装店。

爱丁堡：鼓舞人心的首府

几个世纪以来，苏格兰的首府爱丁堡一直鼓舞着市民和游客。如今，这座美丽的城市成为商业、艺术、科学和学术界创新的背景。

每年大约有五百多万人参观爱丁堡地区，享受着不同的经历——从夜生活到文化到户外活动。许多人爱上这座城市，被这座城市的生活质量、强大的经济实力和独特氛围所吸引，他们重返这里居住或投资。

爱丁堡是座充满活力的城市，景色迷人，遍布举世瞩目的建筑。东、西、中洛锡安各自为城区添加自己鲜明的个性——从北贝里克的迷人海岸线到引人注目的彭特兰丘陵。

城市中心的世界遗产遗址结合了中世纪的老城区、乔治亚风格的新城区和获奖的现代建筑。

鼓舞人心的印象

爱丁堡给人留下美好的第一印象——然后变得更好。其壮观的城堡和岩石、古典的圆柱和尖塔的天际线为终年持续进行的文化节目提供了背景。爱丁堡只是欧洲大都市之一。

Edinburgh Castle　爱丁堡城堡　　　　Charlotte Square　夏洛特广场

爱丁堡当然是个适合漫步的城市。爱丁堡城堡在众多的城市景观中十分突出，是每位游客必去之地。接下来是皇家大道，即爱丁堡老城的尖塔，这条历史街道连接了城堡和荷里路德宫大厦。附近的维多利亚街通向跳蚤市场，从那里可以欣赏城堡的全景。

另一种爱丁堡氛围——典雅的十八世纪新城——可以从夏洛特广场初见端倪，独特的鹅卵石、私人花园和对称的建筑物向北下坡的街区道路可以帮助游客进一步领略其风采。

回到市中心，购物选择多种多样，以各式酒吧和餐厅为主的娱乐和夜生活各领风骚——尝试乔治街、玫瑰街一带——如果你已经"文化超载"了，这里是很好的缓解之地。

爱丁堡的港口利斯，遍布着河流的岸滩和旧仓库，拥有完全不同的性格和众多精美的餐厅。

鼓舞人心的游览

爱丁堡艺术节世界闻名。每年夏天，爱丁堡人口因为国际艺术节和众多其他庆祝电影、文学、电视和爵士乐的节日而增加一倍。夏季，城市街道上回响着来自世界各地的音乐和表演。

冬天，爱丁堡白天明亮、清凉，夜晚漫长、难忘，呈现出神奇的特质。圣诞节对购物者和狂欢者来说是个特殊的时刻。城市街道闪耀着五十万头装饰灯的光芒，创造了一个真正的神奇体验。爱丁堡摩天轮、溜冰场和大陆街头市场增添了节日气氛。爱丁堡冬季节日的高潮是王子街的除夕庆祝晚会，那时，数千人聚集在一起，享受音乐、观看烟花，加入可称为世界上最热闹的新年庆祝活动。

但是，都市给人的鼓舞不只是节日庆祝活动。全年，爱丁堡以其美丽风景、众多艺术馆和博物馆以及人民的热情吸引着游客。城市中心美观、紧凑，步行很容易到达旧城和新城的景点。巴士服务优良，价格便宜，包括机场班车，每天二十四小时运行。

爱丁堡周边地区也遍布文化景点和自然风光。城市充满了迷人的海景和乡村美景。当然，苏格兰以高尔夫球而著名，爱丁堡周围不远处有许多世界著名的球场，包括2002年举办公开锦标赛的缪尔菲尔德高尔夫球场。东洛锡安的约翰·缪尔路沿途优美的自然风光吸引了众多步行者和观鸟人士。

邓巴的贝尔哈文湾吸引着冲浪者,彭特兰丘陵吸引着徒步旅行者和登山者。

鼓舞人心的生活

爱丁堡这座紧凑、友好的城市为当地居民提供了一个国际大都市的所有设施。居民享受着国家艺术馆和博物馆,从大型连锁到精品专卖的各种商店,城市餐厅和酒吧提供的各色世界美食应有尽有。

爱丁堡的海边重新焕发生机,为城市生活提供了新视野。这种创新性的发展将提供高质量住房、商业、教育和娱乐场所,它结合了迷人的水边和公园环境与城市生活的喧嚣。

很多人选择住在城市中心或中心附近,住在传统的石头"房屋"(公寓楼)或乔治亚风格的联排别墅里。周边地区提供的住房从一室公寓到带花园的家庭住宅,可以满足人们的各种不同口味。爱丁堡拥有丰富的绿色空间。市中心有荷里路德公园的原生态火山遗址,还有美丽的茵维莱斯公园。皇家植物园以其科研工作而世界闻名,但是对许多游客而言,这里是休闲和欣赏美景的地方。从那里很容易就可到达海边和洛锡安的乡村地区。夜生活、就业、绿色空间和良好学校等综合因素吸引着学生、年轻的专业人士和家庭。

City of Literature—Edinburgh 文学之都爱丁堡

Edinburgh is named by UNESCO as "City of Literature." It has produced many writers such as Walter Scott, Robert Louis Stevenson, and Joanne Kathleen Rowling. The following is a detective story that adds another color to Edinburgh literature.

The Empty House[1]

◎ Arthur Conan Doyle

It was in the spring of the year 1894 that all London was interested, and the fashionable world dismayed, by the murder of the Honourable Ronald Adair under most unusual and inexplicable circumstances. The public has already learned those particulars of the crime which came out in the police investigation, but a good deal was suppressed upon that occasion, since the case for the prosecution was so overwhelmingly strong that it was not necessary to bring forward all the facts. Only now, at the end of nearly ten years, am I allowed to supply those missing links which make up the whole of that remarkable chain. The crime was of interest in itself, but that interest was as nothing to me compared to the inconceivably sequel[2], which afforded me the greatest shock and surprise of any event in my adventurous life. Even now, after this long interval, I find myself thrilling as I think of it, and feeling once more that sudden flood of joy, amazement, and incredulity which utterly submerged my mind. Let me say to that public, which has shown some interest in those glimpses which I have occasionally given them of the thoughts and actions of a very remarkable man, that they are not to blame me if I have not shared my knowledge with them, for I should have considered it my first duty to do so, had I not been barred by a positive prohibition from his own lips, which was only withdrawn upon the third of last month.

It can be imagined that my close intimacy with Sherlock Holmes had interested me deeply in crime, and that after his disappearance I never failed to read with care the various problems which came before the public.

---

① 选自 *The Complete Sherlock Holmes*, Doubleday / Penguin Books, 2009。
② 结局，后果。

And I even attempted, more than once, for my own private satisfaction, to employ his methods in their solution, though with indifferent success. There was none, however, which appealed to me like this tragedy of Ronald Adair. As I read the evidence at the inquest, which led up to a verdict of wilful murder against some person or persons unknown, I realized more clearly than I had ever done the loss which the community had sustained by the death of Sherlock Holmes. There were points about this strange business which would, I was sure, have specially appealed to him, and the efforts of the police would have been supplemented, or more probably anticipated, by the trained observation and the alert mind of the first criminal agent in Europe. All day, as I drove upon my round, I turned over the case in my mind and found no explanation which appeared to me to be adequate. At the risk of telling a twice-told tale, I will recapitulate[1] the facts as they were known to the public at the conclusion of the inquest.

The Honourable Ronald Adair was the second son of the Earl[2] of Maynooth, at that time governor of one of the Australian colonies. Adair's mother had returned from Australia to undergo the operation for cataract[3], and she, her son Ronald, and her daughter Hilda were living together at 427 Park Lane. The youth moved in the best society—had, so far as was known, no enemies and no particular vices. He had been engaged to Miss Edith Woodley, of Carstairs, but the engagement had been broken off by mutual consent some months before, and there was no sign that it had left any very profound feeling behind it. For the rest of the man's life moved in a narrow and conventional circle, for his habits were quiet and his nature unemotional. Yet it was upon this easy-going young aristocrat that death came, in most strange and unexpected form, between the hours of ten and eleven-twenty on the night of March 30, 1894.

---

[1] 总结。
[2] 伯爵。
[3] 白内障。

Ronald Adair was fond of cards-playing continually, but never for such stakes as would hurt him. He was a member of the Baldwin, the Cavendish, and the Bagatelle card clubs. It was shown that, after dinner on the day of his death, he had played a rubber of whist① at the latter club. He had also played there in the afternoon. The evidence of those who had played with him—Mr. Murray, Sir John Hardy, and Colonel Moran—showed that the game was whist, and that there was a fairly equal fall of the cards. Adair might have lost five pounds, but not more. His fortune was a considerable one, and such a loss could not in any way affect him. He had played nearly every day at one club or other, but he was a cautious player, and usually rose a winner. It came out in evidence that, in partnership with Colonel Moran, he had actually won as much as four hundred and twenty pounds in a sitting, some weeks before, from Godfrey Milner and Lord Balmoral. So much for his recent history as it came out at the inquest.

On the evening of the crime, he returned from the club exactly at ten. His mother and sister were out spending the evening with a relation. The servant deposed② that she heard him enter the front room on the second floor, generally used as his sitting-room. She had lit a fire there, and as it smoked she had opened the window. No sound was heard from the room until eleven-twenty, the hour of the return of Lady Maynooth and her daughter. Desiring to say good-night, she attempted to enter her son's room. The door was locked on the inside, and no answer could be got to their cries and knocking. Help was obtained, and the door forced. The unfortunate young man was found lying near the table. His head had been horribly mutilated③ by an expanding revolver bullet, but no weapon of any sort was to be found in the room. On the table lay two banknotes for

---

① 惠斯特（扑克牌游戏的一种）。
② 宣誓证明。
③ 损伤。

ten pounds each and seventeen pounds ten in silver and gold, the money arranged in little piles of varying amount. There were some figures also upon a sheet of paper, with the names of some club friends opposite to them, from which it was conjectured① that before his death he was endeavouring to make out his losses or winnings at cards.

A minute examination of the circumstances served only to make the case more complex. In the first place, no reason could be given why the young man should have fastened the door upon the inside. There was the possibility that the murderer had done this, and had afterwards escaped by the window. The drop was at least twenty feet, however, and a bed of crocuses② in full bloom lay beneath. Neither the flowers nor the earth showed any sign of having been disturbed, nor were there any marks upon the narrow strip of grass which separated the house from the road. Apparently, therefore, it was the young man himself who had fastened the door. But how did he come by his death? No one could have climbed up to the window without leaving traces. Suppose a man had fired through the window, he would indeed be a remarkable shot who could with a revolver inflict so deadly a wound. Again, Park Lane is a frequented thoroughfare; there is a cab stand within a hundred yards of the house. No one had heard a shot. And yet there was the dead man, and there the revolver bullet, which had mushroomed out, as soft-nosed③ bullets will. Such were the circumstances of the Park Lane Mystery, which were further complicated by entire absence of motive, since, as I have said, young Adair was not known to have any enemy, and no attempt had been made to remove the money or valuables in the room.

All day I turned these facts over in my mind, endeavouring to hit upon some theory which could reconcile them all, and to find that line of

---

① 推测。
② 番红花。
③ （子弹）软头的。

least resistance which my poor friend had declared to be the starting-point of every investigation. I confess that I made little progress. In the evening I strolled across the Park, and found myself about six o'clock at the Oxford Street end of Part Lane. A group of loafers[1] upon the pavements, all staring up at a particular window, directed me to the house which I had come to see. A tall, thin man with coloured glasses, whom I strongly suspected of being a plain-clothes detective, was pointing out some theory of his own, while the others crowded round to listen to what he said. I got as near him as I could, but his observations seemed to me to be absurd, so I withdrew again in some disgust. As I did so I struck against an elderly, deformed man, who had been behind me, and I knocked down several books which he was carrying. I remember that as I picked them up, I observed the title of one of them, *The Origin of Tree Worship*, and it struck me that the fellow must be some poor bibliophile[2], who, either as a trade or as a hobby, was a collector of obscure volumes. I endeavoured to apologize for the accident, but it was evident that these books which I had so unfortunately maltreated were very precious objects in the eyes of their owner. With a snarl of contempt he turned upon his heel, and I saw his curved back and white side-whiskers disappear among the throng.

空屋[3]

◎ 阿瑟·柯南·道尔

1894年的春天，可敬的罗诺德·阿德尔在最不寻常和莫名其妙的情况下被人谋杀的案子，引起全伦敦的注意，并使上流社会感到惊慌。在警方调查中公布的详细案情大家都知道了，但有许多细节被删去了。

---

[1] 游手好闲者。
[2] 藏书家。
[3] 出自 http://ishare.iask.sina.com.cn/download/explain.php?fileid=6778596。

这是因为起诉理由非常充足，没有必要公开全部证据。只是到现在，将近十年之后，才允许我来补充破案过程中一些短缺的环节。案子本身是耐人寻味的，但比起那令人意想不到的结局，这点趣味在我看来就不算什么。在我一生所经历的冒险事件中，这个案子的结局最使我震惊和诧异。即使过了这么长的时间，现在一想起它来就叫我毛骨悚然，并且使我重温那种高兴、惊奇而又怀疑的心情，当时这心情像突然涌来的潮水一般，完全淹没了我的神志。让我向那些关心我偶尔谈起的一个非凡人物的言行片段的读者大众说一句话：不要责怪我没有让他们分享我所知道的一切。如果不是他曾亲口下令禁止我这样做，我会把这当作首要义务。这项禁令是在上个月三号才取消的。

我和夏洛克·福尔摩斯的密切交往使我对刑事案发生了浓厚的兴趣，这是可以想象到的。在他失踪以后，凡是公开发表的疑案，我都仔细读过，从不遗漏。为了满足个人兴趣，我还不止一次地试用他的方法来解释这些疑案，虽然不很成功。但是，没有任何疑案像罗诺德·阿德尔的惨死那样把我吸引住。当我读到审讯时提出的证据并据此判决未查明的某人或某些人蓄意谋杀罪时，我比过去更清楚地意识到福尔摩斯的去世给社会带来的损失。我肯定这件怪事中有几点一定会特别吸引他。而且这位欧洲首屈一指的刑事侦探，以他训练有素的观察力和敏捷的头脑，很可能弥补警方力量之不足，更可能促使他们提前行动。我整日巡回出诊，脑子里却想着这件案子，找不到一个自己认为是理由充分的解释。我甘冒讲一个陈旧故事的风险，把审讯结束时已公布过的案情扼要地重述一遍。

罗诺德·阿德尔是澳大利亚某殖民地总督梅鲁斯伯爵的次子。阿德尔的母亲从澳大利亚回国来做白内障手术，跟儿子阿德尔和女儿希尔达一起住在公园路427号。这个年轻人出入上流社会，就大家所知，他并无仇人，也没有什么恶习。他跟卡斯特尔斯的伊迪丝·伍德利小姐订过婚，但几个月前双方同意解除婚约，嗣后也看不出有多深的留恋。他平日的时间都消磨在一个狭小、保守的圈子里，因为他天性冷漠，习惯于无变化的生活。可是，就在1894年3月30日夜里十点至十一点二十分之间，死亡以最奇特的方式向这个悠闲懒散的青年突然袭来。

罗诺德·阿德尔喜欢打纸牌，而且不断地打，但赌注从不大到有损于他的身份。他是鲍尔温、卡文狄希和巴格特尔三个纸牌俱乐部的会员。他遇害的那天，晚饭后在卡文狄希俱乐部玩了一盘惠斯特。当天下午他也在那儿打过牌。跟他一起打牌的莫瑞先生、约翰·哈代爵士和莫兰上校证明他们打的是惠斯特，每人的牌好坏差不多，阿德尔大概输了五镑，不会更多。他有一笔可观的财产，像这样的输赢决不至于对他有什么影响。他几乎每天不是在这个俱乐部就在那个俱乐部打牌，但是他打得小心谨慎，并且常常是赢了才离开牌桌的。证词中还谈到在几星期以前，他跟莫兰上校作为一家，一口气赢了哥德菲·米尔纳和巴尔莫洛勋爵四百二十镑之多。在调查报告中提到的有关他的近况就这些。

在出事的那天晚上，他从俱乐部回到家里的时间是整十点。他母亲和妹妹上亲戚家串门去了。女仆供述听见他走进二楼的前厅——就是他经常当作起居室的那间屋子。她已经在屋里生好了火，因为冒烟她把窗户打开了。一直到十一点二十分梅鲁斯夫人和女儿回来以前，屋里没有动静。梅鲁斯夫人想进她儿子屋里去说声晚安，发现房门从里边锁上了。母女二人叫喊、敲门都不见答应。于是找来人把门撞开，只见这个不幸的青年躺在桌边，脑袋被一颗左轮子弹击碎，模样很可怕，可是屋里不见任何武器。桌上摆着两张十镑的钞票和总共十一镑十先令的金币和银币，这些钱码铺了十小堆，数目多少不一。另外有张纸条，上面记了若干数目字和几个俱乐部朋友的名字，由此推测遇害前他正在计算打牌的输赢。

现场的详细检查只是使案情变得更加复杂。第一，举不出理由来说明为什么这个年轻人要从屋里把门插上。这有可能是凶手把门插上了，然后从窗户逃跑。由窗口到地面的距离至少有三十英尺，窗下的花坛里正开满了番红花。可是花丛和地面都不像被人踩过，在房子和街道之间的一块狭长的草地上也没有任何痕迹。因此，很明显是年轻人自己把门插上的。假使有人能用左轮手枪从外面对准窗口放一枪，而且造成这样的致命伤，这人必定是个出色的射手。另外，公园路是一条行人川流不息的大道,离这所房子不到一百码的地方就有马车站。这儿已经打死了人,还有一颗像所有铅头子弹那样射出后就会开花的左轮子弹和它造成的立刻致死的创伤,但当时却没有人听到枪声。公园路奇案的这些情况,由于找不出动机而变得更加复杂,因为,正如我前面所讲的,没人听说年轻的阿德尔有任何仇人,他屋里的金钱和贵重物品也没人动过。

我整天反复思考这些事实,竭力想找到一个能解释得通的理论,来发现最省力的途径,我的亡友称它为一切调查的起点。傍晚,我漫步穿过公园,大约在六点左右走到了公园路连接牛津街的那头。一群游手好闲的人聚在人行道上,他们都仰起头望着一扇窗户。他们给我指出了我特地要来瞧瞧的那所房子。一个戴着墨镜的瘦高个子,我非常怀疑他是个便衣侦探,正在讲他自己的某种推测,其他人都围着听。我尽量往前凑过去,但他的议论听起来实在荒谬,我有点厌恶地又从人群中退了出来。正在这时候我撞在后面一个有残疾的老人身上,把他抱着的几本书碰掉在地上。记得当我捡起那些书的时候,看见其中一本书名是《树木崇拜的起源》。这使我想到老人必定是个穷藏书家,收集一些不见经传的书籍作为职业或者作为爱好。我极力为这意料不到的事道歉,可是不巧给我碰掉的这几本书显然在它们的主人眼里是非常珍贵的东西。他讨厌地吼了一声,转身就走。我望着他弯曲的背影和灰白的连鬓胡子消失在人群里。

Who Is Arthur Conan Doyle?

☞ 1859–1930.

☞ Scottish physician and writer, most noted for his stories about the detective

Sherlock Holmes.

☞ His other works include science fiction stories, plays, romances, poetry, non-fiction and historical novels.

☞ From 1876 to 1881, he studied medicine at the University of Edinburgh, and began writing while studying.

☞ Notable works are *Stories of Sherlock Holmes* and *The Lost World*.

☞ In 1903, he published his first Holmes short story "The Adventure of the Empty House."

☞ Holmes was featured in a total of 56 short stories and four Conan Doyle novels.

Chapter 6   London

London is a modern Babylon.
—Benjamin Disraeli

Quotes Featuring London

- I'm leaving because the weather is too good. I hate London when it's not raining.
  —Groucho Marx

- When it's three o'clock in New York, it's still 1938 in London.
  —Bette Midler

- I don't know what London's coming to—the higher the buildings the lower the morals.
  —Noël Coward

- Hell is a city much like London—
  A populous and a smoky city;
  There are all sorts of people undone,
  And there is little or no fun done.
  —Percy Bysshe Shelley

Key Words

Rainy weather, the British Museum, London Bridge, and Westminster Abbey.

Questions

1. Which landmark in London impresses you most?
2. What color do you think features London? And why?
3. What's the difference between London in Dickens' description and that in your mind?

London Today 今日伦敦

The article offers a general picture of London. The focus is especially on its culture and landmarks.

London Today[①]

◎ Donna Dailey and John Tomedi

The landscape of London has changed immensely since Dr. Samuel Johnson—writer, lexicographer[②], and man about town—made this observation in the mid-eighteenth century. But his words still hold true in spirit, for London today offers a wealth of experiences: historical sites, theatre, music and entertainment, fine food, and outstanding museums and galleries containing everything from classical art to popular culture.

---

① 选自 *Bloom's Literary Place—London*, by Donna Dailey and John Tomedi, with Introduction by Harold Bloom, Philadelphia: Chelsea House Publishers, 2005，略有删改。
② 词典编纂者。

With a population of over seven million in the metropolitan area, London is Europe's largest city. Many visitors come here looking for merry old England and end up discovering the world. While the capital is the repository of British history and culture, it is also a diverse city with a dynamic mix of residents and visitors from all around the globe. In different parts of the city a typical Londoner is as likely to wear a sari[①] or a chador as a business suit. The ethnic mix embraces 37 different groups, each with more than 10,000 people. Some of the best-selling and most highly acclaimed contemporary British novels have been written by young London writers who came from the Caribbean, Pakistani, and Indian communities.

Class and Culture

The old British obsession with class, explored by authors from Jane Austen to Evelyn Waugh, is now largely confined to the musings of journalists in newspaper columns. And London is a veritable Babel[②] of accents: some talk "posh," others Cockney, and others mockney—a somewhat snide label for those affecting a *de rigueur* working class accent. Being fashionable in London today is about attitude and not origins.

Most Londoners embrace the variety that different races and cultures bring to the city, and are as happy to have a curry or kebab after an evening at the pub as fish and chips. London has long since outgrown its reputation as a culinary wasteland. Celebrity British chefs have inundated[③] popular culture; there's usually a chef peering out of bookshop windows from the cover of his latest bestseller.

Eating out has become the great London pastime. There is a fantastic range of restaurants serving every kind of cuisine and every budget. But

---

① 莎丽，印度妇女的服装。
② 巴别塔，《圣经》中记载的一座半途而废的工程。
③ 淹没。

nothing can outshine that great British institution, the pub. It is still the heart and soul of London social life. One can seek out the old-fashioned pubs that have retained their original character. Some noteworthy pubs date back to the 17th century and were frequented by writers from Charles Dickens to Oscar Wilde—pubs such as the Anchor, the George Inn, and Dr Johnson's local, Ye Olde Cheshire Cheese.

The Landmarks of London

Several of London's top attractions lie along the Thames between these two axes. One of the best introductions to the city is to take a river boat cruise from Tower Bridge to Westminster Pier[①]. At the eastern end is the massive Tower of London, whose construction was begun by William the Conqueror in the 11th century and which remains one of the few medieval buildings in the city. For much of its history it was a place of terror, where enemies of the Crown were imprisoned, tortured, and often beheaded. Today's jovial[②] guardians, the red-and-black-coated Beefeaters, regale[③] visitors with tales of the Tower on free, guided tours. The Crown Jewels, the priceless regalia used at coronations of the British monarchy, are also housed within these formidable walls.

Opposite the Tower are some of the wharves[④] of the old City port, now converted into fashionable apartments, restaurants, and a shopping gallery. The nondescript outline of London Bridge surprises many visitors, who confuse it with the more flamboyant[⑤] Tower Bridge. Historically, however, London Bridge outshines its more noticeable Victorian neighbor. It was the only bridge across the Thames until 1750, and in Shakespeare's day it was lined with houses and shops. Near the bridge's northern end,

---

① 码头。
② 快活的。
③ 逗人欢乐。
④ 码头。
⑤ 浮华的。

hidden by modern buildings, is the Monument to the Great Fire, which started nearby.

Farther along the south shore is the Tate Modern①, which opened in 2000 in the former Bankside Power station. This enormous edifice② makes a superb exhibition space for an international collection of modern art. It also gave the original Tate Gallery at Millbank room to breathe in its reincarnation③ as Tate Britain, which houses the world's largest collection of British art spanning five centuries. Opposite the Tate Modern, the Millennium Bridge is the latest crossing to span the Thames. This pedestrian-only walkway affords an impressive view from the river to the dome of St. Paul's Cathedral.

Farther ahead across the river is London's premier arts complex, the South Bank Center. The minimalist, concrete-block architecture seems dated now, but it houses some of the country's finest institutions: the Royal Festival Hall, the National Theatre, the Hayward Gallery and the National Film Theatre.

Next comes the city's newest and most exciting attraction, the London Eye. When it was built for the millennium, many feared this giant Ferris wheel would blot the landscape and spoil the stately view of Westminster. But a ride in this amazing structure soon silenced its critics. As the wheel rotates slowly above the river, its glass capsules provide a view over London that is simply stunning. It affords a new perspective on the cityscape and its buildings.

London's most famous symbol, Big Ben, is plainly in sight from the Eye. The great bell in its handsome clock tower looms over the Houses of Parliament, and is heard round the world on daily broadcasts of the BBC.

Magnificent Westminster Abbey is as much a national monument as

---

① 泰特现代美术馆。
② 建筑。
③ 再生。

it is a place of worship. Kings and queens are crowned and buried here, and many of the country's great literary figures have been commemorated in Poet's Corner. Its superb medieval architecture encloses lavish monuments, simple tombs, and many national treasures.

The neon-lit Piccadilly Circus is the anchor of London's main shopping district. Three major shopping thoroughfares①—Piccadilly, Regent Street, and Oxford Street—enclose some of the most expensive real estate in the city between here and Hyde Park.

In essence, London is a collection of villages that were knitted together as the city sprawled. It's hard to fathom② that in Jane Austen's day, the now-central Bloomsbury was an airy village well outside the city. For a time it was synonymous with the publishing world, and is home to one of the country's greatest treasures, the British Museum. Its outstanding collections span the globe from prehistoric times through ancient civilizations to the present day.

One of the best features of London is the amount of parkland within the confines of its bustling, urban environment. Kensington Gardens adjoins Hyde Park, creating a vast swath of green in central London. Regent's Park, at the top of Baker Street just beyond the fictional address of Sherlock Holmes, forms a bolt-hole③ to the north of the center. Countless smaller parks and leafy squares are dotted throughout the city.

Almost anyplace of interest to visitors in London is accessible by public transport. The London Underground, better known as the Tube, is generally the quickest way across the city, and there is a comprehensive network of buses. The red-doubled-decker buses so familiar from films and postcards can often provide good sightseeing from the upper deck.

---

① 街区。
② 领悟。
③ 螺栓孔。

今日伦敦[①]

◎ 唐娜·戴利　约翰·汤姆迪

十八世纪中期,伦敦人塞缪尔·约翰逊博士就曾说过伦敦是个日新月异的城市。他说得没错,如今伦敦依然如此,万花筒一般,令人目不暇接:名胜古迹、剧院、音乐厅、娱乐中心、美食,还有收藏丰富的博物馆以及从古典艺术到流行文化无所不包的美术馆。

伦敦是欧洲最大的城市,仅市区人口就有七百多万。很多游客到伦敦是为了一睹古英国快乐的容颜,但结果往往是他们在这里发现了整个世界。伦敦不仅是英国的历史和文化宝库,而且也是一个多民族的城市,其居民和游客来自世界各地。典型的伦敦人可能是西装革履,也可能身着莎丽(印度妇女的服装)或长袍。伦敦人分属三十七个不同的种族,每个种族的人口都超过一万。一些好评如潮的当代英国畅销小说出自于加勒比海、巴基斯坦和印度裔的年轻伦敦作家之手。

阶级和文化

古英国存在着明显的阶级差别。简·奥斯汀、伊夫林·沃等许多作家都曾探讨过这个话题,但如今只有在报纸专栏里才可以见到记者们对这个问题的思考了。伦敦人操着各种各样的方言,伦敦简直就是一座现代的巴别塔。有些人谈吐时尚优雅,有些人一口地道的伦敦土话,还有一些人则装模作样地使用着工人阶级的社交用语。如今,在伦敦一个人时尚与否跟其出身无关,时尚是一种生活态度。

[①] 出自张玉红、杨朝军译:《伦敦文学地图》,上海:上海交通大学出版社,2011年。

Tower of Babel 巴别塔

　　大多数伦敦人认为不同种族和文化丰富了他们的生活。晚上在酒吧吃过鱼和炸薯条之后再来一份咖喱饭或烤肉串只会增加他们的生活乐趣。伦敦早就甩掉了"美食荒原"的恶名。英国名厨的影子在流行文化中随处可见。一名厨师从他最新出版的畅销书上抬起头来,透过书店的窗户朝外凝视,这样的景象在伦敦已是司空见惯。

　　下馆子已经成了伦敦人最享受的休闲活动。在伦敦,餐饮业极其发达,餐馆众多,菜式多样,从豪华大酒店到简陋的大排挡,从世界名菜到地方小吃,无所不有。无论是商务宴请还是朋友小聚,都可以找到合适的饭店。尽管如此,酒吧仍是英国餐饮业一颗璀璨的明珠,是英国人社交活动的中心。有些老式酒吧仍保留着古色古香的风貌,其中有些"名吧"的历史甚至可以追溯到十七世纪,那时候,查尔斯·狄更斯、奥斯卡·王尔德等作家是这些酒吧的常客,如安可酒吧、乔治客栈、约翰逊博士酒家、老柴郡奶酪。

伦敦的地标

伦敦的好几个旅游点都集中在这两个轴心之间沿泰晤士河的区域。最佳旅游路线之一是从伦敦桥乘游船一路游览到威斯敏斯特教堂码头。东端是气势恢宏的伦敦塔,十一世纪威廉征服英国时始建,是当今尚存的为数不多的中世纪建筑之一。在其历史上,大部分时候伦敦塔都是令人毛骨悚然之地：英国王室的敌人被囚禁在这里，遭受非人的折磨，最后往往被斩首示众。现如今那里的卫兵却是春风满面，身着红黑两色上衣的导游还会为游客免费讲解伦敦塔的故事。在伦敦塔令人望而生畏的高大围墙内还珍藏着英国历代国王加冕典礼时所佩戴王冠上的珠宝，以及价值连城的加冕仪式服装和其他物品。

The Thames and the London Eye　泰晤士河和伦敦眼

Westminster Abbey　威斯敏斯特大教堂

伦敦塔对面是老城区的一些码头，如今已建成了时尚的现代公寓、餐馆和购物中心。伦敦桥四不像的轮廓曾令很多游客惊叹，往往把它与浮华的塔桥混为一谈。纵观历史，不难看出伦敦桥要比其相邻的惹眼的维多利亚时代建造的塔桥要重要得多。1750年以前，伦敦桥是泰晤士河上唯一的一座桥梁。在莎士比亚时代，桥两边都林立着民房和商铺。靠近桥的南端，伦敦大火纪念碑掩映在现代化建筑群之中。当时那场大火就是在这附近烧起来的。

沿着南岸再往前是泰特现代美术馆。这座于2000年开始开放的美术馆是在河畔发电站的旧址上建造起来的。这幢宏伟的大楼为来自世界各地的现代艺术品提供了宽敞明亮的展览空间。这也使原泰特美术馆得以变身为泰特英国美术馆。泰特英国美术馆是世界上收藏五百年来英国艺术品最丰富的美术馆。泰特现代美术馆对面的千禧桥是泰晤士河上最新的大桥。这座桥上禁止机动车辆通行，游人可以一边在桥上散步，一边尽情欣赏泰晤士河之风情，欣赏圣保罗大教堂的圆顶。

河对面再往前是伦敦首屈一指的艺术大厦——南岸艺术中心，这座钢筋混凝土建筑现在似乎已经过时了，但大楼内设有英国顶尖的艺术机构，如皇家节日音乐厅、国家大剧院、海沃德美术馆和国家电影剧院。

接下来是伦敦最新也是最激动人心的旅游景点——"伦敦眼"。"伦敦眼"是为迎接新千年而建造的。在建造之初，很多人担心这个巨大的摩天轮会破坏周围的景致，会破坏威斯敏斯特教堂庄严肃穆的氛围，但是只要坐上这摩天轮转上一圈就足以令那些抨击它的人马上改变自己的看法。摩天轮缓缓地在泰晤士河上空旋转，透过吊舱上的玻璃朝外望去，伦敦的美景尽收眼底，真是令人心旷神怡！摩天轮是游客观赏伦敦都市风情和高楼大厦的又一扇窗口。

从"伦敦眼"摩天轮上可以清楚地看到伦敦最著名的象征——大本钟。放置在漂亮的钟楼里的大本钟俯瞰着议会大楼。每天，钟声都会随着英国广播公司的广播而传到世界各个角落。

Big Ben　大本钟

宏伟壮丽的威斯敏斯特教堂不仅是做礼拜之地，而且也是一座国家纪念碑。国王和王后在这里加冕，百年之后也安葬在这里。另外还有很多英国文学史上的名人的骨灰也安葬在这里的诗人角，以供后人凭吊。在威斯敏斯特教堂这座精美绝伦的中世纪建筑里，既有豪华气派的纪念碑，也有简陋的坟冢。同时，威斯敏斯特教堂也是很多国宝的珍藏之地。

霓虹灯闪烁的皮卡迪利广场是伦敦主要商业街的中枢。伦敦三大商业街，即皮卡迪利大街、摄政街和牛津街上的房地产是从这里到海德公园这一区域最贵的。

Piccadilly Circus　皮卡迪利广场

The British Museum　大英博物馆

　　实际上，现在的伦敦是在不断向外扩展的过程中由很多村庄连缀而成的。很难想象，在简·奥斯汀的时代，现在已成为市中心的布鲁姆斯伯里当时只不过是个偏远的村庄，离伦敦还有相当远的距离。这个地方曾一度是出版业的代名词，如今却坐落着有"国家宝库"之称的大英博物馆。大英博物馆的收藏极其丰富，藏品来自世界各地，从史前时代、古代文明一直到现在。

　　在喧嚣的都市当中保留有大片的绿地，这是伦敦的特色之一。肯辛顿花园与海德公园毗邻，在伦敦市中心形成了大片绿色地带。离小说中神探福尔摩斯家不远的贝克街尽头是摄政公园，它就像是通往中心北部的换气孔。不计其数的小公园和绿树成荫的广场点缀着这个现代化大都市。

　　在伦敦，乘坐公共交通可以到达几乎所有的景点。通常情况下，地铁是这个城市最快捷的交通工具，同时这个城市还有四通八达的公共汽车网络。坐在在电影和明信片上经常可以看到的红色双层大巴的上层，可以尽情观赏沿途的风景。

Memories of London 记忆伦敦

The city of London left deep memories on the writer. She talked about weather, transportation, scenery and politics of London.

Memories of London[①]

◎ Ida B. Wells

The thermometer has been at freezing point several times the past week in town and there has been frost in the country. Last May when I was here, everybody said there had not been such a mild and lovely spring for twenty years; this time it is said there has not been a time within memory of the oldest inhabitant when May was so cold and rainy as now. I fully agree with the American tourist who, when asked about the English climate, remarked that "they had no climate—only samples." The only other English thing I do not like is the railway carriage. They can change the one if they cannot the other. To me, the narrow railway compartments, with seats facing each other, knees rubbing against those of entire strangers, and being forced to stare into each other's faces for hours, are almost intolerable and would be quite so, were the English not uniformly so courteous as they are, and the journeys comparatively short. But primitive as are these railway carriages, I as a Negro can ride in them free from insult or discrimination on account of color, and that's what I cannot do in many States of my own free (?) America. One other thing about English railways must strike the American traveler, the carefulness with

---

① 选自"Memories of London" in *Always Elsewhere*, edited by Alasdair Pettinger, London: Cassell, 1998。

which human life is guarded. The lines of railways are carefully enclosed on both sides by stone wall or hedge the entire length, and never cross a roadway as they invariably do in America. The railway always goes under the roadway through a tunnel or over it on a bridge. Passengers are never allowed to cross the tract from one side of the station to the other—there is always a bridge or subway. As a consequence, accidents to human life are most rare occurrences, and I begin to understand how aghast the British was to see our railway and streetcar tracks laid through the heart of our towns and cities and steam engines and cable cars dashing along at the rate of thirty miles per hour. Even in London the only rapid steam or cable locomotion is under ground.

They call the streetcars here tramways, or tram-cars, and I puzzled over it very much until I learned that a man named Outram first hit upon the experiment of rolling cars or trucks on tracks—this was before the invention of the steam engine—and all cars so propelled without the aid of steam were called Outram cars. This has since been shortened. The first syllable of the name of the inventor has been dropped, and they are known as trams. I have found many Englishmen who do not know the origin of the word, yet are surprised that the green American does not at first know what he means by trams.

London has been in the throes[①] of a cab strike for two weeks, but beyond making it safe for pedestrians there seems little notice taken of it. The hansom[②] is the only rapid means of general locomotion in London, save the Underground Railway, and there were thousands plying every hour of the day and night. They never slacken the pace when crossing the street, because there are so many streets they would always be stopping. So that between the omnibuses and cabs, persons took almost as much risk in crossing a street as they do in Chicago from the cable cars. The strike

---

① 剧痛。
② 汉孙式马车，一种双轮供两人乘坐的马车。

has taken more than half the usual number of cab off the street, and the pedestrian is enjoying the result; for this two-wheeled friend of the weary—the hansom—has rubber tires and as it rolls along an asphalt pavement, there is only the sound of the horses' hoofs, and the cab is upon you before you know it.

    London is a wonderful city, built, as everybody knows, in squares—the residence portion of it. The houses are erected generally on the four sides of a hollow square, in which are the trees, seats, grass and walks of the typical English garden. Only the residents of the square have the entrée to this railed in garden. They have a key to this park in miniature, and walk, play tennis, etc., with their children, or sit under the trees enjoying the fresh air. The passerby has to content himself with the refreshing glimpse of the green grass and inviting shade of these trees which make such a break in the monotony of long rows of brick and stone houses and pavements. The houses are generally ugly, oblong structures of mud-colored brick, perfectly plain and straight the entire height of the three or four stories. This exterior is broken only by the space for windows. The Englishman cares little for outside adornment—it is the interior of his home which he beautifies.

    There is also the charm of antiquity and historic association about every part of the city. For instance, I am the guest of P.W. Clayden, Esq.[①], editor of the *London Daily News*. His house is near Bloomsbury Square, in the shadow of St. Pancras Church, an old landmark, and from where I am now writing, I look out the windows of the breakfast-room across to Charles Dickens' London home. We are also only a few squares—five minutes' walk—from the British Museum.

    I have been too engrossed in the work which brought me here to visit the British Museum (although I pass it every day), the Royal Academy or

---

① 先生，esquire 的缩写。

Westminster Abbey, which every American tourist does visit. I have been to the Houses of Parliament twice, and also to Cambridge University. My first visit to the British Parliament was under the escort of Mr. J. Keir Hardie, M.P.① Mr. Hardie is a labor member and he outrages all the propriety by wearing a workman's cap, a dark flannel shirt and sack coat—the usual workingman's garb—to all the sittings. He is quite a marked contrast to the silk-hatted, frock-coated members by whom he is surrounded. The M.P.'s sit in Parliament with their hats on, and the sessions are held at night. A great deal of ceremony must be gone through to get a glimpse of the British lawmaking body at work. A card of permit must be issued by a member for admission to the galleries, and it is a mark of honor to be conducted over the building by one. Mr. Hardie himself had to secure a card to permit me to enter the House of Lords and look upon a lot of real live lords, who, according to the trend of public opinion, should no longer be permitted to sit upon their red-feathered sofas and obstruct legislation. There is a special gallery for women, and the night I stood outside the door and peered into the House of Commons I noticed about the speaker's chair a wire netting which extended to the ceiling. Behind this there were what I took to be gaily dressed wax figures, presumably of historic personages. Imagine my surprise when I was told that was the ladies' gallery, and it was only behind this cage that they were allowed to appear at all in the sacred precincts② hitherto devoted to men.

　　The question of removing the grille③ was again brought in Parliament this year, as it has been for several years past, but nothing came of it. An amusing incident happened two weeks ago when two ladies, strangers, had applied for permission to visit the House. A member of Parliament left them, as he thought, at the door while he went into the

---

① 议员，member of Parliament 的缩写。
② （教堂的）界域。
③ 格栅，铁栅。

chamber for the necessary card. Unaware that women were never permitted to enter, and the doorkeeper being for the moment off guard, they followed the member of Parliament up the aisle nearly halfway to the speaker's chair, when they were discovered and hurriedly taken out. They are said to be the first ladies who were ever on the floor of the House during a sitting.

  Mr. Hardie interviewed me for his paper, the *Labor Leader*, and explained much that was strange while we had tea on the beautiful terrace overlooking the Thames at 6 o'clock that evening. British M.P.'s are not paid to legislate and unless they are gentlemen of means they pursue their different avocations① meanwhile. An M.P. does not necessarily reside in the district he represents; he may be, and most always is, an entire stranger to his constituents until he "stands" for election. M.P. Naoriji, a native of India, is representing a London constituency. He is the gentleman about whom Lord Salisbury said: "The time has not come yet for a British constituency to be represented in Parliament by a black man." The English people resented this attempt to draw a color line and promptly returned Naoriji to Parliament, and Lord Rosebery, the present Prime Minister, gave him a dinner on the eve of his election.

伦敦记忆

◎ 艾达·B. 韦尔斯

过去的一周，伦敦的温度几次降到冰点，英国已经出现了霜冻。去年五月我在这里时，大家都说，二十年来从来没有过这样温和、美丽的春天；而这次，据说即使最年长居民的记忆中，也不曾有过像这样寒冷和阴雨的五月。我完全同意那个美国游客的观点，当被问及英国气

---

① 副业。

候时，他说："英国没有气候——只有不同的天气样本。"还有另外唯一一件英国的事情令我不喜欢，那就是他们的火车车厢。如果无法改变气候，这件事是他们可以改变的。对我来说，坐在狭窄的火车车厢里，面对着座位对面的乘客，膝盖摩擦着对面完全陌生人的膝盖，被迫好几小时盯着对方的脸看，这几乎令人无法忍受，如果不是所有英国男人都无一例外彬彬有礼，使得旅途似乎缩短了一些，那么这的确令人忍无可忍。但是，尽管火车车厢很原始，作为一个黑人，我可以随便乘坐火车，不会因为肤色不同受到侮辱或歧视，这是在我自己国家许多自由（？）州府所无法做到的事情。还有一件关于英国铁路的事情肯定会令美国游客震惊，那就是生命得到细心的呵护。整条铁路沿线两侧都用石墙或隔断仔细封闭起来，永远不会发生在美国经常发生的横穿铁路的事件。铁轨总是通过隧道从下面穿过道路，或者由桥梁从上面穿过道路。从来不允许乘客从火车站的一边跑到另一边——总有过街天桥或地下通道。因此，发生人身事故极其偶然。我开始明白，当英国人看到我们国家的铁路和电车轨道穿越城镇中心铺设，蒸汽机车和电缆车以每小时三十英里的速度狂奔时是多么地吃惊了。在伦敦，即使唯一的快速蒸汽机车或缆车也是在地下行驶。

这里，人们称电车为 tramway 或 tram-car，我感到非常困惑，直到我了解到，一个名叫 Outram 的人首先想到了在铁轨上行驶汽车或卡车的实验——这是在发明蒸汽机之前——所有这样不借助蒸汽驱动的汽车都被称为 Outram car，之后简称为 tram-car。发明人名字的第一个音节被省略掉，现在称为 tram。我发现许多英国人都不知道这个词的来历，然而他们感到吃惊的是绿色环保的美国人竟然起初也不知道 tram 是什么意思。

伦敦已经在出租车罢工的伤痛中捱过了两个星期，但是，除了确保行人安全，似乎没有人在意。除了地铁，马车是唯一快速的交通方式，从早到晚每个小时都有成千辆马车跑来跑去。穿过马路时，它们从不放慢速度，因为要穿过那么多条街道，如果放慢速度就总得停下来。因此，在公共马车和出租车之间穿梭，行人过马路所冒的风险不亚于穿行于芝加哥出租车之间的风险。罢工已经使超过平时一半的出租车停工，行人可以享受由此带来的结果；对于疲惫之人的这个两轮朋友——马车——橡胶轮胎滚动在沥青路面上，只有马蹄声，车到你面前你才知道车来了。

众所周知，伦敦是一个美丽的城市，依居住区域的方形广场而建。房子一般建在空旷广场四周，里面有树木、座椅、绿草和典型的英式花园走道。只有本区的居民可以进入围有护栏的花园。他们有钥匙进入这种小公园，与孩子们一起散步、打网球等，或者坐在树下享受清新的空气。幽幽绿草、诱人的树阴，树木打破了长排砖房、石头房子和路面的沉闷，路人只能以看看这些令人耳目一新的景色满足自己。房子一般都很难看，泥色砖墙的长方形结构，平淡无奇的三四层楼房。除了窗户，外墙已经破损了。英国人寥有问津外墙装饰——他们只注重美化自己家的室内。

城市的每一部分都有古香古色的韵味和历史意义。例如，我是 P.W. 克莱登先生的客人，他是《伦敦每日新闻》的编辑。他住在布卢姆斯伯里广场附近，老地标圣潘克拉斯教堂后面，从我写作的地方向外望去，透过早餐房的窗户，可以看到查尔斯·狄更斯的伦敦故居。我们离大英博物馆也只隔几个广场——步行也就五分钟的路程。

Charles Dickens' House　查尔斯·狄更斯故居

我一直太专注于工作，所以朋友才带我来到这里参观大英博物馆

（虽然我每天经过这里）、皇家艺术学院，或者还有每位美国游客必去的威斯敏斯特大教堂。我已经去过国会大厦两次，也去过剑桥大学两次。第一次参观国会大厦有 J. 凯尔·哈迪先生陪同，议员哈迪先生是名工党成员，他违反礼仪，身穿工人的日常装束——戴着工人帽，穿着一件深色绒布衬衫和麻布外套——出席所有会议。与他周围那些头戴丝绒帽身穿礼服外套的人形成鲜明对比。议员们戴着帽子坐在议会大厅里，会议在晚上举行。一定要经过许多仪式过程才能对英国立法工作窥见一斑。必须由议员颁发许可证才能允许进入议会的旁听席，由议员带领参观大楼是荣誉的象征。哈迪先生自己必须拿到许可证才能带我进入上议院，在那里看到许多现实生活中的议员。根据公众民意所向，不允许议员们坐在红色羽绒沙发上阻挠立法。有一个女性专用的旁听席，那天晚上，我站在门外朝下议院看，注意到发言人椅子周围有金属网一直通到天花板。在这背后，我想是一些穿着艳丽的蜡像，大概是些历史人物。想象一下，当有人告诉我那是女士旁听席，只有在这个防护网后面才允许她们出现在到目前为止完全属于男士的神圣领地，那时我是多么地吃惊。

The Houses of Parliament　国会大厦

去除防护网的问题今年再次在议会提出,过去几年每年都被提起,但都无疾而终。两周前发生了一件有趣的事情,两位陌生女士已经申请参观议会。一位议员让她们等在门口,自己进去领许可证。她们不知道不允许女性入内,看门人当时脱岗,于是她们跟随那名议员沿着走廊几乎走到了通往发言人坐席的半途中,就在这时,有人发现了她们,赶忙将她们请出。据说,她们是首次在开会期间进入议会的女士。

那天晚上六点钟,我们在俯瞰泰晤士河的美丽露台上喝茶,哈迪先生代表他的报纸《工党领袖》采访了我,给我解释了许多奇怪现象。英国议员立法没有报酬,除非他们是有钱人,否则他们需要同时从事不同的职业。一名议员不一定住在他所代表的区域;对于他的选民来说,在他作为候选人"站出来"之前,他可能完全是陌生人,这种情况屡见不鲜。纳欧瑞吉议员是个土生土长的印度人,他代表伦敦的一个选区。关于这位男士,约索尔兹伯里勋爵这样说:"在议会中,英国选区由一个黑人代表的时代还没有到来。"英国人很反感这种试图以肤色区分人的做法,他们立刻让纳欧瑞吉重返议会,现任首相罗斯伯里勋爵在选举前宴请了他。

London in Literature 文学伦敦

The writer describes London in the morning in great detail at his time of 19th century.

The Street—Morning[①]

◎ Charles Dickens

The appearance presented by the streets of London an hour before sunrise, on a summer's morning, is most striking even to the few whose

---

① 选自 *London in Dickens' Time*, edited by Jacob Korg, Englewood Cliffs, N.J.: Prentice-Hall, Inc., 1960.

unfortunate pursuits of pleasure, or scarcely less unfortunate pursuits of business, cause them to be well acquainted with the scene. There is an air of cold, solitary desolation about the noiseless streets which we are accustomed to see thronged at other times by a busy, eager crowd, and over the quiet, closely-shut buildings, which throughout the day are swarming with life and bustle, that is very impressive.

The last drunken man, who shall find his way home before sunlight, has just staggered heavily along, roaring out the burden of the drinking song of the previous night: the last houseless vagrant whom penury① and police have left in the streets, has coiled up his chilly limbs in some paved corner, to dream of food and warmth. The drunken, the dissipated, and the wretched have disappeared; the more sober and orderly part of the population have not yet awakened to the labours of the day, and the stillness of death is over the streets; its very hue seems to be imparted to them, cold and lifeless as they look in the grey, sombre light of daybreak. The coach-stands in the larger thoroughfares are deserted: the night-houses are closed; and the chosen promenades② of profligate③ misery are empty.

An occasional policeman may alone be seen at the street corners, listlessly gazing on the deserted prospect before him; and now and then a rakish-looking cat runs stealthily across the road and descends his own area with as much caution and slyness—bounding first on the water-butt, then on the dust-hole, and then alighting on the flag-stones—as if he were conscious that his character depended on his gallantry④ of the preceding night escaping public observation. A partially opened bedroom-window here and there, bespeaks the heat of the weather, and the uneasy slumbers

---

① 救济所。
② 散步的场所。
③ 放荡的。
④ 勇敢。

of its occupant; and the dim scanty flicker of the rushlight, through the window-blind, denotes the chamber of watching or sickness. With these few exceptions, the streets present no signs of life, nor the houses of habitation.

An hour wears away; the spires[①] of the churches and roofs of the principal buildings are faintly tinged with the light of the rising sun; and the streets, by almost imperceptible degrees, begin to resume their bustle and animation. Market-carts roll slowly along: the sleepy wagoner impatiently urging on his tired horses, or vainly endeavouring to awaken the boy, who, luxuriously stretched on the top of the fruit-baskets, forgets, in happy oblivion, his long-cherished curiosity to behold the wonders of London.

Covent-garden market, and the avenues leading to it, are thronged with carts of all sorts, sizes, and descriptions, from the heavy lumbering wagon, with its four stout horses, to the jingling costermonger[②]'s cart, with its consumptive donkey. The pavement is already strewed with decayed cabbage-leaves, broken hay-bands, and all the indescribable litter of a vegetable market; men are shouting, carts backing, horses neighing, boys fighting, basket-women talking, piemen expatiating[③] on the excellence of their pastry, and donkeys braying. These and a hundred other sounds form a compound discordant enough to a Londoner's ears, and remarkably disagreeable to those of country gentlemen who are sleeping at the Hummums[④] for the first time.

Another hour passes away, and the day begins in good earnest.

---

① 尖顶。
② 街头卖水果和蔬菜的小商贩。
③ 详述。
④ 原意为考文特花园的土耳其浴室,后来指此浴室附属的旅馆。

街头——清晨

◎ 查尔斯·狄更斯

夏日早晨日出前一小时,伦敦街头呈现的景象最引人注目,甚至对于那些寻求快乐无果的少数人,或者几乎差不多同样不幸的希望做成生意的人士,也是如此,这使他们熟悉这里的场景。安静的街道上,弥漫着寒冷、孤独、凄凉的空气,在其他时候,我们习惯于看到街道上熙熙攘攘,拥挤着忙碌、焦急的人群,此刻平静、紧闭的大楼里,整天充斥着生活的喧嚣,那真令人印象深刻。

最后一个醉汉会在日出前找到回家的路,这时刚刚蹒跚走来,狂吼着前一天晚上的醉酒歌;救济所和警察局留在街道上的最后那个无家可归的流浪者,在某个柏油马路的街角蜷缩着自己冰冷的四肢,梦想着食物和温暖。醉酒的、流浪的、不幸的人已经不见了;较为清醒、有序的人士还没有醒来开始一天的劳作,街道上死寂一片;街道的色调似乎要表现此景,破晓时分灰暗、黯淡的光线使街道看起来冷冰冰的,毫无生气。大街上的汽车站空无一人;旅馆关门了;娱乐场地空空如也。

偶尔,街道的拐角处孤零零出现一名警察,百无聊赖地凝视着自己眼前空旷的场景;有时,一只淘气的猫悄悄跑着穿过马路,尽可能小心谨慎地俯下身——先跳上水桶,然后跳到垃圾坑,然后跳到石板路——好像他知道自己的性格取决于前一天晚上自己逃避公众注视的勇敢。四处是半开着的卧室窗户,诉说着天气的炎热以及住户的睡眠不宁;通过百叶窗透出摇曳微弱的灯芯草烛光,表示这是景观房,或者有病人在此。除此之外,街道上没有生命迹象,也没有房子表明有人居住。

一小时过去了;教堂的尖顶和大楼的房顶依稀映出冉冉升起的太阳光辉;不知不觉地,大街小巷开始恢复了各自的喧嚣和活力。四轮马车缓缓地向前驶去:昏昏欲睡的车夫不耐烦地催促着疲惫的马,或者徒劳地努力唤醒那个男孩，那个男孩无拘无束四脚朝天地沉睡在水果筐上，高兴中忘了自己一直想看看伦敦景观的好奇心。

考文特花园市场，通向市场的大街，挤满了各类大小不同、外形各异的车辆，有四匹大马拉着的笨重大车，有驴拉的叮当作响的小贩车。路面上散落着腐烂的白菜叶、碎草带，以及所有菜市场都有的难以准确说出名字的垃圾；男人们在大声喊叫，车在后退，马在嘶鸣，男孩子们在打斗，提着篮子的妇女在聊天，馅饼商滔滔不绝地说着自己糕点的如何美味可口，驴在大叫。这些声音和其他一百种声音形成了足以让伦敦人听上去感到不和谐的复合音，特别对于那些第一次睡在土耳其浴室的乡村绅士来说，这种声音尤为不和谐。

又过了一个小时，新的一天真真切切地开始了。

Who Is Charles Dickens?

☞ 1812–1870. He was born in Portsmouth, England.

☞ English writer and social critic, the greatest novelist of the Victorian period.

☞ He left school to work in a factory after his father was thrown into debtors' prison.

☞ He edited a weekly journal for 20 years, wrote 15 novels and hundreds of short stories and non-fiction articles, lectured and performed extensively.

☞ Major works: *David Copperfield*, *Oliver Twist*, *Bleak House*, *A Tale of Two*

Cities, *Great Expectations*, *Dombey and Son*, and *Hard Times*.
- His works are characterized by attacks on social evils, injustice, and hypocrisy.
- His writing style is marked by a profuse linguistic creativity.
- He was an active member of many organizations including the National Association of Colored Women.
- He was regarded as the "literary colossus (巨人)" of his age.

Chapter 7   Paris

When good Americans die, they go to Paris.
—Oscar Wilde

Quotes Featuring Paris

- When Paris sneezes, Europe catches cold.
  —Prince Metternich
- Good talkers are only found in Paris.
  —Francois Villon
- You can't escape the past in Paris, and yet what's so wonderful about it is that the past and present intermingle so intangibly that it doesn't seem to burden.
  —Allen Ginsberg
- A walk about Paris will provide lessons in history, beauty, and in the point of life.
  —Thomas Jefferson
- The last time I saw Paris, her heart was warm and gay, I heard the laughter of her heart in every street café.
  —Oscar Hammerstei

Key Words

Cathedrals, sidewalk cafés, wide and luxurious boulevards.

Questions

1. What do you think is the most representative feature of Paris that distinguishes it from other European cities?
2. How do you understand the statement that cafes are Paris's window to the world?
3. How did Paris in Hugo's description differ from what it is now?

Paris Today 今日巴黎

The article provides its readers with a general picture of life and tourist attractions in Paris.

Paris Today[①]

◎ Mike Gerrard

Whether it's April in Paris or Paris in the fall, the French capital has inspired writers at all times of year throughout its history. It is known as one of the most beautiful and romantic cities in the world, dubbed the City of Light, and perhaps only Venice can rival its effect on visitors. No one can fail to be enchanted by that first sight of the Eiffel Tower[②]. Paris's

---

① 选自 *Bloom's Literary Places—Paris*, by Mike Gerrard, with Introduction by Harold Bloom, Philadelphia: Chelsea House Publishers，2005，略有删改。
② Eiffel Tower: 埃菲尔铁塔，镂空结构铁塔，1889 年建成，位于巴黎战神广场，得名于它的桥梁设计工程师居斯塔夫·埃菲尔。

many long-renowned structures, such as the Louvre[①] and the Arc de Triomphe[②], contrast in a variety of ways with the city's more modern sights, such as the Pompidou Center[③], putting the rich history of the city into dramatic relief: this new arts center literally turned architectural convention inside-out and created quite a stir when it was first built in 1977, with its normal interior features—including escalators and air ducts—all colorfully visible on the outside. Perhaps the strength of the city's traditions in all the arts provide its painters and poets, its fashion designers and filmmakers, with the incentive and the authority required to take the kind of risk and Pompidou exemplifies.

The Pompidou Center is just one example of Parisian innovativeness, and in fact, Paris gave us the expression *avant-garde* to describe anything that is forward thinking. At the same time, however, Parisians remain true to their traditions, preserving even in their everyday conversation certain niceties of social decorum. For example, it is considered rude not to greet someone with *bonjour* (good day) or *bonsoir* (good evening) before starting a conversation. And the most eccentric productions of Paris's avant-garde are often in a sense the most radically respectful of the traditions from which they depart.

Paris also has a long tradition in tourism, and the city is full of attractions; its many art galleries and museums are especially famous. Paris is an easy city to get around in, with an inexpensive metro (subway) system that goes almost everywhere. Often people prefer to walk, however, because the city is compact and it offers so many beautiful sights,

---

① 卢浮宫，世界上最古老、最大、最著名的博物馆之一，始建于 1204 年，宫前的金字塔形玻璃入口，是华人建筑大师贝聿铭设计。
② Arc de Triomphe: 凯旋门，为纪念战争胜利而建，始建于法国皇帝拿破仑一世政权的鼎盛时期的 1806 年。
③ Pompidou Center: 蓬皮杜中心，现代艺术博物馆，1977 年建成，外部钢架林立、管道纵横，是一座设计新颖、造型特异的现代化建筑。

especially by the banks of the River Seine[①], which runs right through the center of Paris.

Popular Districts

One of the most popular districts for visitors these days is the Marais[②], about one mile southeast of the Louvre along one of the city's most famous streets, the rue de Rivoli. The Marais is one of the city's oldest quarters and contains perhaps the city's loveliest square, the place des Vosges[③]. There are also numerous museums, including the Victor Hugo Museum in the author's former home, right on the place des Vosges.

Almost two miles (3 km) due north of the Louvre is another district that most visitors usually, and understandably, want to see: Montmartre[④]. This slightly elevated area, a kind of village almost, has long been the home of the city's artists. The painters Henri Toulous-Lautrec, Vincent Van Gogh, Edar Degas, and Maurice Utrillo have all called this district home. Many of them frequented the clubs and cabarets that also flourished there, including the infamous Moulin Rouge[⑤], which still exists today. Also in Montmartre is the church of Sacre-Coeur, another notable Paris landmark. From the front of the church is a splendid view across the city, making it a popular spot on weekends.

The magnificent Notre-Dame Cathedral[⑥] is the other great church that tourists typically flock to see. Construction on it was begun in 1163 and completed in 1330. When it later fell into disrepair, Victor Hugo was

---

① River Seine: 塞纳河，法国北部大河，巴黎在该河一些主要渡口上建立起来。

② 玛莱区，又译作"玛黑区"，巴黎的一个区，遍布各种风格的酒吧、另类书店、情趣商店等。

③ the place des Vosges: 孚日广场，巴黎最古老的广场，作为皇家广场（Place Royale）修建于1605~1612年。

④ 蒙玛特区，以艺术氛围和历史而闻名。

⑤ Moulin Rouge: 红磨坊，位于蒙马特高地脚下道地的法国式歌舞厅，屋顶上装有闪烁着红光的大叶轮。

⑥ Notre-Dame Cathedral: 巴黎圣母院，位于法国巴黎市中心的教堂建筑，建造于1163~1250年，属哥特式建筑形式，有小说、电影、音乐剧等以此为名。

instrumental in raising funds and campaigning to have it restored. He also wrote a book about the cathedral, whose French title, *Notre-Dame de Paris*, is lesser known than the English translation, *The Hunchback of Notre-Dame*.

Notre-Dame dominates the Ile de la Cite, one of the two small islands that stand in the River Seine. The smaller Ile St-Louis is full of atmospheric backstreets, while the Ile de la Cite contains not only the Notre-Dame Cathedral, but also the church of Sainte-Chapelle. It has one of the world's finest collections of stained glass, the Conciergerie. This church was also used as a prison at the time of the French Revolution and as the headquarters of the city's police force. Close by is the Police Judiciaire, the Paris detective force where Georges Simenon's famous fictional detective, Inspector Maigret, was based.

The Landmarks of Paris

About two mile (3 km) due west of the Ile de la Cite, past the golden dome of the Dome Church where Napoleon Bonaparte is buried, is Paris's most famous landmark: the Eiffel Tower. It was built for the Universal Exhibition in 1889, and despite its astonishing enormity—it stands 1,051 feet (320 m) high—it was only intended as a temporary structure. The tower was quite controversial, but history has silenced its early detractors, and the immense metal structure has been the signature symbol of Paris ever since. Scores of anecdotes are connected to the tower in one way or another, and even the numbers associates with it, because of its sheer size, can themselves be astonishing.

The view from the top of the tower is worth the inevitable wait for the elevator ride, with the whole city spread out all around. Just one mile due north is the city's other great landmark: the Arc de Triomphe. The triumphal arch was begun in 1806, the year after Napoleon led the French to victory against the Austro-Russian Army at the Battle of Austerlitz. One of the friezes on the side of the arch commemorates this victory, showing French troops drowning the enemy by breaking the ice on a lake.

    The arch itself was not, in fact, a great triumph for Napoleon. When he married in 1810, after divorcing his childless wife Josephine just a year earlier, he had wanted to lead his new bride through the arch and on to the wedding celebrations at the Louvre Palace. Construction had been delayed, however, and the emperor had to settle for a model of the arch instead. The real structure was not completed until 1836, and four years later Napoleon's body passed under the arch during his own funeral procession. Today, the Arc de Triomphe is the site of the Tomb of the Unknown Soldier, with its everlasting flame. In addition, the arch serves as a focal point for political rallies and major national events, such as the Tour de France.

The Picturesque Streets of Paris

The official name of the square (actually a circle) where the Arc de Triomphe is located is the place de Charles de Gaulle, named after France's great leader of the late 20th century. This square is also known as l'Etoile (the Star), because no fewer than 12 streets converge there like the points of a star. One of these streets is the broad avenue de Champs-Elysees[①], which leads in a straight line to the place de la Concorde. On its far side, and in line with the Arc de Triomphe, is the Arc de Triomphe du Carrousel, which stands outside the Louvre.

    Opposite from l'Etoile runs the avenue de la Grande Armee, which is in direct line with one of the city's wonderful modern structures, the Grande Arche at La Defense. La Defense is a business and government district complete with shops and restaurants. It is also the site of stunning modern architecture. None is more remarkable than the Grande Arche, a

---

① avenue de Champs-Elysees: 香榭丽舍大街，被誉为巴黎最美丽的街道，有很多奢侈品商店和演出场所。

futuristic cube that echoes the designs of the city's other two arches. The Grande Arche is so massive that the entire Notre-Dame Cathedral could fit underneath it.

今日巴黎[1]

◎ 迈克·杰勒德

无论是四月份,还是在秋季,法国的首都巴黎一直都是作家们的灵感之地。它是公认的世界上最漂亮、最浪漫的城市之一,被誉为"光明之城"。在对游客的影响力上,也许只有威尼斯堪与之媲美。人们无不是第一眼见到埃菲尔铁塔就为之折服。巴黎很多久负盛名的建筑(如卢浮宫和凯旋门)与城内的现代景观(如蓬皮杜中心)在诸多方面形成鲜明对比,更加彰显出城市的悠久历史:蓬皮杜这个新艺术中心实际上颠覆了建筑传统,在 1977 年落成时引起巨大轰动。通常的内部构造(包括楼梯和管道)都色彩鲜艳地展示在外部。也许,巴黎艺术传统的强大力量为其画家和诗人、时尚设计师和电影制作人提供了冒险的动力和信心,蓬皮杜就是一个很好的实例。

The Pompidou Center　蓬皮杜中心

---

[1] 出自齐林涛、王淼译:《巴黎文学地图》,上海:上海交通大学出版社,2011 年。

蓬皮杜中心只是巴黎创新精神的一个例子，事实上，巴黎还创造了一个词语"前卫"（avant-garde），用来描述所有的超前思维。但另一方面，巴黎人又忠实于他们的传统，甚至在他们的日常交谈中也保持着社会规范的某些繁文缛节。例如，与人交谈前应先以"早安"或"晚上好"打声招呼，否则就会被视为粗鲁。巴黎前卫的最怪诞的产物通常都极尊重其赖以生存的传统。

旅游业在巴黎也历史悠久，城中景点遍布，其中，为数众多的艺术馆和博物馆尤为有名。巴黎地铁四通八达，价格适宜，游玩极为方便。但人们通常更喜欢步行，因为城市不大，而美景太多。塞纳河从巴黎城正中流过，两岸美景尤为集中。

热门区域

如今最受游客欢迎的区域之一是玛莱区。沿巴黎最为有名的街道之一里沃利街前行，玛莱区就位于卢浮宫东南约一英里处，是巴黎最古老的住宅区之一，并拥有也许算是全城最漂亮的广场——孚日广场。区内博物馆不计其数，其中，维克多·雨果博物馆就在孚日广场一带雨果的故居之中。

The Louvre 卢浮宫　　　　The Place des Vosges 孚日广场

卢浮宫正北约两英里处是另一个多数游客通常都想去的区域——蒙马特区，这倒在情理之中。这一略显严肃的区域几乎可算是一个村庄，长期以来一直是巴黎艺术家的聚居地。画家亨利·图卢兹·洛特雷克、文森特·凡高、埃德加·德加和莫里斯·郁特里洛都称此区为家。夜总会和酒店在这一区也很繁荣,很多艺术家经常光顾,其中包括今天犹存的臭名昭著的红磨坊。区内还有另一处巴黎有名的地标性建筑圣心大教堂。在教堂前可以饱览全城,因此周末很是热闹。

宏伟的巴黎圣母院是另一个游人经常蜂拥而至的教堂。其建造始于 1163 年,1330 年建成。后来年久失修,维克多·雨果筹集经费,发动宣传,竭力将其修复。他还写了一本关于这个教堂的小说,书的法文名为 Notre-Dame de Paris,其英文译名则更为有名:The Hunchback of Notre-Dame。

巴黎圣母院矗立于塞纳河中的两个小岛之一西岱岛上。另一个岛圣路易岛要更小一些,岛上尽是偏街小巷,而西岱岛上不仅有圣母院,圣礼教堂也坐落在这里。教堂内精美的彩色玻璃堪称世界一流。该教堂在法国大革命时期被用作监狱和巴黎警方总部。不远处是巴黎司法警察局,巴黎侦查队伍所在之处。乔治·西梅翁著名侦探小说中的检察官迈格雷的故事就以此处为背景展开。

巴黎地标

西岱岛正西方向约两英里,越过圆顶教堂(拿破仑·波拿巴埋葬于此)的金色圆顶,就是巴黎最为有名的标志性建筑:埃菲尔铁塔。铁塔乃是 1889 年为世界博览会而建,尽管有着惊人的庞大体形——塔高 1051 英尺(320 米)——建造之时却计划只作为一个临时建筑。当时铁塔颇受争议,但历史平息了早先的非议,这个巨大的金属建筑也从此成为巴黎的标志。有关铁塔的轶事有许多,因其体形庞大,仅与之相关的数字本身就足以令人惊叹。

乘坐电梯上塔顶难免需要等候,但塔顶风光会让你感觉不虚此等:在铁塔上可以俯瞰整个巴黎。往正北约一英里处是城市的另一处地标:凯旋门。凯旋门动工修建于 1806 年,拿破仑此前一年带领法国军队在奥斯特里兹战役中大胜奥俄联军。门柱上的雕带之一展示了法国军队打破湖面坚冰、溺死敌人的场面,纪念的就是这一胜利。

事实上,凯旋门对拿破仑而言却并非一个巨大胜利。1810 年,与未曾生育的前妻约瑟芬离婚才一年,他再次结婚。他本想带着新娘穿过凯旋门到卢浮宫去参加婚礼庆典,但建造工作迟缓,皇帝不得不建了一个凯旋门的模型取而代之。真正的凯旋门直到 1836 年才完工,四年之后,拿破仑本人的葬礼举行,遗骸从凯旋门下经过。今天,凯旋门是无名烈士墓址,并燃有不灭的火焰。此外,凯旋门还是政治集会和全国性重大活动(如环法自行车赛)的中心。

The Eiffel Tower　埃菲尔铁塔　　The Arc de Triomphe　凯旋门

风景如画的巴黎街道

凯旋门所在的广场(广场呈圆形)的正式名称是夏尔·戴高乐广场,以二十世纪后期法国卓越领袖的名字命名。广场也被称为星形广场,因为多达十二条街道如同一颗星的各角在此交汇。其中一条就是可以直达协和广场的香榭丽舍大街。在大街的另一端,与凯旋门相望的是坐落于卢浮宫外的小凯旋门。

星形广场对面是万军林荫大道,大道直接连通巴黎壮观的现代建筑之一拉德芳斯宏伟拱形门。拉德芳斯是拥有商铺和餐馆的商业区和政府区。它还是令人叹为观止的现代建筑所在地。宏伟方拱门引人注目,无与伦比。其新潮的立方体结构,正与巴黎的另外两个拱门的设计相呼应。宏伟方拱门如此巨大,即使把整个巴黎圣母院置于其下都不成问题。

The Avenue de Champs-Elysees 香榭丽舍大街

Paris Impression 印象巴黎

The author describes his visit to Paris, especially the moments of frequenting cafes and seeing French girls. He also compares what he is seeing with the impression he had about Paris.

Doing Paris with Breyten[①]
© Lewis Nkosi

1

Paris in Summer! In the white light of August we grew dim with heat. We sat at Cafe Le Select on Boulevard Montparnasse[②] watching the girls

---

① 选自 "Doing Paris with Breyten" in *Always Elsewhere*, edited by Alasdair Pettinger, London: Cassell, 1998。Breyten Breytenbach（1939-），布雷滕·布雷滕巴赫，作者游览巴黎时的导游，南非作家、画家、政治活动家。

② Boulevard Montparnasse: 蒙巴纳斯大道，曾在法国文化艺术史上领过几十年风骚，如今风韵尤存，依然能引起许多人怀旧眷念的街区。

arrive and depart. At the end of the first week it seemed to me that we had done nothing but watch girls arrive and depart from the cafes. They bore themselves gravely against the wild light of August, against the very motionless stillness of summer, their elegantly French bodies hallowed① in a nimbus② of startlingly white brightness, sometimes arriving delicately at the crowded cafe, pausing briefly near the entrance to survey the perpetually shifting scene, then in a carefree moment of sudden, inscrutable③ decision, stepping firmly toward an empty seat; and silhouetted④ men who had hoped against hope that this "careless, unemphatic⑤" body would deposit itself in the empty, adjacent seat would watch it go by, growing lax⑥ with despair.

Though they pretended otherwise in their cultivated French ennui the girls' departures seemed to me even more spectacular! They would get up from the tables with an air of utmost gravity, pushing back their chairs with little scraping sounds; then carefully weighing their bodies against the concentrated vision of lascivious⑦ males, they would pick their way adroitly⑧ among tables and chairs, all the time cajoling⑨ the eye with an amazing hip-rolling motion that instantly informed the cafe with an atmosphere of an absurdly desolate regret for some thing we all felt to have been within reach but which we had failed to notice or possess.

It seems to me that French girls do not walk at all. Their movement is a perpetual dance, a subtle abandonment of the body to the gay crowded activity of the street. In no other city have I seen girls walk like that. As

---

① 神圣化。
② 光轮，气氛。
③ 不可理解的。
④ 显示轮廓的。
⑤ 不作强调的。
⑥ 散漫的。
⑦ 好色的。
⑧ 巧妙地。
⑨ 哄骗。

days went by it seemed somehow that every walk away from a cafe was a wealthy event to be solemnly witnessed and marvelled at. The swaying hips, the quivering quick narrow breasts inadequately sheltered behind low-necked sweaters, the sly subtle mutilation① of air by bare arms and bronzed legs which shocked by their eager surrender to the bawdy②, fatal, joy of sensual movement—Sex: however, unconscious and reluctant these momentous motions and casual passings, they brought the slumbering sexual images naturally to mind. Something dark and ancient was being celebrated every time a French girl walked away from a cafe. In my mind these girls awakened memories of Zulu③ women balancing incredible cargo on their sturdy, beautiful necks and the effortless manner in which they negotiated their way up the incline of a hill. To walk like that a girl has to lose all fear of the body and be on terms of absolute trust with it.

　　Paris is of course a city hopeless obscured by history, and yet forever accessible, even to those who have never seen it, through its history. It is obscured because so much has been written about Paris that it is no longer possible for anyone to arrive in the city for the first time without looking at it through glasses coloured by a wealth of fiction and literary romance. For Africans who neither had the literary technique nor much use for documented history, it is awesomely astounding to see how much of eighteenth and nineteenth century Paris still abides to intrude into the twentieth century. It is an intimation of a past forever engraved in stone, secreted in darkened ageless building and weather-bitten statuary.

　　My first encounter with Paris was in my early boyhood in Durban④, South Africa, even before I had raised any hopes of ever walking her streets in some distant future.

---

① 切断。
② 低级下流的。
③ 祖鲁族，非洲的一个民族，主要居住在南非。
④ 德班，南非第二大城市。

Having discovered at an early age that I wanted to write I began a systematic raid of the libraries during which I was continuously but graciously rebuffed by embarrassed English lady librarians, until, one day, in angry desperation, I cornered a mobile library for non-whites in (of all places) Red Square, that scene of many stormy political meetings, during which my rights to read were hotly demanded and unjustly disputed. In those first books I borrowed I was introduced for the first time to the literary embodiment of European history by the works of Dumas, Flaubert, Balzac and Hugo, and I began my first journey to France and to Paris. I grasped at the Collins classics primarily because for any alum boy the neat leather-bound books looked invaluably posh[①] and expensive; the vocabulary gave me as much pleasure as it gave me trouble; but such is the power of adventure and romance on a boy's imagination that I struggled through the novels with an array of dictionaries until I had garnered a formidable word-list that astonished my essay master. It is to the credit of Dumas' compulsive readability that I pursued his three musketeers[②] through their daily assignations until, many books later, they were no longer sufficiently young or agile to carry them out; whereupon I turned my attention to the rising fortunes of their offspring till the day I ran out of Dumas' novels. Hugo's *Les Miserables*[③] reduced me to tears and for years I was haunted by the spectre of poor starving wretches in dark narrow streets. It was a picture of Paris that was only counterbalanced by that other Paris of Louis XIV and his powdered, coiffured, glittering courtiers.

My Paris is therefore stubbornly eighteenth and nineteenth century—a city of horses and cobble streets, a city of revelry[④], intrigue,

---

① 精美的。
② 火枪手，大仲马的《三个火枪手》中的人物。
③ *Les Miserables*:《悲惨世界》。
④ 寻欢作乐。

romance, violent revolution and desperate sexual liaisons; a city of duels and dark assignations. For me Dumas and Hugo have ruined forever the actual city; I can't possess the Paris of 1965 without possessing the literary ruins another Paris irrecoverably lost in the shadow of dream and romance. Asleep in the Paris hotel room of 1965 I can still hear the horses of Porthos and D'Artagnan cantering in the midnight streets outside and the dark narrow lanes of Victor Hugo's Paris are still there, fearful with the squandered secrets of yesterday. In fact so possessed is my imagination that when I see a French lady pouring out tea I stare instinctively and apprehensively at the large stone on her finger, for the nineteenth century novelist taught me to expect a thimbleful[①] of poison to be stored up inside that gleaming stone, the contents of which might be emptied into somebody's cup at the flicker of the modest eyelashes.

It is perhaps understandable that when I encountered my real Paris for the first time in 1963 I felt that I had been inexcusably let down. It seemed to me that the beautiful city of my dreams had fallen before advancing hordes of American tourists whose pockets bulged with dollars. Each time or nearly each time I put my hand under the cafe tables in St Germain-des-Pres it came into contact with lumps of chewing gum left there by American coeds from Louisville Kentucky or wherever they are supposed to come from! French people on the other hand were skinning everyone within range of the cash register. One night in Montmartre we had to protest loudly that we were no American tourists though we spoke English before a third had to be taken off the price of the drinks! That—the meanness and the bad weather—finally proved too much for me and I was glad to leave for the quiet of Normandy. It was only during the subsequent visits that I saw the Paris which I had not permitted myself to see during that first encounter. I suppose for everyone there is still enough

---

① 极少量的。

of the old Paris to cherish the city—there is the air of informality and freedom, the much storied Parisian indifference to what people do with their lives, the inimitable① style of the French woman and the much enduring beauty of the city's architecture.

2

The first time I saw Paris was in the summer of 1963 when I was on my way back to Africa. An American television company had signed me on as an interviewer for a series of programmes of African writers. In the hope of tracking down M. Leopold Senghor, the poet-president of the Senegalese Republic, M. Leon Damas, the Martinique poet, and French critics specialising in the field of African literature, we flew into Paris on a Thursday in the evening of August 1, 1963. It was a trying time for me; after the hustle and bustle② of London interviews my nerves were shot; I was feeling—well, yes—feeling very black, very irritable, demanding of Paris that it should be everything it was rumoured to be—and more! I find that the entry I made in the ill-kept diary on that occasion tells a grim story of nerves, dark depression and disappointment:

> *The drive to the air terminus (Invalides) was disappointing. Paris is so bleak and drab, it remains me of Ronnie Segal's description of it: "an old whore in a dirty shabby corset③." It started to rain while we were on our way to the terminus. Then we had to wait for a taxi while it poured down on us. Saw my first French policeman wearing a black cape over his dark uniform. Certainly not as tall and forbidding as policemen look elsewhere. Looks rather like an actor impersonating the*

---

① 不可效仿的。
② hustle and bustle: 熙熙攘攘。
③ 紧身胸衣。

police ...

On that first, dark rainy drive into the city the outer edges of Paris had seemed to me no more than a "vast post-war slum" and it took me somewhat longer to discover that soft, rose-hued Paris of imperishable beauty and ineluctable[①] romance. It was during the four days I spent in the city in the April of 1964 which confirmed the grievous error I had made on that first dark encounter with Paris. Then this year, through the kindness of a friend, my wife and I were left in possession of a three-roomed apartment on Rue Brezin, very near Montparnasse, from which we made daily sorties into the Quarter. The apartment we occupied was up on the fifth floor, with balconies overlooking a small park and square. Climbing up the narrow winding staircase every day was an arduous task, but one which we soon grew to appreciate after the French police who had been called out one night to suppress a party that had become too boisterous[②] left without firing a shot. It seemed to them a long way to travel to the fifth floor on that winding old-fashioned stairway; so they contented themselves with shouting warnings and threats from the street below.

It was a beautiful apartment and we slept with the windows open. Lying in bed at night it was possible gaze across the empty square at the buildings opposite, which were then shrouded[③] in darkness save for the lighted windows that looked like rectangular shapes of muted, coloured lights against the darkened night sky. Watching Paris from the balcony at night always made me feel as though we were suspended in a void of darkness over the city. In the morning, before we were fully awake, French voices were already assailing the peace in the shopping street

---

① 不可避免的。
② 狂躁的。
③ 覆盖。

below; and in the park, across the street, white and Negro children frolicked① in outbursts of energy and noise which were not dissimilar to random explosions of cannon fire. Indeed, the children captured the quarter early in the morning and did not break their siege until late forenoon when they were completely dazed by the sun. The adults, on the other hand, sat contentedly on benches, placed inside the park, their faces uplifted to the sun in a dutiful pose of worshipful adoration. By nine o'clock in the rear balcony the sun was already hot enough to sunbathe; occasionally, I came out in pajamas to see a young woman, nude as a spear, standing at the balcony window of the apartment across the courtyard, her glossy, shadowless, white skin yellowed to dull gold by the rising sun; her form, so casual, so seemingly free, was always too stark not to be startling; and yet there was nothing erotic about it; I am perhaps making too much of a small incident; but it seemed to me that despite the rapid embourgeoisement② of much that is radical and independent in Parisian life, that nude woman symbolised what is still the essence of Paris—a certain worldliness and freedom which attract new waves of exiles to this city every year, young people in flight from the inhibiting provincialism of their own native cities.

3

All day long at the Cafe Select, on Boulevard Montparnasse, people arrived, mostly young men and women, to sit at the tables, sunning themselves like lizards. A number of them came to stare and be stared at, and for this purpose dark glasses were worn like armour. When the sun dipped down behind the buildings on the western fringe the migration began to the Coupole across the street. The Dome, the Coupole, and the Select are just three of the Montparnasse cafes which used to be

---

① 嬉戏。
② 资产阶级化。

frequented by some of the leading figures of the so-called Lost Generation; and it was surprising to me to find that after two successive generations, writers and artists who now find it unthinkable to be seen at places like Deux Magots, still haunted these cafes in Montparnasse; and the impression they conveyed was always that of beleagured[①] artists manning the last front against the creeping inroads of the French bourgeoisie and dollar-laden tourists.

The Coupole, which is full almost every day round about midnight, looks like a large medieval banqueting hall with murals which were painted by famous artists before they became too famous to paint for nothing. We found Giacometti, the internationally famous sculptor, there one night, brooding over a piece of white paper upon which he had been doodling[②]. "In this quarter," a young painter told me, "it is still a shock to hear anyone introduced as a businessman." Like many historic places the Coupole is now threatened with demolition and there are romours that an American-owned business establishment is to be set up in its place.

At the Select across the street announcements are made at intervals through the loudspeaker system, summoning famous personalities to the telephone. At one time it is a well-known French theatre critic; the next moment it is the small, doll-like, blonde actress of the *nouvelle vague* films; blue eyes, skin like honey and white-fringed conical breasts visible for all the world to see under the plunging neckline of her mustard sweater and scanty[③] bra.

What immediately shocks someone coming from London is to find this casual acceptance of the proximity of glamour and fame and the complete lack of hostility toward the artist. For ages the artist has been part of the community and no one reacts any more. In London any

---

① 围困。
② 乱画。
③ 缺乏的，单薄的。

confession that one writes, paints or sculpts is treated as cause either for mirth①, pity or as reason for the profoundest distrust. It is also generally assumed that any famous artist who visits a popular pub—except the obscure country places—is either not serious or is shamelessly cadging② for publicity. For a sculptor of Henry Moore's stature to be seen frequenting a pub in Soho would stimulate so much doubt about his sense of propriety as to be actually damaging to his reputation. That is because the relationship between the artist and his society in England is still essentially one of suspicion and distrust. Yet in Paris, there was Giacometti, to be seen almost every night either at the Coupole or the Dome, and his present there was treated by the cafe crowd with respectful but most casual interest.

Our own guide into the Latin Quarter of 1965 was Breyten Breytenbach, a South African painter and poet who has lived in Paris for five years and speaks fluent French. Breyten is something rare among Afrikaners: he has pushed his rebellion against the Afrikaner's narrow parochialism③ to a point where, without making any political gestures, he has been able to mix and be accepted by some very left-wing artists in Paris. His estrangement from his own Afrikaner people was perhaps sealed when he married a Vietnamese girl, the daughter of a former Vice-President of South Vietnam. On one score at least the decision could not have been very difficult to make, for Yolande Breytenbach is a ravishing beauty; and being Paris-born she combines naturally and gracefully the occidental and the oriental sides of her upbringing.

Each day then we carried to the cafe our neat stack of notebooks, papers and pens which we heroically supposed were mightier than swords and each day we suffered cruel defeat in the face of other more numerous,

---

① 欢乐。
② 乞讨，索要。
③ 地方观念。

diversionary interests. How any writer has been able to work in a Paris cafe is the kind of mystery that I cannot hope to unravel. Yet it seems that the lonely and the homeless, the dwellers in cold-water flats, the romantic searchers and the predatory, have, each in his own season, sometimes found it necessary to annex a Paris cafe as a place in which to work, to rendezvous, or simply to become part of the daily drift to nowhere. I know of no other city where it is so easy to drift and more difficult to work.

For an African in Europe the Paris cafe is what gives street life its tang, sharpness and point. At the Coupole one night a young Dutch painter told me: "I've visited London from time to time; I'm afraid I cannot live there. For a painter there is no community, no place to meet other painters, and everything closes so early!" He shrugged his shoulders and surveyed the boulevard which at the hour of midnight was swirling with September crowds. It is true, of course, that we have the English pub in London; but the business hours are so restrictive that they only compel the sleepless, neurotic artist as well as the potential sexual offender to roam the street aimlessly after hours. "Time gentlemen, please," a cry in which the English take such secret pride, is a cruel mindless surrender to self-inflicted pain and discomfort. After 11 p.m. in London you really have no place in which to meet your friends except in some noisy discotheque[①] or dreary expensive night club or some sad, indescribably pretentious restaurant.

Perhaps the observation is no longer fresh, but after spending two months in Paris it was possible to discover anew just how effectively the cafe has served Parisian society as the focus of the city's social life. The rich may have Maxim's but the poor have the cafe in which it is possible to lunch on a sandwich and cheap red wine while calmly enduring the withering scornful gaze of the *garcon*[②]. I am also certain that not only are

---

① 迪斯科舞厅。
② 侍者。

Chapter 7 Paris • 157 •

the sins of murder, adultery and theft conceived mostly at the cafe table, but important books, plans for revolutionary warfare and the assassination of national figures thousands of miles away from French soil continue to be plotted at the cafe table.

In the space of one morning at the Cafe Select we had spoken to an African student from Kenya, a Negro musician from Martinique, a coloured painter from the United States. Walking by to buy English newspapers from a kiosk① I caught a glimpse of a member of the Pan-Africanist Congress (South Africa) concealed behind his dark glasses; then sat down with a French girl who was a member of the Liberatory Committee of Portuguese Guinea and then chatted with a London representative of the African National Congress recently flown in to collect some paintings for his London exhibition. Indeed, I would not have been surprised to find a member of Dr. Verwoerd's government similarly anchored in a nearby seat. Paris is truly a city of exiles and the cafe is its window to the world. Here it is well-nigh② impossible for any young woman to nourish her dreams of solitude or to indulge small private griefs and disappointments without being offered a shoulder to cry on. And any Frenchman, however puny, imagines that his shoulder is broad enough to offer to any young woman in distress.

In London I have often been appalled by the depth of loneliness to which single girls from the provinces are condemned, especially if they are shy and retiring by nature. There is no way whatever to meet boys in an atmosphere of freedom, without feeling a sense of commitment, save by attending numerous, insupportably dull, parties from which any girl is lucky to emerge with a bumbling oaf③ who is capable of defending the cause of human reason in tolerably good English. As a consequence, any

---

① 售货亭。
② 几乎。
③ 呆子，畸形儿。

"decent" English girl who finds herself approached by a strange man in the street feels it her more obligation to reach under her tweed skirt for a former Girl Guide whistle. Talk about "sexual revolution"; it would be more accurate to describe it as "sexual panic"!

One can understand, of course, why it is now generally believed that because French girls are friendly they are just as ready for a tumble①. In Paris, especially in a cafe, there is no opprobrium② which attaches to a girl for speaking to a complete stranger, an attitude which appeals enormously to a great many Africans like myself, brought up to feel that it is failing in one's social obligation to sit next to a young woman without paying her some gallant③ attention, however unprepossessing she looks. I was therefore happily surprised by the freedom of Paris! Here at the crowded or almost empty cafe, dreams are finally harvested or nullified④: the golden woman in your trouble feverish dreams arrives mercifully on the appointed hour to sit in full view at the table across from yours. Naturally, it may take a certain amount of ingenuity and hard talk to convince her that you are indeed the Prince destined to sweep her off her feet; but at least the woman of your fantasies is not forever imprisoned in some obscure dream of a super Mayfair⑤ night club or country estate, forever fleshless and inaccessible to your sweaty, tobacco-stained fingers!

4

When evening came and the dense heat of a summer day had changed into a bracing sensual coolness of a Paris evening, we rode a cab from St Michel to Rue Brezin, collecting liquor bottles as we went along. The old woman hauled the bottles down from the shelves as we pointed them out

---

① 混乱。
② 耻辱。
③ 献殷勤的。
④ 使抵消。
⑤ 伦敦的上流住宅区。

at the shop; then as we seized them, ready to leave, she held our attention with a fretful① insistent desire to talk. "You're lovers?" she said. "Young love is a beautiful thing, no?" The French girl and I laughed, but did not explain that we were not lovers because it seemed a good thing to give flesh to the old woman's nostalgia for a departed youth. After the damp fog of England's racism it was also refreshing to find an old woman who was able to take inter-racial love so much for granted; indeed, this was a prelude to a bright, orgiastic② night of dance, talk and drinking which went on for a little quieter but still wanton③ enough, sharpened at times by intellectual contention. After a long evening of theoretical debate with someone a French girl gave up on the English language: "I'm too tired to think in English!" Raymond Kunene, the Zulu poet, shuttled between the bookshelves and the dance floor, was seen at one time executing a spectacular war dance which brought a passionate exaltation to the face of an old Negro painter, Beauford Delaney, for twelve years self-exiled from the United States. "I came to Paris for a weekend and stayed for twelve years!" Now drawn to the madcap frolic of that Zulu dance Beauford Delaney looked both sombre and fervid④, sad and ecstatic, already beginning to ask himself what Africa meant to him, which is to say he had already started on that long journey into the dark night of the Negro psyche where every question leads to the nightmare of slave ships. But if there is anything that Paris teaches it is that exile is the modern condition; and yet for the Negro and the African this is also the century of reunion; here in the warm intimate hour of midnight; with the city slumbering in the darkness, exile spoke to exile, the South African to the doubly exiled American Negro, and out there at the cafe tables one knew there were

---

① 烦躁不安的。
② 狂欢的。
③ 放肆的。
④ 充满激情的。

others just as exiled, just as quick, just as reckless, just as driven, each knowing the truth of his loneliness only in the private cells of his body, or in the illuminated faces of those who had similarly suffered. Dancing, jumping up and down, fierce in dispute, gaiety and sadness was finally their portion. "Aren't they jus' beautiful people!" Delaney enthused.

与布雷滕游巴黎

◎ 刘易斯·恩科西

1

夏日的巴黎！八月刺眼的骄阳使我们看不清周围事物。我们坐在蒙巴纳斯大道的菁英咖啡厅，看着女孩们来来去去。第一周周末，对我来说似乎我们什么事情也没做，只是看着女孩们在咖啡厅出出进进。她们对八月的微风、夏天的静谧感到厌烦，她们优雅的法国人身体在异常明快的氛围里显得神圣化，有时高雅地光临熙熙攘攘的咖啡厅，在入口处稍作停留，环顾着永远喧闹的场面，然后在无忧无虑间变得令人难以捉摸，突然作出决定，步伐坚定地走向某个空座位；男人们希望这个"轻松、欢快"的身影可能会坐在自己身边，希望落空后，他们会眼巴巴地看着女孩从自己身边走过，倍感绝望而变得越发懒散。

Le Select Cafe　菁英咖啡厅

虽然女孩们在自己特有的法式懒散掩盖下假装并非如此，但是她们的离去似乎对我来说更为壮观！她们表情严肃起身离桌，悄无声息地将椅子推回原处，然后小心翼翼地出现在男人好色目光的聚焦下，灵巧地穿过桌椅，眼睛一直闪着勾人的神情，夸张地扭动着髋关节，这个动作令咖啡厅里充满了令我们都觉得有些事情绰手可得但却因为没有注意到或没能拥有而莫名其妙感到遗憾的气氛。

在我看来，法国女孩根本不是在走路。她们走路的动作永远是在跳舞，轻巧地将身体沉浸于街头活动拥挤的欢快人群中。在其他任何一个城市我都没有看到有女孩这样走路。一天天过去了，好像每次路过咖啡厅都是一件需要严肃对待并惊叹的重大事件。摇曳的臀部、低领衫下颤动的丰满乳房、裸露的手臂和古铜色的大腿肆意在空中晃动，急于展示着淫秽、欢快的肢体动作——性感；然而，在不经意间和不情愿间，她们做着这些重要动作而随意走过，带来了沉睡已久的脑海中自然形成的色情形象。每次法国女孩从咖啡厅走过，都是在宣扬一些晦涩、古老的东西。这些女孩唤醒了我的脑海里关于祖鲁妇女的记忆，她们用自己结实、漂亮的脖颈驮着重物并保持平衡，轻松地行走于上坡的山路。像巴黎女孩那样走路必须得不惧自己的身体，对自己有绝对的自信。

当然，巴黎这座城市留下了挥之不去的历史痕迹，因为有了历史，即便从来没有见过巴黎的人都可以了解这座城市。历史模糊了城市，因为有太多关于巴黎的故事，所以，任何人初到巴黎，都会不可避免地透过小说和文学中大量浪漫描写的有色眼镜看巴黎。对非洲人来说，他们既没有掌握法国文学背景也没有太多地翻阅历史文献，当看到这么多十八、十九世纪的历史仍然伺机入侵二十世纪的巴黎，对此感到非常震撼。历史永远地被镌刻在石头上，藏于不见天日的古建筑物里和经过日月洗礼的雕像中。

初次与巴黎相遇是在南非的德班，那时我还是个孩子，甚至想都没想过将来会有机会走在巴黎的街道上。

从小就发现自己有写作欲望，于是开始长时间泡在图书馆里系统地阅读，期间不断遭到英国女图书馆员和蔼而断然的拒绝，直到有一天，在生气和绝望中，我被轰到了一座在红场为非白人开设的流动图书馆（所有地方都有），在许多场面热烈的政治集会中，我强烈要求获得读书的权利，但都被不公正地驳回了。在借阅的第一批图书中，我第一次读到了以文学形式表现的欧洲历史：大仲马、福楼拜、巴尔扎克和雨果的作品，于是开始了自己的法国和巴黎的初次游历。我惊叹于柯林斯的经典作品，主要因为对任何生活在贫民窟的孩子而言，方方正正皮革装帧的图书看上去那么高贵、奢华；那些词汇在带给我乐趣的同时也带我给同样的烦恼；但这正是冒险文学和浪漫文学对一个孩子想象力产生的影响，我借助各种字典拼命阅读这些小说，直到掌握了足以令作文老师吃惊的词汇。大仲马的小说引人入胜，可读性强，正因为如此，我才得以追随他的三个火枪手的刀光剑影，直到读了若干部作品以后觉得没有什么新意了，他们在我心目中不再年轻不再灵巧，也就不再随时随地带着这些书看了；那时，我将注意力转向他们以后的多部作品，直到读完大仲马的所有小说。雨果的《悲惨世界》令我伤心落泪，多年来，黑暗狭窄街道上饥饿、贫困的可怜人形象挥之不去。这就是巴黎的画面，这样的画面只有靠路易十四的另一个巴黎以及他那些涂脂抹粉、穿着考究、容光焕发的朝臣才能与之形成鲜明对比。

因此，我心目中的巴黎定格在十八、十九世纪——城里的马车走在石子路上，狂欢、迷人、浪漫之城，充斥着暴力革命和淫乱的性关系；那也是决斗和秘密幽会之城。对我来说，大仲马和雨果永远毁了巴黎的实际形象；1965年我对巴黎的印象无法摆脱也无法挽回地迷失于文学废墟中描写的梦幻、浪漫阴影中的另一个巴黎。1965年躺在巴黎的旅馆，我仍可以听见外面波尔多斯和达尔达尼央的马车在街上慢跑的声音，维克多·雨果笔下巴黎的狭窄街巷还在那里，其间充满了昨日的秘密而令我感到害怕。事实上，我的想象已经魔障了，看到一位法国女士倒茶时，本能地心中充满悬念，盯着她手指上的那枚大宝石，因为那位十九世纪的小说家曾经告诉我，那块熠熠发光的石头里面可能藏有微量毒药，一眨眼间毒药可能会倒进某人的茶杯。

或许可以理解当我在1963年第一次真正与巴黎相遇，我感到自己之前无端地对巴黎太失望了。对我来说,梦中的美丽城市在一群群钱包鼓鼓的美国游客光临前已经衰落了。每次或者说几乎每次我把手放在圣日耳曼德普雷教堂门前咖啡厅的咖啡桌下面,都能摸到来自肯塔基州路易斯维尔或其他什么地方的美国女大学生留下的一团团口香糖!而法国人则在收银台范围之内对此嗤之以鼻。有一天晚上在蒙马特,我们不得不大声抗议,虽然我们说英语,但是我们不是美国游客!之后,他们才将饮料价格便宜了三分之一。店主的小气和坏天气最后证明对我来说太过分了,我很高兴去往安静的诺曼底。只是在随后游览巴黎期间,我才看见自己刚到时没有看到的事物。我想,对每个人来说,巴黎有足够需要珍藏的历史——随意、自由的氛围,被写进许多故事的巴黎人无所谓的生活的态度,法国女人那无与伦比的姿态以及城市建筑经久不衰的魅力。

2

初次见到巴黎是在 1963 年夏天返回非洲的路上。一家美国电视公司与我签约制作一部关于非洲作家的系列节目。抱着追随塞内加尔共和国诗人总统 M. 利奥波德·桑戈尔、马提尼克诗人 M. 里昂达马斯以及非洲文学领域的法国评论家足迹的希望,我们在 1963 年 8 月 1 日星期四的晚上飞抵巴黎。对我来说,这是个难熬的时刻;伦敦喧嚣的采访后,我的神经已经精疲力竭了;我感到——是的——感觉郁闷、烦躁,于是对巴黎分外苛刻,觉得巴黎就应该跟传说中的一模一样——而且还要更好。我发现自己零落的日记记录了当时精神紧张、忧郁沮丧、灰心失望的时刻:

> 驱车前往机场真令人失望。巴黎如此黯淡、乏味,令我想起了罗尼·西格尔描述的巴黎:"一个穿着破旧紧身胸衣的老妓女"。路上开始下雨。然后,大雨倾盆,而我们不得不等出租车。我第一次看到法国警察,他们身穿深色制服,上面披着黑色雨衣,看上去不像别处的警察那样高大、令人敬畏,而更像冒充警察的演员……

第一次黑夜冒雨开车进入巴黎，在我看来，城市边缘那些地区只不过是个"战后巨大的贫民窟"，花了好长时间我才发现巴黎温柔、玫瑰色的不朽魅力和骨子里的浪漫。1964年4月，我在巴黎待了四天，这四天证实了那次与巴黎初次黯然邂逅我犯了个严重的错误。随后，今年我和妻子有机会由于朋友的慷慨住进了靠近蒙巴纳斯位于布拉钦街一套三居室公寓，这样我们可以每天光顾蒙巴纳斯区。我们住的公寓在五楼，有阳台可以俯瞰楼下的小公园和广场。每天爬上狭窄迂回的楼梯是一项艰巨的任务，但是，很快爬楼梯就变成了一件令我们喜欢的事情，因为有一天晚上，楼里的聚会声音太吵，有人叫来法国警察，他们没开一枪就处理好问题，然后离开了。对他们来说，爬上弯曲老式楼梯五层的路似乎很长；因此，他们只好从街道上大喊着发出警告和威胁。

这是一座漂亮的公寓，我们睡觉时开着窗户。晚上躺在床上，凝视着空旷广场对面的大楼，漆黑一片中还有几个窗户亮着灯，看起来好像是无声长方形里的彩灯映衬在夜幕笼罩的黑暗之中。夜晚从阳台俯瞰巴黎，总使我感觉自己仿佛悬浮在城市上空空旷的黑暗中。早上，我们还没有完全醒来，法国人的说话声已经打破了楼下购物街的平静；街道对面的公园里，白人孩子和黑人孩子淘气地戏水打闹，发出的噪音不亚于火炮突然发出的爆炸声。确实，孩子们一早占领了这块地盘，直到接近中午时眼睛被照得看不清东西他们才回家。而大人们则心满意足地坐在公园的长凳上，脸朝着太阳微微扬起，摆出一副对太阳尽职尽责的崇拜姿势。九点钟，房屋后面的阳台已经热到足以享受日光浴了；偶尔，我穿着睡衣走出来，看到一个年轻的裸体女人，站在院子对面公寓的阳台窗户前，她那富有光泽、白皙的皮肤被冉冉升起的太阳映成暗金色；她的外形表现得如此随意，如此无拘无束，看到此无不令人吃惊；然而，这一切似乎与色情无关。或许我太在意小事，但在我看来，尽管巴黎人激进、独立的生活快速地资产阶级化，那个裸体女性的象征意义仍是巴黎的本质——有些世俗、自由，每年吸引着一波波新的流亡人士来到巴黎，吸引着逃离自己本地生活的城市年轻人。

3

在蒙巴纳斯大道上的菁英咖啡厅，从早到晚不断有人来，大多是年轻的男男女女，他们坐在桌边，像蜥蜴一样晒着太阳。有些人凝视别人，有些人被别人凝视，为此，他们戴着的墨镜像穿着的铠甲一样。太阳西下，落到了西边大厦的后面，圆顶咖啡厅热闹起来。圆顶、多摩和菁英只是蒙巴纳斯若干咖啡厅中的三家，所谓"迷惘的一代"的一些领头人物经常光顾那里；看到连续两代之后，作家、艺术家仍然经常光顾蒙巴纳斯的咖啡厅，我对此很吃惊，现在这些人很难想象自己会出现在像双偶咖啡厅这样的地方；他们给人的印象总是身陷囹圄的艺术家坚守在最后的前沿阵地，阻止法国资产阶级和口袋里揣满美元的游客的蚕食鲸吞。

圆顶咖啡厅几乎天天爆满到午夜时分，看上去就像一个中世纪的宴会大厅，布置着由著名艺术家一名不文时绘制的壁画。我们发现有一天晚上国际著名雕塑家贾科梅蒂在那思忖着一张他曾涂鸦的白纸。"在这里，"一个年轻画家告诉我，"如果有人被以商人的身份介绍给别人，听起来仍然很令人震惊。"像许多历史悠久的名胜古迹一样，圆顶咖啡厅也面临被拆除的危险，有传言称，这里要建一家美国企业。

街道对面的菁英咖啡厅，每隔一段时间都会通过扬声器系统广播通知，召唤名人接电话。有一次，有人找一位著名的法国戏剧评论家。还有一次，有人找一位小巧的像洋娃娃一样金发碧眼的新潮电影演员；蓝眼睛，像蜂蜜一样的皮肤，全世界都可以看到她那低领芥末色毛衣和薄薄胸罩里面白色流苏装饰的圆锥形乳房。

随意接受魅力和名气而完全没有对艺术家的敌意，这种现象令来自伦敦的游客立刻感到震惊。多年以来，艺术家一直是社区的一部分，没有人再有什么反对意见。在伦敦，任何艺术的表白，无论是写作、绘画还是雕塑，都被认为会成为笑柄、令人怜悯，或者成为内心不信任的原因。人们还普遍认为，除了黑暗的乡村场所以外，光顾流行酒吧的任何一位有名艺术家都是或者不太严肃，或者无耻地希望吸引公众的注意。对于像亨利·摩尔这样的雕塑家，如果在苏荷酒吧经常看到他的身影，会令人怀疑他做事没有分寸，这样实际上会损害他的名誉。这是因为在英国艺术家和社会的关系本质上仍然存在怀疑和不信任。然而，在巴黎，几乎每天晚上在圆顶或多摩都可以看到贾科梅蒂，他的出现会引起咖啡厅顾客的敬意和不太特别的兴趣。

Les Deux Magots　双偶咖啡厅

La Coupole　圆顶咖啡厅

The Dome　多摩咖啡厅

我们1965年游览拉丁区的导游名叫布雷滕·布雷滕巴赫，他是一位南非画家、诗人，已经在法国生活五年了，能说一口流利的法语。布雷滕具备一些非洲人罕见的特质：他一直推进反抗非洲人的狭隘主义的运动，已经达到了不必做出任何政治姿态就能与一些非常左翼的巴黎艺术家混在一起并为他们所接受的程度。他与自己非洲同胞的隔阂或许因他娶了一位越南女孩而定格。那个女孩是南越南前副总统的女儿。约兰德·布雷滕巴赫美得令人陶醉，这一点至少使布雷滕不是那么难作决定；约兰德出生在巴黎，她自然而优雅地在成长过程中结合了东西方的特质。

每天，我们都把一摞整齐的笔记本、纸和笔带到咖啡厅，我们英勇地认为文字比武力更强大，每天，当我们面对其他各种不同旁门左道的兴趣时，我们都会遭受残酷的打击。一个作家如何能在巴黎咖啡厅里工作是一个令我无法解开的谜。然而，孤独的人、无家可归的人、住在没有热水供应公寓里的人、寻找浪漫和捕捉猎物的人士，似乎每个人都各得其所，有时发现有必要将巴黎咖啡厅作为另一个工作、幽会的场所，或者只使其成为每天四处游荡的一个落脚点。我知道，其他任何一座城市都不能这么容易四处游荡，这么不容易投入工作。

对于一个在欧洲的非洲人来说，巴黎咖啡厅提供了街头生活的饮品，也赋予了这种生活独特魅力和意义。一天晚上在圆顶，一位年轻的荷兰画家告诉我："我总去伦敦，但恐怕无法生活在那里。对画家而言，没有社区，没有场所与其他画家相识，所有的店铺都早早打烊了！"他耸耸肩，看看林荫大道，时值九月的午夜，街上还有一群群人匆匆走过。当然，在伦敦也有英式酒吧，但是，营业时间非常严格，使得那些失眠的、神经质的艺术家以及伺机作案的性罪犯在酒吧打烊后漫无目的地在街上游荡。"先生们，时间到了，你们请吧"，这样的声音里英国人暗自骄傲，不经意间残酷地给自己造成了痛苦和不适。晚上十一点以后，在伦敦你真的没有地方会朋友，除了在一些嘈杂的迪斯科舞厅或者沉闷、昂贵的夜店，或者一些令人伤感且自命不凡的餐厅。

或许，观察到这些已经不再新鲜，但是，在巴黎逗留两个月之后，有可能重新发现巴黎的咖啡厅如何成功将巴黎人社团作为城市社会生活的焦点进行服务。有钱人可能喝麦馨咖啡，而穷人也可以在此消费，要个三明治、廉价的红酒当作午餐，同时忍受着侍者轻蔑的目光。我还可以肯定的是，坐在咖啡桌周围不光可以筹划罪恶的谋杀、通奸和盗窃，而且还可以构思重要的著作、绘制革命战争计划，以及在远离法国几千英里的土地上暗杀国家重要人物的计划。

一天早上，在菁英咖啡厅，我们与一位来自肯尼亚的非洲学生交谈，他是个来自马提尼克岛的黑人音乐家，也可以说是来自美国的黑人画家；散步去一家便利店买份英文报纸，我瞥见泛非大会（南非）的一名成员，他戴着深色墨镜隐藏自己的身份；然后与一位法国女孩坐下来，她是葡萄牙几内亚解放委员会的成员；然后，又与一位最近飞来巴黎为自己的伦敦展览搜集绘画作品的非洲国民大会伦敦代表交谈。确实，如果我发现维沃尔德博士的政府官员坐在周围，也不会感到任何吃惊。巴黎确实是流放人士之城，咖啡厅是巴黎的世界之窗。这里，任何年轻女子几乎都不可能滋养自己孤独的梦想，也无法沉浸于自己微不足道的悲伤和失望中，因为总有肩膀供她伏在上面哭泣。任何法国男人，无论多么渺小，都会想象自己的肩膀足够宽厚，足以让任何伤心女子倚靠。

在伦敦，常常看到来自伦敦以外地区的单身女孩因无尽的孤独受到谴责，特别是如果她们生性害羞和内向，为此我感到非常震惊。除了参加无数平淡的聚会，女孩们在自由的气氛中遇见男孩，她们没法不感到一种责任感，任何女孩都很幸运，身边不乏装腔作势的呆子，他们用还算流利的英语为人性原因辩护。因此，任何"体面"的英国女孩如果发现街上有陌生男人朝自己走来，感觉自己更有义务应该将手伸到斜纹软呢裙下，拿出早就放在里面的女孩专用警报笛。谈论"性革命"，更准确地应该称之为"性恐慌"！

当然，人们能够理解，为什么现在普遍认为因为法国女孩友好所以她们就容易栽跟头。在巴黎，特别是在咖啡厅，没有人会因为女孩与陌生人说话而谴责她，这种态度对许多像我这样的非洲人很有吸引力，我们这些非洲人从小到大都觉得如果坐在一名女孩旁边，无论这个女孩长相多么一般，如果不大胆地关照她，就是没有履行好自己的社会责任。因此，巴黎的自由令我感到惊喜。这里，在人头攒动或几乎空无一人的咖啡厅，梦想终于或者实现或者破灭：令你不安狂躁的梦中金色女人，亲切和蔼地在约定时间在众目睽睽之下坐到你的对面。

当然，使她相信你确实就是命中注定抱起她的白马王子，还需要一些聪明才智和艰难谈判；但是，至少梦中情人不会永远囚禁在一些超级上流社区的夜总会或乡村庄园里，永远是无血无肉，永远在你那汗渍的烟草熏黄的手指渴望不可及的模糊梦想之中。

4

夜幕降临，夏日白天的热浪已经变成了拥抱巴黎夜晚的凉意，我们乘坐出租车从圣米歇尔到布拉钦街，一路搜集酒瓶子。我们在商店里指着那些瓶子，有个上年纪的妇女从货架上将它们拿下来；然后，当我们拿起那些瓶子准备离开时，她急于希望与我们交谈，这引起了我们的注意。"你们是情侣？"她问。"年轻人相爱是一件很美好的事，哈？"我和那个法国女孩笑了，但是没有解释我们不是情侣，因为给这个老妇人逝去的青春提供些怀旧的素材似乎是件好事。英国种族主义的阴霾之后，有老妇人能将不同种族之间的相爱看作如此理所当然的事情，真令人耳目一新；确实，这是舞蹈、谈话和喝酒欢快、疯狂之夜的前奏，这些活动虽然较为安静，但仍然足够放纵，有时可以得到精神上的满足。一个法国女孩一晚上长时间与人理论后，放弃了使用英语："我烦透了用英语思考！"祖鲁诗人雷蒙·库内在书架和舞池之间穿梭，有一次，有人看见他在跳一种场面壮观的战争舞蹈，这令一位从美国流亡生活在巴黎十二年的老黑人画家波福特·德莱尼神采飞扬、欣喜若狂。"我来巴黎度周末，却在这儿待了十二年！"现在，被那个狂妄、嬉戏的祖鲁舞蹈吸引，德莱尼看上去既忧郁又狂热，既悲伤又欣喜，他已经开始问自己非洲对他意味着什么，也就是说，他已经开始了那段走进黑人心理黑夜的漫长旅途，每一个问题都可以令人想到买卖奴隶航海行程的噩梦。但是，如果巴黎教给了人们什么，那就是流亡是现代社会的一种情况；然而，对黑人和非洲人来说，现在也是团聚的世纪；在这里，在这午夜温暖亲密的时刻；城市沉睡在黑暗之中，流亡人士彼此倾诉，南非人与过着双重流亡生活的美国黑人交谈，而人们知道，在外面的那些咖啡桌旁，还有其他这样的流亡人士，也是一样没有根基，无所谓，一样被放逐，每个人都知道他在身体里或者在那些同样痛苦的人们神采奕奕的面颊上，隐藏着的寂寞的真相。跳舞、跳上跳下、雄辩、欢乐和悲伤最终都是他们生活的一部分。德莱尼热情地说："难道他们不是很可爱的人吗！"

Paris in Literature　文学巴黎

Victor Hugo offers his readers a bird's-eye view of Paris. This picture of hundreds of years ago is different from the present Paris. Historical traces are written into Hugo's description.

A Bird's-Eye View of Paris[①]

◎ Victor Hugo

And if you would receive from the old city an impression the modern one is incapable of giving, go at dawn on some great festival—Easter or Whitsuntide[②]—and mount to some elevated point, whence the eye commands the entire capital, and be present at the awakening of the bells. Watch, at a signal from heaven—for it is the sun that gives it—those thousand churches starting from their sleep. First come scattered notes passing from church to church, as when musicians signal to one another that the concert is to begin. Then, suddenly behold—for there are moments when the ear, too, seems to have sight—behold, how, at the same moment, from every steeple[③] there rises a column of sound, a cloud of harmony. At

---

① 选自 *The Hunchback of Notre-Dame*, Volume 3, Chapter 2, New York: Barnes & Noble Classics, 2004.
② 圣灵降临节，为纪念耶稣复活后差遣圣灵降临而举行的庆祝节日，为复活节后第七个星期日，次日星期一放假。
③ 尖塔。

first the vibration of each bell mounts up straight, pure, isolated from the rest, into the resplendent① sky of morn; then, by degrees, as the waves spread out, they mingle, blend, unite one with the other, and melt into one magnificent concert. Now it is one unbroken stream of sonorous sound poured incessantly from the innumerable steeples—floating, undulating②, leaping, eddying over the city, the deafening circle of its vibration extending far beyond the horizon. Yet this scene of harmony is no chaos. Wide and deep though it be, it never loses its limpid clearness; you can follow the windings of each separate group of notes that detaches itself from the peal③; you can catch the dialogue, deep and shrill by turns, between the bourdon④ and the crecelle; you hear the octaves leap from steeple to steeple, darting winged, airy, strident from the bell of silver, dropping halt and broken from the bell of wood. You listen delightedly to the rich gamut, incessantly ascending and descending, of the seven bells of Saint-Eustache⑤; clear and rapid notes flash across the whole in luminous zigzags, and then vanish like lightning. That shrill, cracked voice over there comes from the Abbey of Saint-Martin; here the hoarse and sinister growl of the Bastille⑥; at the other end the boom of the great tower of the Louvre. The royal carillon⑦ of the Palais scatters its glittering trills on every side, and on them, at regular intervals, falls the heavy clang of the great bell of Notre-Dame, striking flashes from them as the hammer from the anvil. At intervals, sounds of every shape pass by, coming from the triple peal of Saint-Germain-des-Prés. Then, ever and anon, the mass of sublime sound opens and gives passage to the stretto of the Ave-Maria

---

① 华丽灿烂的。
② 波动的，起伏的。
③ 钟声。
④ 低音。
⑤ 圣厄斯塔什教堂，建于 1532 年到 1637 年间，以圣母院为典范。
⑥ 巴士底狱，一座曾经位于法国巴黎市中心的坚固监狱，建造于十二世纪，当时是一座军事城堡，十九世纪的浪漫主义历史学家把巴士底狱当作法国专制王朝的象征。
⑦ 钟琴。

chapel, flashing through like a shower of meteors. Down below, in the very depths of the chorus, you can just catch the chanting inside the churches, exhaled faintly through the pores of their vibrating domes. Here, in truth, is an opera worth listening to. In general, the murmur that rises up from Paris during the daytime is the city talking; at night it is the city breathing; but this is the city singing. Lend your ear, then, to this tutti[①] of the bells; diffuse over the ensemble the murmur of half a million of human beings, the eternal plaint of the river, the ceaseless rushing of the wind, the solemn and distant quartet of the four forests set upon the hills, round the horizon, like so many enormous organ-cases; muffle in this, as in a sort of twilight, all of the great central peal that might otherwise be too hoarse or too shrill, and then say whether you know of anything in the world more rich, more blithe, more golden, more dazzling, than this tumult of bells and chimes—this furnace of music, these ten thousand brazen[②] voices singing at once in flutes of stone, three hundred feet high—this city which is now but one vast orchestra—this symphony with the mighty uproar of a tempest.

巴黎鸟瞰[③]

◎ 维克多·雨果

假若你想得到一个古代巴黎的印象，那是现代巴黎不能给予你的，那就请在一个盛大节日的早晨，当太阳从复活节或者从圣灵降临节升起的时候，攀登到一个可以俯瞰这首都全景的高处，去倾听晨钟齐鸣吧。

---

① 合唱。
② 黄铜的，声音响亮刺耳的。
③ 选自 http://www.woyouxian.com/b06/b060402/balishengmuyuan_cn33.html。

A Bird's-Eye View of Paris
巴黎鸟瞰

Notre-Dame of Paris
巴黎圣母院

  去看看天空一角的颜色——那是阳光照射成的，去听听成千座教堂一下子颤动起来，起先是一阵丁当声从一座教堂响到另一座教堂，好像音乐家们宣告演奏就要开始一样。突然之间，你看吧（因为耳朵有时好像也有视觉呢），看看同时从每座钟楼里升起一根根声音的圆柱，一片片和声的云烟。最初，每只钟的振动笔直地、简单地升起来，也可以这么说，它不和其他钟的振动相混，一直升到早晨灿烂的天空里。随后它们逐渐愈来愈搅在一起，混在一起，成为一个壮丽的大合奏。现在只有一大片响亮的颤音不断地从无数钟里升起，在城市上空飘浮、波动、跳跃、回旋，并且把它那震耳欲聋的颤音扩散到远远的天边去。但这和声的海洋并不是一片混乱，它既深沉又辽阔，而且不失其明朗性。你可以看见成群的音符从每只钟里蜿蜒而出，跟随着这木铃和巨钟的时而尖厉时而低沉的和鸣，你可以看见各种八度音程从一座钟楼跳到另一座钟楼，你可以看见它们飞越地、轻捷地、响亮地从银钟里出来，落到木钟里就变得嘶哑而破碎。在它们之中，你会特别赞赏圣厄斯达谢教堂的七口钟忽起忽落、变化多端的音阶，你看见从每个方向跑来了清亮而急剧的音符，作了三四个光辉的转折，又像光一样消逝了。那边是圣马尔丹寺院尖锐而薄弱的歌声，这边是巴士底狱悲惨而枯竭的调子，另一边是卢浮宫大钟塔的歌唱性男低音。王宫的御钟不断向各个方向抛掷它那华丽的颤音，圣母院钟塔上沉重的钟声均匀地落在它上面，使它像一块铁砧在铁锤下闪出了火花。你时时还听见来自圣日尔曼·代·勃雷大寺院的钟乐三重奏的各种声调，这一雄壮的乐声逐渐散开，让路给突然升起的圣母颂——它像一顶用星星缀成的冠冕一般凸现出来。在下面，在这个大合奏的最深处，你可以模糊地分辨出教堂内部的歌声从拱顶颤动着的洞孔里传出来，这实在是一部值得一听的歌剧。一般说来，巴黎在白天发出的种种声音，是这座城市在讲话；夜晚的声音，是这座城市在叹息；而刚才提到的那些声音，则是这座城市在歌唱。把你的耳朵朝向这些钟的合奏吧，听听那五十万人的絮语，那河水永恒的呜咽，那风无休止的叹息，那天边山岭上四座森林像管风琴那样遥远而低沉的四重奏。听听那最中心的排钟吧，它那最尖细和最沙哑的声音怎样融化成为一种中等的响度。你说，世界上还有什么能比这钟声和铃声的汇合，比这个音乐的大熔炉，比这支在三百英尺高的云端里同时吹响的石笛，比这座像乐队似的大城市，比这像暴风雨在咆哮似的大合奏更为壮丽、更为辉煌、更为灿烂的呢？

The Storming of the Bastille　攻占巴士底狱

Who Is Victor Hugo?

☞ 1802–1885.
☞ French poet, novelist, and dramatist, the most well-known of all the French Romantic writers.
☞ Best-known works: novels of *The Hunchback of Notre-Dame* (1831) and *Les Miserables* (1862), and poetry of *Les Contemplations* and *La Legende des Siecles*.
☞ He was involved in politics as a champion of Republicanism, and forced into exile from 1855 to 1870 due to his political stances.
☞ His work touched upon the political and social issues and artistic trends of his time.
☞ He finally returned to his Paris in 1870, and hailed as a national hero.
☞ He was elected to the National Assembly and the Senate.
☞ He was revered as a towering figure in literature, a statesman who shaped the Third Republic and democracy in France.
☞ He was buried in the Pantheon.

Chapter 8   Prague

Prague is the Paris of the '90s.
—Marion Ross

Quotes Featuring Prague

- Prague isn't just a city, but an entity of some kind.

—Sezin Koehler

- Prague never lets you go ... this dear little mother has sharp claws.

—Franz Kafka

- If European cities were a necklace, Prague would be a diamond among the pearls.

—Anonymous

- The ancient splendor and beauty of Prague, a city beyond compare, left an impression on my imagination that will never fade.

—Richard Wagne

Key Words:
History, castles, Prague University, Franz Kafka, and civilization.

Questions
1. How does the essay "Prague" show that Prague is a city in-between the east and the west?
2. In what way is Prague a city of Kafka?
3. The Great Wall of China is supposed to be a symbol of civilization. How does Kafka's essay "The Great Wall of China" subvert this deep-rooted idea?

Visiting Prague 游览布拉格

Prague, a city that links Western and Eastern Europe, features itself in both western capitalist and eastern socialist ways. The following essay gives full play to both of these aspects.

Prague[1]

◎ Nicolas Guillen

The traveller visiting Czechoslovakia for the first time gets the impression of walking into a huge museum which had gathered its strength and animation under the influence of a subtle but obdurate[2] will. For Americans (including those from the North), such a feeling is even keener

---

[1] 选自 "From New York to Moscow, via Paris" in *Always Elsewhere*, edited by Alasdair Pettinger, London: Cassell, 1998。

[2] 顽固的。

because the life of our continent is like the cry of a new-born baby alongside the venerable stones on which the European spirit generally resides. Paris? Well … Paris is a multiple city, and being so, it receives into its bosom all kinds of different currents, which the boulevard or the Academy, the dancehall or the atelier① channel into a universal stream. Ancient and modern—"audacious, cosmopolitan"—it is still the centre of bourgeois culture, whose brilliant colours recall those of some organic matter in the process of decomposition.

But Prague, which is a very European city, is not Paris … which is very Parisian. In the oldest part of town, spread out along the Moldau②, the centuries seem to sleep their durable history, a history of stone: that history which eventually becomes an examination platitude. The whole Czech country is suffused with the memory of Charles IV—"the first European on the Bohemian throne"—whose dynamism as a builder broadened the vision of the local spirit which had persisted from the time when the city was little more than a fort surrounded by the shacks of Jewish fishermen.

Reminders of feudalism are everywhere; not of course in people's behavior—and even less so now, but very much so in the historical documentation, in the severe and noble past, dominant in the atmosphere of that marvellous set of relics.

When we fly over Bohemia or over Slovakia, our eyes are caught not just by the constant repetition of the urban pattern—luminously white cottages with red roofs—mute witnesses to a past medieval splendour. Later, they figure in profuse number in the "programme of visits," enough to become something of a fairly pleasant nightmare. Jorge Amado, the Brazilian novelist, rejected them outright. "I prefer," he said, "to see life: I want to know what Czechoslovakia is like today …"

---

① 工作室。
② 摩尔道河。

The country—150 thousand square kilometres and 13 million inhabitants—is populated by two distinct groups, the Czechs and the Slovaks, whose political organization stems from the ninth century, under the Great Moravian Empire. The empire was finally destroyed by the invasion of the Magyars, who dominated Slovakia for a thousand years—until 1918—while Bohemia developed under German influence.

Such a difference in origin is of course noticeable in the character of the two peoples. When I was in Bratislava, the Slovak capital bathed by the waters of the Danube①, they said to me:

"Do you know how to tell a Czech from a Slovak?"

"No."

"It's very simple. When a Czech gets drunk, he climbs on the table and goes to sleep; when a Slovak gets drunk he climbs on the table and dances ..."

The Slovaks put it down to their Hungarian blood that they're happier and more lively than the Czechs—who pride themselves on being serious, hardworking and studious; the former are Catholics, the latter Protestants; the Czechs drink beer, the Slovaks wine ...

As a result of the First World War, Czechoslovakia emerged in 1918 as an independent republic, free at last of its traditional bonds. Then came the Nazi occupation, which provoked a dramatic liberation movement. Since last year, through the revolutionary events of February, it has been transformed into a popular democracy. Today it is a huge socialist experiment, of which I certainly saw some signs during my stay in the country.

I remember, for example, that after dinner at the Hotel Paris in Prague, somebody mentioned the Workers' Diplomatic School ...

"What's that?" I asked, somewhat surprised.

---

① 多瑙河。

"Just what it sounds like. We are undertaking an interesting experiment: the creation of a diplomatic corps drawn from the working class. Would you like to visit these workers in their school and see for yourself the future diplomats?"

"You bet! Let's go straight away!"

We didn't go immediately, but two days later. One morning a young man and a very charming young woman came to pick me up at the hotel, and invited me to follow them. Before long the car we travelled in was going up the slope into Prague Castle, which overlooks the city. In an instant we were in front of an ancient building—an old feudal palace—on the top floor of which was what we were looking for, the *Delnicka Diplomaticka Skola*, that is to say, the Workers' Diplomatic School … A staircase, a small room, and then another, which was the office of the director, Yanku Vladimir, a young man with blue eyes, blond hair and an intelligent face.

"All this is brand new," he warned me, through the interpreter, Miss Reinhaltova. "The school was opened on the 13th of June this year, so it's not yet a month old …"

"Do you have many students?"

"Fifty-four."

"Classes?"

"Every day. It's a boarding school. The students live here and come from different parts of the Republic. They've been selected from the workers who have given most proof of their love of the study of social problems. Each factory proposes a certain number of candidates, who are rigorously examined and selected …"

"How long does the course last?" I asked again.

"A year. When the academic studies finish, they go on to the Ministry of Foreign affairs, where they make contact with what we might call the core of their career."

"Apart from political and technical disciplines, what other subjects do they follow?"

"Czech literature, world literature; figurative arts, music, history, geography. Some aspects of general culture, which they'll extend later."

"Do they study French?"

"No; English and Russian."

After I'd filled several pages of my notebook, Yanku Vladimir gently interrupted me:

"My dear friend, time passes and something important is still missing. The students are waiting for you …"

"For me?"

"For you … They've been waiting for an hour and I fear they may be getting impatient. Besides, it seems as if they are going to give you a little something to do."

We went out into a short corridor that led us to the classroom. We went in and the students, three girls among them, got noisily to their feet. The director then told me that the students wanted to ask me some questions about Cuba.

I willingly agreed, of course, surrendering myself to the voracity of those young people, in whose eyes our country perhaps appeared enveloped in a distant mist out of which poked the swaying and golden tips of the coconut palms.

But the questions were not of touristic or picturesque variety. How did Cuba get its independence? Do the blacks and whites mix socially? Are the workers organized? A real regulation bombardment[①] … I'd hardly replied to one question before another was posed. Many of them had their notebooks and took careful notes.

Finally they wanted me to recite them a poem.

---

① 轰炸。

"But you won't be able to understand it!" I replied.

They stuck to their guns. They wanted to "hear Spanish verse." I read them the poem, and then had to give them a summary, which Miss Reinhaltova translated for them.

Another day I visited Prague University, where I was taken by Jaroslav Kuchvalek, who teaches Spanish language and literature in the Faculty of Philosophy. I went to his class and spoke to his students, young men and women. Among the latter were some singularly beautiful girls, who sang, to their own guitar accompaniment, songs in a very good Spanish, which didn't surprise me since Kuchvalek, their teacher, speaks it perfectly, and even with a marked Madrid accent … What was amusing was that after my talk they made me sing myself, and in "plainsong," that's to say with no accompaniment, since I've never played an instrument.

Until the Nazis arrived (killing off all cultural expression), university teaching in Czechoslovakia had a formalist character, theoretical and academic. When the country was liberated in 1945, the old establishment that the invaders had closed down was opened again. Except that a great wind of healthy suspicion was beating at its walls. Progressive student leaders, like Kazimour, first, and then Pelikan, played a role similar to that of Mella's at Havana University, although none of them met the tragic fate of the inspirational Cuban student.

It was also in that same Prague University that I witnessed one night an event in which I took a lively interest. In a huge room, one of the biggest there, a motley[①] crowd squashed together: soldiers, students, teachers, workers, but also no lack of young middle-class people. And for what? A poetry reading. A competitive reading in which six or seven poets participated and where every poem and even every line was judged, and

---

① 混杂的。

which was the occasion for a heated discussion.

The poets were on a kind of stage, presided over by the famous Vitezslav Nezval, author of the *Nocturnal Poems*, among which is the already classic one devoted to the North American inventor, Edison.

Naturally it was impossible for me to follow the lines of the debate in Czech, but a Spanish-speaking friend kept me in touch with the gist of the discussion. The heart, or nub, or that discussion was as follows: What new directions are currently opening up for national poets as a result of the revolutionary transformation taking place in Czechoslovakia? It was curious to observe the interest with which the audience, made up of such diverse parts, followed the intricacies of a discussion which had at its centre subtle literary speculations. The name of Nezval was often heard, and you could see him turning in his seat or protesting passionately in a language which, although it was unintelligible to me, was impressive in its fluency.

Through his lyrical[①] learnings, Nezval belongs to the generation of Czech poets grouped together in the school known as Poetism, active since 1922. He was really its most important figure, as he would later be in Czech surrealism. Although he is a man committed to the political change that took place a year ago in his country, there is still in his writing many of the formalist elements characteristic of both schools. This year Nezval published a new book—*The Big Clock*—which in the judgement of his critics contains many poems written in a style that is "taboo." Poets of the new generation admired him, but don't imitate him. Young Czechs know his earlier poems by heart, but demand that he now sings of the new times with more conviction. The author of *Nocturnal Poems* doesn't refuse, but maintains that poetry conceived within socialist realism should not mean simple propaganda or sloganizing ... as produced by the youngsters who

---

① 抒情的。

criticize his. And Nezval draws support from the words of the Minister of Information himself, Kopecky, who, talking about them, wrote without any beating about the bush: "They think that it's enough to scatter through the poem without rhyme or reason our most current expressions, such as 'shock troops,' 'brigades,' 'political meetings,' 'national committees,' 'tractors,' 'combine harvesters,' etc., for such abortions to be called poetry …"

布拉格

◎ 尼古拉斯·古伦

初次参观捷克斯洛伐克的游客感觉好像走进了一座大型博物馆，在微妙而冷静的意志影响下博物馆凝聚了能量和活力。对来自美洲（包括来自北美）的游人来说，这种感觉更为强烈，因为美洲大陆的生活就像沿着富含欧洲精神的古老石头发出的新生婴儿的哭声。巴黎怎么样？嗯……巴黎是座多样化的城市，正因为如此，巴黎接受各种不同流派的思想，无论林荫大道还是学术学院、舞厅或者工作室都汇成统一的潮流。在巴黎，古老与现代并存，"大胆创新、国际化"，那里仍是资产阶级文化中心，它那绚丽的色彩令人想起分解过程中的一些有机物质。

但是布拉格是座很欧洲的城市，它不是巴黎……却极具巴黎的特点。伏尔塔瓦河流域是城市最古老的部分，几个世纪以来似乎都沉睡在自己绵延不断的历史中，这是沉淀在石头里的历史：最终成为老生常谈的历史。整个捷克国家充满着对查尔斯五世——"波西米亚王位的欧洲第一人"——的记忆，他作为建设者的活力扩展了这座城市本土精神视野，这种精神从布拉格还仅是犹太渔民窝棚包围的堡垒时就一直存在。

封建主义的遗迹无处不在；当然，不在人们的行为举止中——甚至现在更加如此，而在历史记载中、在严肃而高尚的过去中、在那些令人称奇的文物所主宰的氛围中，这种情况尤为如此。

当飞越波西米亚或斯洛伐克时，我们的眼睛不仅被不断重复的城市格局所吸引——红色屋顶的明亮白色小屋——静静地见证着中世纪曾经的辉煌。后来，这些小屋还充斥于无数"游览计划"中，足以成为一些既令人愉快又如同噩梦般的东西。巴西小说家豪尔赫·阿马多含沙射影地反对如此。他说，"我喜欢观察生活：我想知道捷克斯洛伐克今天是什么样子……"

捷克斯洛伐克国土面积十五万平方公里，人口一千三百万，由捷克人和斯洛伐克人两个不同的群体组成，他们的政治组织源于九世纪的大摩拉维亚帝国。帝国最终因马扎尔人的入侵而灭亡，马扎尔人统治斯洛伐克一千年，直到1918年，而波西米亚在德国的影响下发展起来。

当然，这种起源的不同在两类人的性格中可以很容易看出来。当我在斯洛伐克首府布拉迪斯拉发沐浴在多瑙河中时，他们问我："你知道如何区分捷克人和斯洛伐克人吗？"

"不知道。"

"非常简单。当捷克人喝醉时，他们爬上桌子，然后呼呼大睡；当斯洛伐克人喝醉时，他们爬上桌子，然后翩翩起舞……"

斯洛伐克人将此归于自己的匈牙利血统，他们比捷克人生性更快乐、更活跃，捷克人引以为豪的是他们的认真、勤奋和好学；斯洛伐克人是天主教徒，捷克人是新教徒；捷克人喝啤酒，斯洛伐克人喝葡萄酒……

作为一战结果，1918年捷克斯洛伐克成立独立的共和国。终于摆脱了传统束缚，可接着又是纳粹占领，这激起了强烈的解放运动。自去年以来，通过"二月革命"事件，捷克斯洛伐克已改造为一个民主国家。今天，捷克斯洛伐克正在作着关于社会主义的巨大尝试，我在捷克斯洛伐克逗留期间看出了一些迹象。

比如，记得在布拉格的巴黎饭店吃完饭，有人提到工人外交学校……

我感到有些吃惊，问道："工人外交学校是什么？"

"就是字面表达的意思。我们正在进行一次有趣的尝试：创造一个来自工人阶级的外交使团。你想去学校访问这些工人们并亲自看看这些未来外交官吗？"

"当然了！我们马上去！"

我们没有马上去，而是两天后去的。一天早晨，一位年轻男士和一位非常迷人的年轻女士来旅馆接我，并邀请我跟他们一起。不久，我们乘坐的汽车沿着俯瞰城市的布拉格城堡的斜坡往上行驶。转眼间，我们来到一座古建筑面前，那是一座旧的封建宫殿，宫殿的顶层就是我们要找的地方，即工人外交学院……楼梯、小房间，然后又是一间小房间，那是扬库·弗拉基米尔主任的办公室，他是个年轻人，长着蓝眼睛、金黄的头发和一张睿智的脸。

Prague Castle　布拉格城堡

扬库通过翻译小姐赖因哈尔托娃告诉我说："这一切都是全新的，学校今年六月十三日开学，所以还不到一个月……"

"学生多吗？"

"五十四个。"

"课多吗？"

"每天都有课。这是一所寄宿学校，学生们住在这里，他们来自国内不同地区。他们是从最能证明自己热爱研究社会问题的学生中挑选出来的,每家工厂提供一定数量的候选学生,这些学生经过了严格审查和筛选……"

"要上多长时间的课程?"我又问了一遍。

"一年。专业课程结束后,他们继续去外交部,在那里,他们将接触到我们可以称之为事业核心的事务。"

"除了政治和技术学科,他们还学习什么其他科目吗?"

"捷克文学、世界文学、具象艺术、音乐、历史、地理。他们以后还将学习一些大众文化的课程。"

"他们学法语吗?"

"不学。学英语和俄语。"

在我写满了好几页笔记之后,扬库·弗拉基米尔轻轻地打断了我:"亲爱的朋友,时间不等人,还有些重要事情。学生们在等你……"

"等我?"

"等你……他们已经等了一小时了,我担心他们可能会等得不耐烦。还有,好像他们要你做些事情。"

我们走出房间来到通往教室的短短走廊。走进教室,学生们中有三位女生,学生们吵吵嚷嚷地站了起来,随后主任告诉我,学生们想问我一些关于古巴的问题。

我欣然应允,尽力回答那些年轻人的各种问题,在他们眼里,我们的国家似乎笼罩在遥远的迷雾中,摇曳着椰子树棕榈叶的金边。

但是,他们的问题没有关于旅游或风景类的。古巴如何获得独立的?社会生活中,黑人和白人混在一起吗?有工人组织吗?真是制度的轮番轰炸……我还没来得及回答这个问题,他们又问了那个问题。许多人都拿着笔记本仔细记录。

最后,他们要我背诵一首诗。

我回答说:"但是你们听不懂呀!"

他们坚持要我背诵一首,因为他们希望"听到西班牙语的诗句"。我给他们读了一首诗,然后给他们讲解了大概意思,让赖因哈尔托娃小姐给他们翻译。

又过了一天,在雅罗斯拉夫·库查瓦莱克——他在哲学系教西班牙语言和文学——的带领下，我参观了布拉格大学。我去了他班里，与年轻学生们一起交谈。有些女生特别漂亮，她们用吉他伴奏，自弹自唱，用流利的西班牙语演唱歌曲，对此，我并不感到意外，因为他们的老师库查瓦莱克能讲一口流利的西班牙语，甚至带着明显的马德里口音……有趣的是，与他们谈话后，他们让我独唱，而且是"清唱"，也就是说，没有伴奏，因为我从来没有弹奏过任何乐器。

Prague University　布拉格大学

直到纳粹到来（一切文化表达方式遭到扼杀）之前，捷克斯洛伐克的高等教育教学在理论上和学术上都具有形式主义的特点。当这个国家在1945年获得解放时，侵略者废除的旧体制重新开放，尽管对旧体制刮起了一定的怀疑之风。进步学生领袖，如，先是卡茨摩尔，然后是伯利坎，与哈瓦那大学的梅利亚起到相似的作用，虽然这些学生领袖没有遭遇那些情绪激昂的古巴学生的悲惨经历。

有天晚上，也正是在这所大学我亲眼目睹了一件很令我感兴趣的事情。在学校的一间大厅里，一群人聚在一起：士兵、学生、教师、工人，其中却也不乏年轻的中产阶级人士。他们为什么聚在一起？朗诵诗歌。他们在进行诵读比赛，有六七个诗人参加，要对每首诗甚至每行诗进行评判，讨论场面颇为热烈。

诗人们站在舞台上，比赛由著名的《夜曲诗集》作者维捷斯拉夫·涅兹瓦尔主持,诗集中有一首献给美国发明家爱迪生的经典诗。

当然,我不可能听得懂捷克语讨论的内容,但是,有一位讲西班牙语的朋友一直给我翻译主要内容。讨论的核心问题如下:作为发生在捷克斯洛伐克革命性变革的结果,对于民族诗人当前有什么新方向?令人好奇的是,来自不同领域的观众们饶有兴趣地倾听着讨论的起伏转折,讨论的中心都是些复杂的文学构想。讨论中经常能听到涅兹瓦尔的名字,你可以看见他或者在自己的座位上左顾右盼,或者情绪激昂地辩驳着,虽然听不懂他在说什么,但是他说得非常流利,令人印象深刻。

通过涅兹瓦尔的诗文倾向可以看出,他属于自1922年活跃于捷克诗坛被称为"诗情主义"的那一代诗人。他确实是位最重要的人物,因为他以后会是捷克超现实主义的一员。虽然他投身于发生在一年前的国家政治变革,但在他作品里仍然还有这两个流派许多典型的形式主义元素。今年,涅兹瓦尔出版了一本新书《大钟》,他的评论者们认为,里面包含有许多以"禁忌"风格写成的诗歌。新一代的诗人欣赏他,但没有模仿他。年轻的捷克人可以背诵他的早期诗歌,但要求他现在更坚定地歌唱新时代。《夜曲诗集》的作者没有拒绝,但仍然坚持认为社会主义现实中构想的诗歌不应该意味着简单的宣传或喊口号……就像那些批评他作品的年轻人创作的诗歌那样。信息部部长科佩基本人发言支持涅兹瓦尔的观点,科佩基谈到诗歌时坦言:"他们认为通过没有韵律或没有道理的诗歌足以粉碎我们的最新表达方式,比如'士兵突击'、'战斗旅'、'政治会议'、'国家委员会'、'拖拉机'、'联合收割机'等,因为这类语言失败才称为诗歌……"

Literary Prague 文学布拉格

Franz Kafka, one of the most influential writers in the early 20th century, was born and spent most of his time in Prague. He questions and subverts the contradictory frame of civilization-barbarism in "The Great Wall of China."

The Great Wall of China[1]

◎ Franz Kafka

The Great Wall of China was finished at its northernmost location. The construction work moved up from the south-east and south-west and joined at this point. The system of building in sections was also followed on a small scale within the two great armies of workers, the eastern and western. It was carried out in the following manner: groups of about twenty workers were formed, each of which had to take on a section of the wall, about five hundred metres. A neighbouring group then built a wall of similar length to meet it. But afterwards, when the sections were fully joined, construction was not continued on any further at the end of this thousand-metre section. Instead the groups of workers were shipped off again to build the wall in completely different regions. Naturally, with this method many large gaps arose, which were filled in only gradually and slowly, many of them not until after it had already been reported that the building of the wall was complete. In fact, there are said to be gaps which have never been built in at all, although that's merely an assertion which probably belongs among the many legends[2] which have arisen about the structure and which, for individual people at least, are impossible to prove with their own eyes and according to their own standards, because the structure is so immense.

Now, at first one might think it would have been more advantageous in every way to build in continuous sections or at least continuously within

---

① 选自 *The Kafka Project* by Mauro Nervi, translated by Ian Johnston, Nov. 2003, http://www.kafka.org/index.php?aid=171。
② 传说，神话。

two main sections. For the wall was conceived[①] as a protection against the people of the north, as was commonly announced and universally known. But how can protection be provided by a wall which is not built continuously? In fact, not only can such a wall not protect, but the structure itself is in constant danger. Those parts of the wall left standing abandoned in particular regions could easily be destroyed again and again by the nomads, especially by those back then who, worried about the building of the wall, changed their place of residence with incredible speed, like grasshoppers[②], and thus perhaps had an even better overall view of how the construction was proceeding than we did, the people who built it.

However, there was no other way to carry out the construction except the way it happened. In order to understand this, one must consider the following: the wall was to be a protection for centuries; thus, the essential prerequisites[③] for the work were the most careful construction, the use of the architectural wisdom of all known ages and peoples, and an enduring sense of personal responsibility in the builders. Of course, for the more humble tasks one could use ignorant day laborers from the people—the men, women, and children who offered their services for good money. But the supervision of even four day laborers required a knowledgeable man, an educated expert in construction, someone who was capable of feeling sympathy deep in his heart for what was at stake[④] here. And the higher the challenge, the greater the demands. And such men were in fact available—if not the crowds of them which this construction could have used, at least in great numbers.

They did not set about this task recklessly[⑤]. Fifty years before the

---

① 构想。
② 蝗虫。
③ 前提，必要条件。
④ at stake: 在危险中，生死攸关。
⑤ 卤莽地。

start of construction it was announced throughout the whole region of China which was to be enclosed within the wall that architecture and especially masonry[①] were the most important areas of knowledge, and everything else was recognized only to the extent that it had some relationship to those. I still remember very well how as small children who could hardly walk we stood in our teacher's little garden and had to construct a sort of wall out of pebbles, and how the teacher gathered up his coat and ran against the wall, naturally making everything collapse, and then scolded us so much for the weakness of our construction that we ran off in all directions howling to our parents. A tiny incident, but an indication of the spirit of the times.

I was lucky that at twenty years of age, when I passed the final examination of the lowest school, the construction of the wall was just starting. I say lucky because many who earlier had attained the highest limit of education available to them for years had no idea what to do with their knowledge and wandered around uselessly, with the most splendid architectural plans in their heads, and a great many of them just went downhill from there. But the ones who finally got to work as supervisors on the construction, even if they had the lowest rank, were really worthy of their position. They were masons who had given much thought to the construction and never stopped thinking about it, men who, right from the first stone which they sunk into the ground, had a sense of themselves as part of the wall. Such masons, of course, were driven not only by the desire to carry out the work as thoroughly as possible but also by impatience to see the structure standing there in its complete final perfection. Day labourers do not experience this impatience. They are driven only by their pay. The higher supervisors and, indeed, even the middle supervisors, see enough from their various perspectives on the

---

① 砌石工程。

growth of the wall to keep their spirits energized. But the subordinate[1] supervisors, men who were mentally far above their small, more trivial tasks, had to be catered to[2] in other ways. One could not, for example, let them lay one building block on top of another in an uninhabited region of the mountains, hundreds of miles from their homes, for months or even years at a time. The hopelessness of such a hard task, which could not be completed even in a long human lifetime, would have caused them distress and, more than anything else, made them worthless for work. For that reason they chose the system of building in sections. Five hundred metres could be completed in something like five years, by which time naturally the supervisors were as a rule too exhausted and had lost all faith in themselves, in the building, and in the world.

Thus, while they were still experiencing the elation[3] of the celebrations for the joining up of a thousand metres of the wall, they were shipped far, far away. On their journey they saw here and there finished sections of the wall rising up; they passed through the quarters[4] of the higher administrators, who gave them gifts as badges[5] of honour, and they heard the rejoicing[6] of new armies of workers streaming past them out of the depths of the land, saw forests being laid low, wood designated as scaffolding[7] for the wall, witnessed mountains being broken up into rocks for the wall, and heard in the holy places the hymns[8] of the pious[9] praying for the construction to be finished. All this calmed their impatience. The quiet life of home, where they spent some time,

---

[1] 下属的。
[2] catered to: 迎合，为……服务
[3] 得意，情绪高涨。
[4] 军营，住处。
[5] 徽章，奖章。
[6] 欣喜，欢呼。
[7] 脚手架。
[8] 赞歌。
[9] 虔诚的。

reinvigorated them. The high regard which all those doing the building enjoyed, the devout① humility with which people listened to their reports, the trust that simple quiet citizens had that the wall would be completed someday—all this tuned the strings of their souls. Then, like eternally hopeful children, they took leave of their home. The enthusiasm for labouring once again at the people's work became irresistible. They set out from their houses earlier than necessary, and half the village accompanied them for a long way. On all the roads there were groups of people, pennants②, banners—they had never seen how great and rich and beautiful and endearing their country was. Every countryman was a brother for whom they were building a protective wall and who would thank him with everything he had and was for all his life. Unity! Unity! Shoulder to shoulder, a coordinated movement of the people, their blood no longer confined in the limited circulation of the body but rolling sweetly and yet still returning through the infinite extent of China.

In view of all this, the system of piecemeal③ building becomes understandable. But there were still other reasons, too. And there is nothing strange in the fact that I have held off on this point for so long. It is the central issue in the whole construction of the wall, no matter how unimportant it appears at first. If I want to convey the ideas and experiences of that time and make them intelligible, I cannot probe deeply enough into this particular question.

First, one must realize that at that time certain achievements were brought to fruition which rank only slightly behind the Tower of Babel, although in the pleasure they gave to God, at least by human reckoning④, they made an impression exactly the opposite of that structure. I mention

---

① 虔诚的。
② 锦旗，三角旗。
③ 分段修建。
④ 认为，猜想。

this because at the time construction was beginning a scholar wrote a book in which he drew this comparison very precisely. In it he tried to show that the Tower of Babel had failed to attain its goal not for the reasons commonly asserted, or at least that the most important cause was not among these well-known ones. He not only based his proofs on texts and reports, but also claimed to have carried out personal inspections of the location and thus to have found that the structure collapsed and had to collapse because of the weakness of its foundation. And it is true that in this respect our age was far superior to that one long ago. Almost every educated person in our age was a mason by profession and infallible① when it came to the business of laying foundations.

But it was not at all the scholar's aim to prove this. He claimed that the great wall alone would for the first time in the age of human beings create a secure foundation for a new Tower of Babel. So first the wall and then the tower. In those days the book was in everyone's hands, but I confess that even today I do not understand exactly how he imagined this tower. How could the wall, which never once took the form of a circle but only a sort of quarter or half circle, provide the foundation for a tower? But it could be meant only in a spiritual sense. But then why the wall, which was still something real, a product of the efforts and lives of hundreds of thousands of people? And why were there plans in the book—admittedly hazy② plans—sketching the tower, as well as detailed proposals about how the energies of the people could be channelled into powerfully new work.

There was a great deal of mental confusion at the time—his book is only one example—perhaps simply because so many people were trying as hard as they could to join together for a single purpose. Human nature,

---

① 绝对正确的，永无过失的。
② 模糊的。

which is fundamentally careless and by nature like the whirling① dust, endures no restraint. If it restricts itself, it will soon begin to shake the restraints madly and tear up walls, chains, and even itself all over the place.

It is possible that even these considerations, which argued against building the wall in the first place, were not ignored by the leadership when they decided on piecemeal construction. We—and here I'm really speaking on behalf of many—actually first found out about it by spelling out the orders from the highest levels of management and learned for ourselves that without the leadership neither our school learning nor our human understanding would have been adequate for the small position we had within the enormous totality.

In the office of the leadership—where it was and who sat there no one I asked knows or knew—in this office I imagine that all human thoughts and wishes revolve in a circle, and all human aims and fulfilments in a circle going in the opposite direction. And through the window the reflection of the divine② worlds fell onto the hands of the leadership as they drew up the plans. And for this reason the incorruptible③ observer will reject the notion that if the leadership had seriously wanted a continuous construction of the wall, they would not have been able to overcome the difficulties standing in the way. So the only conclusion left is that the leadership deliberately chose piecemeal construction. But building in sections was something merely makeshift④ and impractical. So the conclusion remains that the leadership wanted something impractical. An odd conclusion! True enough, and yet from another perspective it had some inherent justification.

Nowadays one can perhaps speak about it without danger. At that

---

① 旋转的。
② 神的。
③ 不腐败的，廉洁的。
④ 临时的，权宜之计的。

time for many people, even the best, there was a secret principle: Try with all your powers to understand the orders of the leadership, but only up to a certain limit—then stop thinking about them. A very reasonable principle, which incidentally found an even wider interpretation in a later often repeated comparison: Stop further thinking about it, not because it could harm you—it is not at all certain that it will harm you. In this matter one cannot speak in general about harming or not harming. What will happen to you is like a river in spring. It rises, grows stronger, eats away powerfully at the land along its shores, and still maintains its own course down into the sea and is more welcome as a fitter partner for the sea. Reflect upon the orders of the leadership as far as that. But then the river overflows its banks, loses its form and shape, slows down its forward movement, tries, contrary to its destiny, to form small seas inland, damages the fields, and yet cannot maintain its expansion long, but runs back within its banks, in fact, even dries up miserably in the hot time of year which follows. Do not reflect on the orders of the leadership to that extent.

Now, this comparison may perhaps have been extraordinarily apt[①] during the construction of the wall, but it has at most only a limited relevance to my present report. For my investigation is only historical. There is no lightning strike flashing any more from storm clouds which have long since vanished, and thus I may seek an explanation for the piecemeal construction which goes further than the one people were satisfied with back then. The limits which my ability to think sets for me are certainly narrow enough, but the region one would have to pass through here is endless.

Against whom was the great wall to provide protection? Against the people of the north. I come from south-east China. No northern people can

---

① 恰当的。

threaten us there. We read about them in the books of the ancients. The atrocities① which their nature prompts them to commit make us heave② a sigh on our peaceful porches. In the faithfully accurate pictures of artists we see the faces of this damnation③, with their mouths flung open, the sharp pointed teeth stuck in their jaws, their straining eyes, which seem to be squinting④ for someone to seize, whom their jaws will crush and rip⑤ to pieces. When children are naughty, we hold up these pictures in front of them, and they immediately burst into tears and run into our arms. But we know nothing else about these northern lands. We have never seen them, and if we remain in our village, we never will see them, even if they charge straight at us and hunt us on their wild horses. The land is so huge, it would not permit them to reach us, and they would lose themselves in empty air.

So if things are like this, why do we leave our homes, the river and bridges, our mothers and fathers, our crying wives, our children in need of education, and go to school in the distant city, with our thoughts on the wall to the north, even further away? Why? Ask the leadership. They know us. As they mull⑥ over their immense concerns, they know about us, understand our small worries, see us all sitting together in our humble huts, and approve or disapprove of the prayer which the father of the house says in the evening surrounded by his family. And if I may be permitted such ideas about the leadership, then I must say that in my view the leadership existed even earlier. It did not come together like some high mandarins hastily summoned⑦ to a meeting by a beautiful dream of the future, something hastily concluded, a meeting which saw to it that the general

---

① 残暴。
② 喘息。
③ 非难，诅咒。
④ 眯着眼看。
⑤ 劈，裂开。
⑥ 深思熟虑。
⑦ 召唤，召集。

population was driven from their beds by a knocking on the door so that they could carry out the decision, even if it was only to set up an lantern in honour of a god who had shown favour to the masters the day before, so that he could thrash[①] them in some dark corner the next day, when the lantern had only just died out. On the contrary, I imagine the leadership has always existed, along with the decision to construct the wall as well. Innocent northern people believed they were the cause; the admirable innocent emperor believed he had given orders for it. We who were builders of the wall know otherwise and are silent.

Even during the construction of the wall and afterwards, right up to the present day, I have devoted myself almost exclusively to the histories of different people. There are certain questions for which one can, to some extent, get to the heart of the matter only in this way. Using this method I have found that we Chinese possess certain popular and state institutions which are uniquely clear and, then again, others which are uniquely obscure. Tracking down the reasons for these, especially for the latter phenomena, always appealed to me, and still does, and the construction of the wall is fundamentally concerned with these issues.

Now, among our most obscure institutions one can certainly include the empire itself. Of course, in Peking, right in the court, there is some clarity about it, although even this is more apparent than real. And the teachers of constitutional law and history in the schools of higher learning give out that they are precisely informed about these things and that they are able to pass this knowledge on to their students. The deeper one descends into the lower schools, understandably the more the doubts about the students' own knowledge disappear, and a superficial education surges up as high as a mountain around a few precepts[②] drilled into them for centuries, sayings which, in fact, have lost nothing of their eternal truth,

---

① 鞭打。
② 戒律，格言。

but which remain also eternally unrecognised in the mist and fog.

But, in my view, it's precisely the empire we should be asking the people about, because in them the empire has its final support. It's true that in this matter I can speak once again only about my own homeland. Other than the agricultural deities① and the service to them, which so beautifully and variously fills up the entire year, our thinking concerns itself only with the emperor. But not with the present emperor. We'd rather think about the present one if we knew who he was or anything definite about him. We were naturally always trying—and it's the single curiosity which satisfies us—to find out something or other about him, but, no matter how strange this sounds, it was hardly possible to learn anything, either from pilgrims②, even though they wandered through much of our land, or from the close or remote villages, or from boatmen, although they have travelled not merely on our little waterways but also on the sacred rivers. True, we heard a great deal, but could gather nothing from the many details.

Our land is so huge, that no fairy tale can adequately deal with its size. Heaven hardly covers it all. And Peking is only a point, the imperial palace only a tiny dot. It's true that, by contrast, throughout all the different levels of the world the emperor, as emperor, is great. But the living emperor, a man like us, lies on a peaceful bed, just as we do. It is, no doubt, of ample proportions, but it could be merely narrow and short. Like us, he sometime stretches out his limbs③ and, if he is very tired, yawns with his delicately delineated④ mouth. But how are we to know about that thousands of miles to the south, where we almost border on the Tibetan highlands? Besides, any report which came, even if it reached us,

---

① 神。
② 圣徒。
③ 肢，臂。
④ 轮廓分明的。

would get there much too late and would be long out of date. Around the emperor the glittering and yet mysterious court throngs[①]—malice[②] and enmity clothed as servants and friends, the counterbalance to the imperial power, with their poisoned arrows always trying to shoot the emperor down from his side of the balance scales. The empire is immortal, but the individual emperor falls and collapses. Even entire dynasties finally sink down and breathe their one last death rattle[③]. The people will never know anything about these struggles and sufferings. Like those who have come too late, like strangers to the city, they stand at the end of the thickly populated side alleyways, quietly living off the provisions[④] they have brought with them, while far off in the market place right in the middle foreground the execution of their master is taking place.

There is a legend which expresses this relationship well. The Emperor—so they say—has sent a message, directly from his death bed, to you alone, his pathetic[⑤] subject, a tiny shadow which has taken refuge at the furthest distance from the imperial sun. He ordered the herald[⑥] to kneel down beside his bed and whispered the message into his ear. He thought it was so important that he had the herald repeat it back to him. He confirmed the accuracy of the verbal[⑦] message by nodding his head. And in front of the entire crowd of those who've come to witness his death—all the obstructing[⑧] walls have been broken down and all the great ones of his empire are standing in a circle on the broad and high soaring flights of stairs—in front of all of them he dispatched his herald. The messenger started off at once, a powerful, tireless man. Sticking one arm

---

① 人群。
② 怨恨。
③ 咯咯声。
④ 食物，给养。
⑤ 可怜的。
⑥ 传令官，使者。
⑦ 口头的。
⑧ 阻塞，妨碍。

out and then another, he makes his way through the crowd. If he runs into resistance, he points to his breast where there is a sign of the sun. So he moves forward easily, unlike anyone else. But the crowd is so huge; its dwelling places are infinite. If there were an open field, how he would fly along, and soon you would hear the marvelous pounding of his fist on your door. But instead of that, how futile are all his efforts. He is still forcing his way through the private rooms of the innermost palace. He will never win his way through. And if he did manage that, nothing would have been achieved. He would have to fight his way down the steps, and, if he managed to do that, nothing would have been achieved. He would have to stride through the courtyards, and after the courtyards the second palace encircling the first, and, then again, stairs and courtyards, and then, once again, a palace, and so on for thousands of years. And if he finally did burst through the outermost door—but that can never, never happen—the royal capital city, the centre of the world, is still there in front of him, piled high and full of sediment①. No one pushes his way through here, certainly not with a message from a dead man. But you sit at your window and dream of that message when evening comes.

That's exactly how our people look at the emperor, hopelessly and full of hope. They don't know which emperor is on the throne, and there are even doubts about the name of the dynasty. In the schools they learn a great deal about things like the succession, but the common uncertainty in this respect is so great that even the best pupils are drawn into it. In our villages emperors long since dead are set on the throne, and one of them who still lives on only in songs had one of his announcements issued a little while ago, which the priest② read out from the altar. Battles from our most ancient history are now fought for the first time, and with a glowing face your neighbour charges into your house with the report. The imperial

---

① 沉积。
② 牧师，神父。

wives, over indulged[①] on silk cushions[②], alienated from noble customs by shrewd courtiers[③], swollen with thirst for power, driven by greed, excessive in their lust, are always committing their evil acts over again. The further back they are in time, the more terrible all their colours glow, and with a loud cry of grief our village eventually gets to learn how an empress thousands of years ago drank her husband's blood in lengthy gulps[④].

That, then, is how the people deal with the rulers from the past, but they mix up the present rulers with the dead ones. If once, once in a person's lifetime an imperial official travelling around the province comes into our village, sets out some demands or other in the name of the rulers, checks the tax lists, attends a school class, interrogates the priest about our comings and goings, and then, before climbing into his sedan[⑤] chair, summarizes everything in a long sermon[⑥] to the assembled local population, at that point a smile crosses every face, one man looks furtively[⑦] at another and bends over his children, so as not to let the official see him. How, people think, can he speak of a dead man as if he were alive. This emperor already died a long time ago, the dynasty has been extinguished, the official is having fun with us. But we'll act as if we didn't notice, so that we don't hurt his feelings. However, in all seriousness we'll obey only our present ruler, for anything else would be a sin. And behind the official's sedan chair as it hurries away there arises from the already decomposed urn[⑧] someone or other arbitrarily endorsed as ruler of the village.

---

① 沉迷于，享受。
② 垫子。
③ 朝臣。
④ 大口。
⑤ 轿子。
⑥ 布道，说教。
⑦ 偷偷地，秘密地。
⑧ 瓮。

Similarly, with us people are, as a rule, little affected by political revolutions and contemporary wars. Here I recall an incident from my youth. In a neighbouring but still very far distant province a rebellion broke out. I cannot remember the causes any more. Besides, they are not important here. In that province reasons for rebellion arise every new day—they are an excitable people. Well, on one occasion a rebel pamphlet① was brought to my father's house by a beggar who had travelled through that province. It happened to be a holiday. Our living room was full of guests. The priest sat in their midst and studied the pamphlet. Suddenly everyone started laughing, the sheet was torn to pieces in the general confusion, and the beggar was chased out of the room with blows, although he had already been richly rewarded. Everyone scattered and ran out into the beautiful day. Why? The dialect of the neighbouring province is essentially different from ours, and these differences manifest themselves also in certain forms of the written language, which for us have an antiquated② character. Well, the priest had scarcely read two pages like that, and people had already decided. Old matters heard long ago, and long since got over. And although—as I recall from my memory—a horrifying way of life seemed to speak irrefutably③ through the beggar, people laughed and shook their head and were unwilling to hear any more. That's how ready people are among us to obliterate④ the present.

If one wanted to conclude from such phenomena that we basically have no emperor at all, one would not be far from the truth. I need to say it again and again: There is perhaps no people more faithful to the emperor than we are in the south, but the emperor derives no benefits from our

---

① 小册子。
② 陈旧的，过时的。
③ 无可辩驳地。
④ 擦掉……的痕迹，忘记。

loyalty. It's true that on the way out of our village there stands on a little pillar the sacred dragon, which, for as long as men can remember, has paid tribute[①] by blowing its fiery[②] breath straight in the direction of Peking. But for the people in the village Peking itself is much stranger than living in the next world. Could there really be a village where houses stand right beside each other covering the fields and reaching further than the view from our hills, with men standing shoulder to shoulder between these houses day and night? Rather than imagining such a city, it's easier for us to believe that Peking and its emperor are one, something like a cloud, peacefully moving along under the sun as the ages pass.

Now, the consequence of such opinions is a life which is to some extent free and uncontrolled. Not in any way immoral—purity of morals like those in my homeland I have hardly ever come across in my travels. But nonetheless a life that stands under no present laws and only pays attention to the wisdom and advice which reach across to us from ancient times.

I guard again generalizations and do not claim that things like this go on in all ten thousand villages of our province or, indeed, in all five hundred provinces of China. But on the basis of the many writings which I have read concerning this subject, as well as on the basis of my many observations, especially since the construction of the wall with its human material provided an opportunity for a man of feeling to travel through the souls of almost all the provinces—on the basis of all this perhaps I may truly state that with respect to the emperor the prevailing idea again and again reveals a certain universal essential feature common to the conception in my homeland. Now, I have no desire at all to let this conception stand as a virtue—quite the contrary. It's true that in the main things the blame rests with the government, which in the oldest empire on

---

① 进贡。
② 火的，激烈的。

earth right up to the present day has not been able or has, among other things, neglected to cultivate the institution of empire sufficiently clearly so that it is immediately and ceaselessly effective right up to the most remote frontiers of the empire. On the other hand, however, there is in this also a weakness in the people's power of imagining or believing, which has not succeeded in pulling the empire out of its deep contemplative[①] state in Peking and making it something fully vital and present in the hearts of subjects, who nonetheless want nothing better than to feel its touch once and then die from the experience.

So this conception is really not a virtue. It's all the more striking that this very weakness appears to be one of the most important ways of unifying our people. Indeed, if one may go so far as to use the expression, it is the very ground itself on which we live. To provide a detailed account of why we have a flaw here would amount not just to rattling[②] our consciences but, what is much more serious, to making our feet tremble. And therefore I do not wish to go any further in the investigation of these questions at the present time.

An Illustration from the Manuscript of Kafka's "The Trial"
卡夫卡的《审判》手稿中的插图

---

① 沉思的。
② 使觉醒。

Pictures from Kafka's Diaries
卡夫卡日记中的图画

Kafka's Manuscript
卡夫卡的手稿

万里长城建造时[1]

◎ 弗朗茨·卡夫卡

中国长城是在其最靠北的地方竣工的。此项工程分别由东南和西南开始，最后交汇在这里。在东西两路筑墙大军中，又在更小的范围里实行这种分段修筑的方法，于是修筑城墙的人就被分成一个个二十人左右的小队，每个小队负责修筑出五百米，然后一个相邻的小队再朝他们修筑同样长的一段。可是当这两段连通之后，却并没有接着这一千米的头继续往下修，更确切地说，这两个小队又被派往完全不同的地区去修筑长城。采用这种方法自然就产生了许多大豁口，它们是逐步缓慢地填补起来的，有些甚至到长城宣布竣工之后才填补上。

是的，据说有些豁口根本未被堵上，虽然这是一种大概只能在围

---

[1] 出自 http://bbs.dahe.cn/read-htm-tid-1474697.htm。

绕这项工程而产生的众多传说中见到的看法，但由于这项工程规模太大，靠自己的眼睛和自己的标准是无法核实这些传说的，至少单个的人做不到。

起初人们认为，无论从哪种意义上说，连起来修，至少两大部分各自连起来修更为有利。谁都在说，谁都知道，修筑长城是出于抵御北方诸族的考虑。然而一道未连起来修筑的长城如何进行抵御？实际上，一道这样的长城不仅无法抵御，而且建筑本身也总是处在危机之中。处在荒凉地区无人看管的一段段墙体很易遭受游牧民族的一再破坏，由于修筑长城使他们受了惊吓，像蝗虫似地飞快地变换着居住地，因此他们大概比修筑者更能了解整体的情况。

尽管如此，这项工程的实施大概只能采用这种实际采用的方法。若要理解这些必须这样考虑：此长城应当成为几个世纪的屏障；绝对认真修筑，各朝各代和各个民族的建筑智慧，修筑者持之以恒的个人责任感，这些都是修造长城必不可少的先决条件。那些粗活可以由无知的民夫完成，男的、女的、少的，都是为了挣大钱而自荐其身，但指挥四个民夫的伍长则应是个有头脑、受过专业建筑教育的人，应是个能从心底体会出此事意义何在的人。要求越高，成效就越高。实际上，虽然当时这种人才的数量满足不了工程所需，但也十分可观。

当时动工并不轻率。在此项工程开工前五十年，在大概已用墙圈起来的整个中国，建筑技术，特别是泥瓦手艺已被宣布为最重要的科学，而其他各业仅仅在与其有关联时才能获得承认。我还十分清楚地记得，还是小孩的时候，我们走路还不稳，就站在先生的小花园里，被要求用卵石砌起一堵墙，当先生撩起长衫撞向那堵墙时，它当然全倒塌了，先生训斥我们砌得不牢，吓得我们哭着叫着四下跑开去找自己的父母。虽是一桩小事，但却典型地反映出那个时代的精神。

我很幸运，当我二十岁完成了初等学校的最高级考试时，正好赶上长城开工。我说幸运，那是因为有许多人早已完成他们所能享受的学业，但多年没有用武之地，胸藏宏伟的建筑构想，但却徒劳地四处奔波，大批地潦倒了。不过那些终于作为工程领导者——尽管属于最低等级——来从事这项工程的人，事实上是堪当此任的。他们是对这项工程进行过许多思考而且还在继续思考的泥瓦匠人，自打第一块基石埋入土中，他们就感到已与这项工程融为一体。当然，除了渴望能够从事最基础的工作，驱使这些泥瓦匠人的还有迫不及待地想看到工程终于完美无瑕地竣工的心情。民夫可没有这种心情，驱使他们的只有工钱。至于高层领导者，甚至中层领导者，为了保持精神方面的强大，他们讨厌工程多方展开。然而对那些地位较低、才智未尽其用的人，则必须采取别的措施，例如不能让他们一连数月、甚至数年在离家千里的荒山野岭一块又一块地砌墙砖，这种辛勤的劳动可能干一辈子也没什么结果，若对它失望就会使他们丧失信心，最重要的是会使他们在工作中愈加失去作用。因此，人们选择了分段修筑的方法。五百米约五年即可完成，此时这些小头目自然已是筋疲力尽，对自己、对工程、对世界都失去了信心。

所以当他们还在为一千米城墙连通典礼而欢欣鼓舞时，就又给派往很远很远的地方。旅途中，他们不时看到一段段竣工的城墙巍峨耸立，路经上司的驻地时，他们得到颁发的勋章，耳中听到的是新从内地涌来的筑墙大军的欢呼声，眼里看到的是为做手脚架而伐倒的森林，一座座石山被敲成了城砖，在各个圣地还能听到虔诚的人们祈求工程竣工的歌声。这一切都缓和了他们焦急的心情。在家乡过了一段平静的生活，他们变得更加健壮。修筑长城的人享有的声誉，人们听他们讲述修长城时的虔诚敬意，沉默的普通老百姓对长城终将完工的信心，这一切又绷紧了他们的心弦。他们像永远怀着希望的孩子一样辞别了家乡，再为民族大业尽力的欲望变得无法抑制。他们还没到时间就从家里出来，半个村子的人一直把他们送出好远好远。每条路上都能看见一队队人、一面面角旗、一面面彩旗，他们从未发现，自己的国家这么辽阔、这么富裕、这么美丽、这么可爱。每个农人都是兄弟，要为他们筑起一道屏障，为此他将用他的一切感激一辈子。多么协调！多么一致！胸贴着胸，一种民间轮舞，血液不再被禁锢在可怜的体内循环之中，而是在无边无际的中国甜蜜地往复流淌。

通过这些分段修筑的方法就变得容易理解了，不过它大概还有种种其他原因。我在这个问题上停留了这么长时间并不奇怪，它是整个长城工程的核心问题，它暂时好像不那么重要。我要介绍那个时代的思想和经历，并让人们理解它们，而我无法深入探究的恰恰是这个问题。

人们大概首先得告诉自己，那时取得了许多成就，它们仅略略逊色于巴别塔的建造，然而在虔诚方面，它们简直就是那项建筑的对立面，至少按照人的打算是这样。我之所以提起这些，是因为在长城工程开始时，有位学者写了本书，十分详细地进行了比较。他在书中试图证明，巴别塔的建造未达目的绝不是由于众人所说的那些原因，或者说，至少首要原因不在众所周知的原因之列。他不仅写文章和报道进行证明，而且还想亲自去实地调查，同时他认为，那项工程失败于根基不牢，而且肯定是失败于根基不牢。然而在这方面我们这个时代远远超过了那个早已逝去的时代。如今几乎每个受过教育的人都是专业泥瓦匠人，在地基问题上都不含糊。

可这位学者根本没有论及这些，他声称，长城在人类历史上将第一次为新的巴别塔打下坚实的基础。也就是说，先筑长城后造塔。这本书当时人手一册，不过说实话，直到今天我还没完全弄明白，他怎么想象出了这座塔。长城并没构成一个圆，而是只构成四分之一或半个圆，难道它能作为一座塔的基础？这只能算作智力方面的平庸。然而作为一种实实在在存在的长城，付出无数艰辛和生命的结果，它到底是为了什么？为何在这部著作里要描绘那座塔的规划，虽然是朦胧模糊的规划，为何要为在这项新的大业中如何统一协调民族的力量提出种种具体建议呢？这本书仅仅是一个例子，当时人们的脑子里极为混乱，也许这恰恰是因为许多人力图尽量聚向一个目标。

人的天性从其根本上来说是轻浮的，犹如飞扬的尘土的天性，它不受任何束缚。如果受到束缚，那它马上就开始疯狂地摇撼束缚它的东西，将围墙、锁链连同自己统统晃得飞向四面八方。

在确定分段修筑时，领导阶层可能并非没有重视与修筑长城截然相反的考虑。我们——在这里恐怕我是以很多人的名义这样说，其实我们是在抄写诏书时才互相认识的，而且我们发现，如果没有最高领导集团，无论是我们的书本知识还是我们的见识，都不足以应付我们在这伟大的整体中担负的那点小小的职责。

在领导集团的密室里———它位于何处以及里面坐着谁,我问过的人谁也不知道,现在仍不知道。大概人的所有想法和愿望都在那间密室里盘旋,而人的所有目标和愿望都在反向盘旋。透过窗户,神界的余辉洒落在领导集团描绘各种规划的手上。全线同时修筑面临着许多困难,领导集团就是真想克服也无力克服,这种说法有主见的观察者是不会接受的。这么一来就有了这样的推断,即领导集团故意实行分段修筑。然而分段修筑仅仅是一种权宜之计,是不合适的。于是就有了这种推断:领导集团要的就是不合适。奇特的推断!毫无疑问,即使从另一方面看它也有一些自身的合理性。

今天说这些大概毫无危险了。当时有许多人暗暗遵循着一条准则,甚至连最杰出的人也不例外,这就是设法尽全力去理解领导集团的指令,不过只能达到某种界限,随后就得停止思考。一个十分理智的准则,它在后来经常提起的一个比喻中又得到了进一步的阐释:并非因为可能会危及于你才让你停止思考,不能完全肯定就会危及于你。在这里简直既不能说会危及,也不能说不会危及。你的命运将与春天的河流一样。它水位上升,更加势壮威大,在其漫长的河岸边更加接近陆地,保持着自己的本性直到汇入大海,它与大海更加相像,更受大海的欢迎。对领导集团的指令的思考就到此为止。然而那条河后来漫出了自己的堤岸,没了轮廓和体形,放慢了向下游流淌的速度,企图违背自己的使命,在内陆形成一个个小海,它毁掉了农田草地,但却无法长久保持这种扩展的势头,只好又汇入自己的河道,到了炎热的季节甚至悲惨地涸干。对领导集团的指令可别思考到这种程度。

这个比喻用在修筑长城期间大概特别恰当,但对我现在的报道的影响至少是十分有限。我的调查只是一种历史调查。已经消散的雷雨云不会再喷射闪电,因此我可以去寻找一种对分段修筑的解释,它要比人们当时所满足的解释更进一步。我的思维能力给我划定的范围可是够窄的,但能纵横驰骋的区域却无边无际。

长城该用来防御谁?防御北方诸族。我来自中国东南部。没有一个北方民族能对我们构成威胁。关于他们我们都是在古人写的书中读到的，他们出于本性犯下的暴行害得我们在宁静的亭子里长吁短叹。在艺术家们一幅幅写实画里，我们看到了那些该罚入地狱的面孔，咧开的嘴巴，插着尖牙利齿的下巴，闭拢的眼睛，似乎特别眼馋将被嘴巴咬碎嚼烂的猎物。如果小孩子调皮捣蛋，只要把这些画拿给他们一看，他们就会哭着扑过来搂住我们的脖子。关于这些北方国家，我们知道的也就这么多。我们从未见过他们，待在自己的村子里，我们永远也见不到他们，即使他们跨上烈马笔直朝我们奔来——国土太大了，他们到不了我们这里，他们将永远留在空中。

既然如此，我们为何要离开家乡，离开这条河这些桥，离开父母，离开啼哭的妻子和急待教诲的孩子，前往遥远的城市求学？我们为何还要想着北方的长城？为什么？去问问领导集团。他们了解我们。总在考虑忧心的大事的领导集团知道我们的事，清楚我们这小小的手艺，他们知道我们全坐在低矮的棚屋里，傍晚父亲当着家人作的祈祷他们或许满意，或许不满意。如果允许我这样想领导集团的话，那我就得说，按照我的观点，这个领导集团早就存在，但却不碰头，大概是受凌晨一个美梦的刺激，朝臣们急急忙忙召开了一次会议，急急忙忙作出决定，到晚上就叫人击鼓将百姓从床上召集起来解释种种决定，尽管那无非就是为了办一次祭神灯会，那神昨天曾向这些先生显示过吉兆，可到第二天街灯刚刚熄灭，他们就在一个昏暗的角落里被痛打了一顿。其实这个领导集团可能一直存在着，修筑长城的决定也一样。无辜的皇上以为是他下诏修筑的长城。我们修过长城的人知道不是那么回事，我们沉默着。

从修筑长城一直到今天，我几乎一直单攻比较世界史——有些问题只有这种方法才能在一定程度上触到它们的神经——我在研究中发现，我们中国人对某些民众和国家的机构无比清楚，而对其他机构又无比模糊。探寻这些原因，尤其是探寻后一现象曾一直吸引着我，如今也一直吸引着我，而这些问题就涉及长城的修筑。

至少皇室就属于我们最不清楚的机构之一。当然在北京，或者说在宫廷侍臣中，对它还清楚一点，虽然这种清楚虚假大于真实。就连高等学府的国家法教师和历史教师也装作对这些事了如指掌，装作能将了解的情况介绍给大学生。学校的等级越低,对自己的知识当然就越不疑心,而浅薄的教育则围着少数几个数百年一成不变的定理掀起扑天盖地的巨浪,它们虽然不失为永恒的真理,但在这种云天雾海中恐怕永远也分辨不出来。

不过根据我的看法,关于皇室的问题该去问问百姓,因为百姓是皇室最终的支柱。当然在这里我又是只能说说我的故乡。除了各位农神以及全年对于其丰富多彩、非常出色的祭祀活动,我们脑子里装的只有皇上,但不是当朝皇上。其实,如果我们了解当朝皇上,或是知道他某些具体的情况,我们脑子里就会装着他。当然我们总想得知这方面的什么事,这是我们仅有的好奇心,然而说起来是那么离奇,要了解到什么几乎是不可能的,从游历众多的朝圣者那里了解不到,从远远近近的村子里了解不到,从不仅在我们的小河里行过船、而且闯过大江大河的船夫那里也了解不到。虽然听到的很多,但从中什么也推断不出。

我们国家如此辽阔,哪个童话也出不了它的国境,上天也才刚刚罩住了它……北京仅仅是一个点儿,而皇宫仅仅是一个小点儿。然而皇帝却反而大得充满这世界的每一层。可当今皇上和我们一样也是人,他像我们一样也要躺在一张床上,那床虽然量时绰绰有余,但可能还是又短又窄。和我们一样,他有时也伸伸胳膊展展腿,十分困倦时就用他那细嫩的嘴打打呵欠。可这些我们怎么会知道,在几千里之外的南方,我们几乎处在西藏高原的边缘。另外,就算每个消息都能传到我们这里,那也到得极晚极晚,早就过时了。皇上周围簇拥着大批显赫却难以看透的朝臣——臣仆和朋友的衣服里面是恶毒和敌意,他们是帝制的平衡体,他们总想用毒箭把皇帝射下称盘。帝制是不朽的,但各个皇帝却会跌倒垮台,即使整个王朝最终也会倒在地上,咕噜一声便断了气。关于这些争斗和苦楚百姓永远不会知道,他们就像迟到的外地人,站在人头攒动的小巷的巷尾,静静地吃着带来的干粮,而前面远处的集市广场中央,正在行刑处决他们的主人。

有那么一个传说,它清楚地反映出了这种关系。皇上,故事就是这么讲的,给你,给你个人,给你这可怜的臣仆,给你这在皇上的圣光前逃之夭夭的影子,皇帝临终前躺在床上偏偏给你下了一道诏。他让传诏人跪在床边,对着他的耳朵低声下了诏。他非常重视这道诏,所以又让传诏人对着他的耳朵重复了一遍。他点了点头表示重复的诏毫无差错。当着所有目睹皇上驾崩的人——一切障碍均被摧毁,在高大宽阔的露天台阶上,站着一圈圈帝国的大人物——当着这所有人的面,皇上把传诏人打发走了。传诏人马上动身。他身强体壮,不知疲倦,一会儿伸出这只胳膊,一会儿伸出那只胳膊,在人群中奋力给自己开路。遇到抵抗时,他就指指胸前,那里有太阳的标记,因而他比任何人都更容易往前走。可拥在一起的人是那么多,他们的住地一眼望不到头。如果面前展现出一片空旷的原野,那他就会疾步如飞,你大概很快就会听到他的拳头擂你的门。但实际上却并非如此,他的汗水会付诸东流。他依旧还在内宫的房间内拼命挤着,他将永远也挤不出来。即使他能挤出来,那也没用,他还得奋力挤下台阶。即使挤下台阶,也还没用,还须穿过好几处院落,穿过院落之后又是一座圈起来的宫殿,又是台阶和院落,又是一座宫殿,如此下去得要几千年。当他终于冲出最外面那道宫门时——然而这种事永远永远也不会发生,京城才出现在他面前,这世界的中心处处塞满了高处落下的沉积物。谁也别想从这里挤出,带着遗诏也不行。然而每当黄昏降临时,你就坐在窗边梦想着那道遗诏。

我们的百姓就是这样看皇上,既那样失望,又是那样满怀希望。他们不知道谁是当朝皇帝,甚至对朝名也心存疑问。学校里依照顺序学着许多这类东西,然而人们在这方面普遍感到疑惑,因而连最好的学生也只能跟着疑惑。早已驾崩的皇上在我们这些村子里正在登基,只在歌中还能听到的那位皇上不久前还颁布了一道诏书,由和尚在祭坛前宣读了它。最古老的历史战役现在才打起来,邻居满脸通红冲进你家送来这个消息。后宫的女人被奢养在锦垫绣枕之中,狡猾的侍从使她们疏远了高尚的品德,权欲膨胀,贪得无厌,恣意行乐,一再重新犯下一桩桩罪行。时间过得越久,一切色彩就越是艳丽得可怕。有一次全村人在悲号中得知,几千年前曾有一个皇后大口大口饮过自己丈夫的血。

百姓就是这样对待过去的君主，但又将当朝君主混进死人堆里。有一次，那是某一代的某一次，一个正在省内巡视的皇室官员偶然来到我们村子，他以当朝皇上的名义提了某些要求，核查了税单，听了学校的课，向和尚询问了我们的所作所为，在上轿之前，他对被驱赶过来的村民长篇大论地训诫了一番，将一切又总结了一遍，这时大家的脸上都掠过一阵微笑，你瞟我一眼，我又瞄他一下，接着都低下头看着孩子，免得让那位官员注意自己。怎么回事，大家暗想，他讲死人就跟讲活人一样，可这位皇上早已驾崩，这个朝代也早已覆亡，官员先生是在拿我们开心吧，不过我们装作并未觉察，以免伤了他的面子。可人们只能真正服从当朝君主，因为其他一切都是罪孽。在匆匆离去的官轿后面，某个被从已经坍塌的骨灰坛中揿起的人一跺脚变成了这个村子的主人。

同样，我们这里的人通常很少与朝政的变更和当代的战争有什么关联。我还记得少年时代的一件事。一个邻省，虽是邻省但相距却十分遥远，暴发了一场暴动。暴动的原因我想不起来了，而且它们也不重要，那地方每天早晨都会产生暴动的理由。那地方的人情绪激动。有一天，一个游遍那个省的乞丐将一份暴动者的传单带到我父亲家里。当时正好逢节，我们家里宾客满堂。和尚坐在正中间仔细看着这份传单。突然大家哄然而笑，传单在你抢我夺中扯碎了，收受了不少东西的乞丐被一顿棍棒赶出了门，大家四散而去，赶着享受那美好的日子。为什么会这样？邻省的方言与我们的完全不同，这种差异也表现在书面语的某些形式上，对我们来说，这些形式带有古文的味道。和尚还没读完两页，大家都已经作出了判断。老掉牙的东西，早就听说了，早就没搁在心里了。尽管——我记得好像是这样——乞丐的话无可辩驳地证实了那种可怕的生活，可大家却笑着晃着脑袋，一个字也不想听了。我们这里的人就是如此乐意抹杀现在。

如果能从这种现象中推断出，我们的心底根本没有皇上，那就离真实不远了。我得反复地说：也许再也没有比我们南方百姓更忠于皇上的百姓了，不过这种忠诚给皇上也带不来益处。虽然我们村口的小柱子上盘着神圣的龙，有史以来就正对着北京方向崇敬地喷吐着火热的气息，但村里的人觉得北京比来世还要陌生许多。难道真有那么个村子，那里房屋鳞次栉比，布满田野，站在我们的小山上怎么看也看不到，房子之间昼夜都站着摩肩接踵的人，真有那么个村镇吗？对我们来说，想象这样一座城市的模样太难了，还不如就当北京和皇上是一回事，或许就是一片云，一片在太阳底下静静漫步在时间长河中的云。

这些看法的结果就是一种比较自由、无羁无绊的生活，但绝不是不讲道德，我在旅途中几乎从未遇到过像我故乡那种纯真的道德。这是一种不受当今任何法律约束、只遵从由古代延续给我们的训示和告诫的生活。

我得避免一概而论，我并不认为我们省上万个村子的情况都是这样，中国的五百个省就更不用说了。不过也许我可以根据我读过的有关这个题目的文字材料，根据我自己的观察——修筑长城期间人的资料尤为丰富，观察者借此机会可以探索几乎所有省份的人的心灵——根据这一切也许我可以说，各个地区关于皇上的主要看法显示出的基本特征与我家乡的总是一致的。我毫无将这种看法作为一种美德的意思。它主要是由统治集团造成的，在世界上最古老的帝国里，统治集团直到今天也没有能力或忽视了将帝制机构训练得如此清晰，以使其影响力能持续不断地直接到达帝国最远的边境。不过另一方面，百姓的想象力或猜测力欠缺也与此有关，帝制仅在北京是活生生的，只在北京才能让当代人感受到，百姓没有能力将它拉到自己这臣仆的胸前，他们的胸膛除了感受一下这种接触并在这种接触中消亡，再也别无所求。

这种看法也许并不是一种美德。更为奇特的是，这种欠缺似乎正是我们民族最重要的凝聚剂之一，是的，如果允许表达得更大胆的话，那就是我们生活于其上的这片土地。在这里详细说明一种指责的理由并不是在震撼我们的心灵，而是在摇撼我们的双腿，这更加糟糕。因此对这一问题的研究我暂时不想再搞下去了。

（周新建 译）

Who Is Franz Kafka?

☞ He was born in Prague in 1883, and died of T.B. in 1924.
☞ German-language writer of novels and short stories.
☞ He attended German Karl-Ferdinands-Universitat, studying chemistry, and later law.
☞ He obtained the degree of Dr. of Law in 1906.
☞ Most of his works were published posthumously.
☞ Best known works: "The Trail," "The Metamorphosis," "The Amerika," and "The Castle."
☞ He burned about 90% of his works.
☞ Under excessive stresses and strains, he suffered from migraines, insomnia, constipation, boils, and other ailments, clinical depression and social anxiety throughout life.

Chapter 9   Rome

All roads lead to Rome.
—Anonymous

Quotes Featuring Rome

🕭 A great city, whose image dwells in the memory of man, is the type of some great idea. Rome represents conquest; Faith hovers over the towers of Jerusalem; and Athens embodies the pre-eminent quality of the antique world, Art.

—Benjamin Disraeli

🕭 Rome—the city of visible history, where the past of a whole hemisphere seems moving in funeral procession with strange ancestral images and trophies gathered from afar.

—George Eliot

🕭 Are we like late Rome, infatuated with past glories, ruled by a complacent, greedy elite, and hopelessly powerless to respond to changing conditions?

—Camille Paglia

Key Words

Historical relics, sayings, Church of St. Peter, and travelogue.

Questions

1. Rome is a city with many well-preserved historical relics. How does your city government protect (or damage) its historical relics?
2. How do you understand the expression "To see Rome is to see everything"?
3. What's your impression on Rome after reading Mark Twain's description of the city?

Rome Today 今日罗马

Rome, an "old" city, is one of the world's most famous and historically and culturally rich cities. No wonder, as Goethe declared, "He who has seen Rome has seen everything."

To See Rome Is to See Everything[①]

◎ Brett Foster and Hal Marcovitz

You, o visitor to Rome, are only the latest of many, many before you.

In the Middle Ages, pilgrims undertook journeys to Rome from the far reaches of Christendom, sometimes taking several months to reach their sacred destination. Once there, they venerated[②] the apostles'[③] relics,

---

① 选自 *Bloom's Literary Places—Rome*, by Brett Foster and Hal Marcovitz, with Introduction by Harold Bloom, Philadelphia: Chelsea House Publishers, 2005。
② 崇拜。
③ 使徒，传教士。

or the legendary places where saints and martyrs met their deaths, or the countless churches of Europe's spiritual capital, the Mother City of the Catholic Mother Church. Alcuin, the great medieval scholar from York, England, who himself visited Rome twice in his life, describes this Rome as the "monumental city" of holy thresholds and "tremulous walls of the brazen temples." The sight of Rome's towers and steeples in the distance often stopped such pilgrims in their tracks, and they would delay their lengthy journeys, often made entirely on foot, to sing "Te Deums" as thanks for safe travels and as praise for the holy city just ahead of them. After a few more miles walking along the Via Flaminia, a Roman thoroughfare built in the third century B.C., the pilgrims would presently enter the northernmost gate, the Porta del Popolo, which today displays its statues of Saints Peter and Paul within an enduring exterior of sixteenth-century grandeur. Consciously resembling a triumphal arch of imperial Rome, the gate also features decorations by the famed Baroque artist Bernini on its inner wall, right beside which in the church Santa Maria del Popolo reside two masterpieces by the late Renaissance painter Caravaggio, the *Conversion of Saint Paul* and the *Crucifixion of Saint Peter*.

An Egyptian obelisk[①], more than 3,000 years old and among the military spoils of the Emperor Augustus, gives the broad, open space of Piazza del Popolo a focal point, one at once steadfast and exotic. Pope Sixtus V relocated the obelisk to this piazza in 1589. It and several other such monuments erected around the city announced the Counter-Reformation church's triumph over paganism[②] (and, by corollary, over more recent Protestant heresies[③]), a gesture of militant bravado[④] that

---

① 方尖塔。
② 异教。
③ 异教。
④ 虚张声势。

Sixtus himself personified well: this pope oversaw one of the most extensive and breathtaking set of urban changes Rome in its long history had ever experienced. Taken all together, then, this initial locale is a fitting, transhistorical hodgepodge①, an emblematic welcome to a city whose chronological variety—and resulting sense of vertigo②—is unmatched by any place in the world. As the Romantic poet Goethe once declared, "He who has seen Rome has seen everything."

Occasionally a modern traveler enters Rome in an altogether more individual, perilous fashion. The British travel writer and photographer Freya Stark, for example, on a "lark③" drove from Perugia to the Eternal City on a Vespa, the ubiquitous, mini-motorcycles that flit all around Rome. Stark, in a letter, vividly captured the chaotic, even Darwinian, environment of Roman motorists: "We got here for tea and risked our lives across Rome where no one thinks of traffic rules but only gives a look to see whether the opposing vehicle is bigger or smaller; of course the Vespa is fair game for anyone to run at!"

Today, however, you are more likely to arrive, like other international visitors to Rome, via the Fiumicino Airport southwest of the city, and once there you may appreciate a little better the Roman winter Pliny's peculiar estimation of the city as the "capital of the world, sixteen miles from the sea." The airport, also known as "Leonardo da Vinci" in honor of Italy's great Renaissance artist, inventor, and early theoretician of flight, is near the Tyrrhenian Coast and Ostia, a well-preserved ancient town and former colony. The Roman Republic conquered Ostia in the fifth century B.C., when it served as a valuable port and defensive site at the mouth of the Tiber River. Pius II, a humanist pope of the early Renaissance, memorably

---

① 大杂烩。
② 眩晕。
③ 骑马越野。

elegized[①] Ostia's ruins, decrepit[②] even then, six and a half centuries ago. It is commonplace to speak of Rome's ever mutable, rising and declining, straw-to-marble-to-dust landscape, through which the unchanging, resolute Tiber serenely passes. But this is not so. Today grasslands surround Ostia, due to the gradual, centuries-long silting of its harbor. More dramatically, a violent flood in 1557 (relatively recently, by geological standards) caused the river to steer a new course away from the Roman outpost[③]. In Rome itself, nineteenth- and twentieth-century urban projects have led to the channeling of the river, usually by concrete embankments, as protection against severe flooding. Thus not even the resolute river has evaded the dizzying sense of change and historical progress that will greet you upon entrance to the city proper.

But first, you may experience an equally dizzying feeling—the feeling that everything at first looks rather more familiar than you had anticipated. Having landed at the thoroughly modern, recently expanded airport, you might take the short trip to Rome by taxi or rental car (the latter by no means recommended!) along a thoroughly modern highway, or more prudently you may wish to take a train: from the international terminal, one can easily catch a shuttle to Ostiense Station, on Rome's southern edge. Again, a sense of the familiar may strike you as you proceed northward. From the train window you'll notice the outlying high-rises, tenements, and general urban sprawl that plague many a modern, world-class city, and that has greatly changed Rome's urban identity following World War II. This atmosphere was captured powerfully, as early as 1948, in Vittorio De Sica's classic neo-realist film, *The Bicycle Thief* (*Ladir di biciclette*). Today more than three million live in the city, which spreads across 580 square miles. You may see hanging from many

---

① 唱挽歌。
② 老朽的。
③ 前哨,国境。

windows—punctuating the visual monotony of sandstone and granite—bright, rainbow-colored flags declaring in Italian (passionately, one imagines!) *Pace!* (*Peace!*) The present, too, necessarily invests itself in the Eternal City, something these flags of protest remind you of, those modestly anonymous responses to a post-millennial, martial[①] age.

From Stazione Ostiense, a succession of long elevators connects you to the Piramide Metro station. (Rome's subway system is called the Metropolitana.) Or perhaps you simply cannot wait any longer to place you own two feet on Italy's *terra aeterna*. If the weather is pleasant (and it likely is, especially if you're fortunate or cunning enough to have traveled in May or September), you may prefer the three-block walk above-ground. And if you are burdened with luggage, rest for a moment at a kiosk on the way, where you are advised to purchase a *scheda* or *carta telefonica*. These inexpensive phone cards will conveniently allow you to make any initial arrangements in the city, although if you're planning a longer stay, you can now rent a *telefonino*, or cell phone, for even greater convenience.

看到了罗马就看到了一切[②]

◎ 布雷特·福斯特　哈尔·马科维奇

到罗马参观的人呐，你是最晚的一个，因为已经有很多很多人先于你到过此地了。

在中世纪，朝圣者从遥远的基督教地区来到罗马。有时需要好几个月的时间才能抵达他们神圣的目的地。一旦到达，他们对那些使徒的遗迹。传说中圣人和殉道者逝去的地方顶礼膜拜，同时也对坐落在欧洲精神首府和罗马天主教宗主城市里那不计其数的教堂推崇至极。

---

① 军事的，战争的。
② 出自郭尚兴、刘沛译：《罗马文学地图》，上海：上海交通大学出版社，2011 年，略有改动。

中世纪英国约克郡的伟大学者阿尔昆一生中两次造访罗马。他把罗马描述为一座圣国中的"不朽之城"。此城拥有神圣无比的大门,一座座黄铜色的圣殿墙壁因回声而不停地震动。朝圣者从远处一看见罗马各式各样的塔楼和教堂的尖塔,都会放缓脚步,驻足遥望,吟唱《感恩颂》,感谢旅途的安全与顺利,赞美前方不远处的圣城。沿着始建于公元前三世纪的罗马弗拉米尼亚大道再走几英里,朝圣者很快就会进入罗马城最北端的大门,波波洛城门。如今,那里伫立着圣彼得和圣保罗的雕像,显示诞生于十六世纪之经久不衰的恢宏。设计者修建波波洛城门时有意识地参照了罗马帝国的凯旋门。城门内墙上的装饰极为独特,出自巴洛克时代著名艺术家贝尔尼尼之手。内墙旁边的波波洛圣母玛利亚教堂里有两幅文艺复兴后期画家卡拉瓦乔的杰作,分别是《圣保罗的皈依》和《圣彼得钉上十字架》。

Piazza del Popolo 波波洛广场

波波洛广场上至今屹立着一座有三千多年历史的埃及方尖石塔,它是奥古斯都皇帝的战利品。这座尖塔一出现在宽敞开阔的广场上,立刻成为关注的焦点。教皇西斯笃五世于 1589 年将这尊方尖塔移至广场。该塔与城内其他几个类似的纪念碑宣告了天主教在反宗教改革的斗争中击败"异教",大获全胜(当然,也必然能战胜近来更多的"异教邪说"),同时,也显示出西斯笃个人在军事上的强大姿态。这位教皇统治期间,罗马经历了历史长河中规模最大、最激动人心的城市变迁。纵观所有这些遗迹,这个起始点就是一幅拼贴画,恰当地融合了跨越多个历史时期的代表性建筑。对于罗马这座城市来说,其年代的多样性是世界上任何一个城市都无法比拟的,而我们现在所处的这个地点就体现了其标志性的欢迎方式。正如浪漫主义诗人歌德所言:"一个人如果看到了罗马,他就看到了一切。"

现代的旅行者偶尔会以更加独特而危险的方式进入罗马城。例如,英国旅行家、摄影家弗芮雅·斯塔克乘坐一种遍布罗马城的小黄蜂小型摩托车,以游戏的方式从佩鲁贾抵达"不朽之城"罗马。斯塔克曾在一封信中形象地描述了罗马机动车驾驶员所面临的混乱境况,那种情况甚至类似于达尔文给我们展现的物种进化时的杂乱无序的状态:"我们到这儿是为了喝茶。来的路上,我们冒着生命危险在罗马城穿行。在这儿,没人在意交通规则。大家只会看一眼对面的车辆以判断其是大是小。当然,在这种情况下,小黄蜂就成为最佳猎物,任何人都能朝它冲过去。"

而现在,你会像来自各个国家的其他游客一样,从城市西南部的菲乌米奇机场到达罗马。一旦踏上罗马的土地,你将更能体会到罗马作家普林尼对这座城市作出的独特评价。它是"离大海十六英里的世界之都"。菲乌米奇机场也被称为"莱昂纳多·达·芬奇"机场,以纪念这位意大利文艺复兴时期伟大的艺术家、发明家及早期飞行理论家。机场毗邻第勒尼安海岸和奥斯蒂亚市。奥斯蒂亚市是一座保存完好的古代城镇,也是曾经的殖民地。罗马共和国于公元前五世纪征服奥斯蒂亚。该城镇位于台伯河入口处,是当时极有价值的港口和防御地点。文艺复兴早期具有人文主义的教皇皮乌斯二世曾于六个半世纪以前创作挽歌,祭奠奥斯蒂亚城里那些早已坍塌的遗迹。人们通常都会谈论到罗马那反反复复、从未间断的起落兴衰,还有种类繁多的地形地貌。只有台伯河安详地流经这片土地,坚贞不渝,从未发生改变。但现如今,情况也并非完全如此。由于几个世纪以来港口泥沙逐渐淤塞,奥

斯蒂亚四周被郁郁葱葱的草地环绕。更为戏剧性的是，1557 年，一场
凶猛的洪水（以地质学的标准来看，时间相对较近）致使河水改道，
远离罗马而去。在罗马城内，十九至二十世纪实施市政工程时在台伯
河上开筑水道，用混凝土砌成大堤，严防重大的洪水袭击。因此，即
便是坚忍不拔的台伯河水也在躲避那令人眼花缭乱的变化和历史进
程，不再环绕于市区的入口处欢迎你的到来。

　　然而，你首先可能同样会感到困惑——感觉周围的一切第一眼看
上去比你预想的要熟悉很多。在近期才完成扩建的极为现代化的机场
着陆之后，你乘坐出租车或自行租一辆汽车（后者决不推荐），沿着完
全现代化的公路很快就能到达罗马。如果你想选择更加安全或稳妥一
些的方式，也可以乘坐火车：在国际终点站，你很容易就能搭乘一列
往返火车，到达位于罗马南部边界的奥斯蒂亚车站。当你向北行进，
一种熟悉的感觉会再次涌上心头。透过车窗，你可以看到远处高楼、
房屋以及城市里杂乱无序的扩建区域。这个问题不但困扰着许多世界
顶级现代化城市，在第二次世界大战后，也极大地改变了罗马城市的
个性。早在 1948 年，维托利奥·德·西卡的新现实主义经典影片《偷
自行车的人》就强有力地表现了该地区当时的环境。如今，三百多万
人居住在市区，共覆盖五百八十平方英里。你或许能够看到许多窗户
外面悬挂着色彩鲜艳的彩虹旗，可以不时调剂一下砂岩和花岗岩造成
的视觉上的千篇一律。这些旗帜像是在用意大利语宣告（可以想象，
语气一定十分激昂）：和平！当前，别样的旗帜也有必要出现在这座"不
朽之城"，即那些抗议旗帜让你想起的事，那是对千年后的战争年代作
出的谨慎而一致的回应。

　　在奥斯蒂亚火车站，一连串的长电梯就可以把你送到金字塔地铁
站（罗马的地铁系统叫做 Metroplitana）。或许，你迫不及待地想踏上
意大利那片永恒的土地。假如天气晴朗宜人（特别是如果你足够幸运
或者恰巧赶在五月或九月份来到这里，很可能有大好的天气），你会更
乐意选择步行三个街区这种方式。如果你随身带有沉重的行李，可以
在途中的售货亭休息片刻，并且最好在那里买一张电话磁卡。这些价
格便宜的电话卡便于你一到罗马就能安排好各种事务。如果你打算长

期逗留，也可以租一部手机，这样会更加方便。

Rome in Literature 文学罗马

Many writers have been to Rome and noted down their experiences there. Mark Twain, an American writer, set out from New York City for Europe, and recorded what he had seen, felt and experienced.

The Innocents Abroad[①]

◎ Mark Twain

What is there in Rome for me to see that others have not seen before me? What is there for me to touch that others have not touched? What is there for me to feel, to learn, to hear, to know, that shall thrill me before it pass to others? What can I discover? —Nothing. Nothing whatsoever. One charm of travel dies here. But if I were only a Roman! —If, added to my own I could be gifted with modern Roman sloth[②], modern Roman superstition, and modern Roman boundlessness of ignorance, what bewildering worlds of unsuspected wonders I would discover! Ah, if I were only a habitant of the Campagna[③] five and twenty miles from Rome! Then I would travel.

…

Of course we have been to the monster Church of St. Peter, frequently.

---

① 选自 The Innocents Abroad, Chapter 26, by Mark Twain, Oxford: Oxford University Press, 1996。
② 懒散。
③ 大平原，指意大利台伯河东南一片平原，在罗马郊外。

I knew its dimensions. I knew it was a prodigious[①] structure. I knew it was just about the length of the capitol[②] at Washington—say seven hundred and thirty feet. I knew it was three hundred and sixty-four feet wide, and consequently wider than the capitol. I knew that the cross on the top of the dome of the church was four hundred and thirty-eight feet above the ground, and therefore about a hundred or may be a hundred and twenty-five feet higher than the dome of the capitol. —Thus I had one gauge[③]. I wished to come as near forming a correct idea of how it was going to look, as possible; I had a curiosity to see how much I would err. I erred considerably. St. Peter's did not look nearly so large as the capitol, and certainly not a twentieth part as beautiful, from the outside.

When we reached the door, and stood fairly within the church, it was impossible to comprehend that it was a very large building. I had to cipher a comprehension of it. I had to ransack[④] my memory for some more similes. St. Peter's is bulky. Its height and size would represent two of the Washington capitol set one on top of the other—if the capitol were wider; or two blocks or two blocks and a half of ordinary buildings set one on top of the other. St. Peter's was that large, but it could and would not look so. The trouble was that every thing in it and about it was on such a scale of uniform vastness that there were no contrasts to judge by—none but the people, and I had not noticed them. They were insects. The statues of children holding vases of holy water were immense, according to the tables of figures, but so was every thing else around them. The mosaic pictures in the dome were huge, and were made of thousands and thousands of cubes of glass as large as the end of my little finger, but those pictures looked smooth, and gaudy[⑤] of color, and in good proportion to

---

① 庞大的。
② 国会大厦。
③ 标准,评估。
④ 彻底搜索。
⑤ 花哨的。

the dome. Evidently they would not answer to measure by. Away down toward the far end of the church (I thought it was really clear at the far end, but discovered afterward that it was in the centre, under the dome,) stood the thing they call the baldacchino①—a great bronze pyramidal frame-work like that which upholds a mosquito bar. It only looked like a considerably magnified bedstead—nothing more. Yet I knew it was a good deal more than half as high as Niagara Falls②. It was overshadowed by a dome so mighty that its own height was snubbed③. The four great square piers or pillars that stand equidistant④ from each other in the church, and support the roof, I could not work up to their real dimensions by any method of comparison. I knew that the faces of each were about the width of a very large dwelling-house front, (fifty or sixty feet,) and that they were twice as high as an ordinary three-story dwelling, but still they looked small. I tried all the different ways I could think of to compel myself to understand how large St. Peter's was, but with small success. The mosaic portrait of an Apostle⑤ who was writing with a pen six feet long seemed only an ordinary Apostle.

But the people attracted my attention after a while. To stand in the door of St. Peter's and look at men down toward its further extremity, two blocks away, has a diminishing effect on them; surrounded by the prodigious pictures and statues, and lost in the vast spaces, they look very much smaller than they would if they stood two blocks away in the open air. I "averaged" a man as he passed me and watched him as he drifted far down by the baldacchino and beyond—watched him dwindle to an insignificant school-boy, and then, in the midst of the silent throng of

---

① 圣体伞。
② Niagara Falls: 尼亚加拉瀑布，位于美国东北部边境纽约州西面。
③ 冷落。
④ 等距离的。
⑤ 使徒。

human pigmies[①] gliding about him, I lost him. The church had lately been decorated, on the occasion of a great ceremony in honor of St. Peter, and men were engaged, now, in removing the flowers and gilt paper from the walls and pillars. As no ladders could reach the great heights, the men swung themselves down from balustrades[②] and the capitals of pilasters by ropes, to do this work. The upper gallery which encircles the inner sweep of the dome is two hundred and forty feet above the floor of the church—very few steeples in America could reach up to it. Visitors always go up there to look down into the church because one gets the best idea of some of the heights and distances from that point. While we stood on the floor one of the workmen swung loose from that gallery at the end of a long rope. I had not supposed, before, that a man could look so much like a spider. He was insignificant in size, and his rope seemed only a thread. Seeing that he took up so little space, I could believe the story, then, that ten thousand troops went to St. Peter's, once, to hear mass, and their commanding officer came afterward, and not finding them, supposed they had not yet arrived. But they were in the church, nevertheless—they were in one of the transepts[③]. Nearly fifty thousand persons assembled in St. Peter's to hear the publishing of the dogma of the Immaculate Conception[④]. It is estimated that the floor of the church affords standing room for—for a large number of people; I have forgotten the exact figures. But it is no matter—it is near enough.

---

① 矮人。
② 栏杆。
③ 教堂的十字形翼部。
④ Immaculate Conception: 圣灵感孕说。

傻子出国记[①]

◎ 马克·吐温

我在罗马看到的,有什么是人家没看到过的呢?我接触得到的,有什么是人家没接触过的呢?我所见、所闻、所感、所受,有什么会使我比人家先惊喜的呢?我能发现什么?什么也不能。随便什么都不能。旅行的一种魅力就此完蛋。但只要我是个罗马人就好了!要是除了天生性格之外,还能赋有近代罗马人的惰性、近代罗马人的迷信、近代罗马人的无比愚蠢,我就会发现多少确确实实的奇景异色,看得我目不暇接呵!啊,只要我是罗马郊外二十五英里路大平原上的居民就行了!那我就出门旅行去。

……

Church of St. Peter 圣彼得教堂

不用说,我们常到巍峨的圣彼得堂。我知道它有多大。我知道它是个巨大建筑。我知道它跟华盛顿的国会大厦差不多一般长——大约

[①] 出自马克·吐温著,陈良廷、徐汝椿译:《傻子出国记》,北京:人民文学出版社,1985年,略有改动。

有七百三十英尺，因此比国会大厦的圆顶要高一百英尺光景，也许是一百二十五英尺。这样我心里就有了个谱。我希望尽可能得出个正确的概念：这教堂到底是怎么副模样。我不禁想知道自己究竟错多少。我竟然大错特错。从外表看来，圣彼得堂几乎不像国会大厦那么大，当然也不及国会大厦二十分之一的漂亮。

　　我们走到门口，完全站在教堂里头，简直无从理解这是个很大的建筑。我得琢磨一下。我得搜索枯肠再找几个比喻。圣彼得堂真庞大。高低大小等于两个华盛顿国会大厦叠在一起。圣彼得堂就是那么大，可看来不见得有那么大，也不会那么大。毛病就在于教堂里头和四下的所有东西，都是一律规模宏大，找不到对比来分个大小——只有游人好作对比，可我没留神看游人。在里头，人就像小毛虫。按照统计数字说起来，执圣水瓶的小孩雕像都大得很，但周围一切东西也大极了。穹顶下的镶嵌图案画真是奇大无比，全是用千千万万块方玻璃拼凑起来的，每块玻璃都跟我小指头尖一般大，不过那些图案看上去光光整整，色彩鲜艳，和穹顶十分相称。显然那些图案大得无法测量。在教堂远端（我还以为明明是在远端，可事后才发现原来是在教堂当中，穹顶底下），屹立着一座所谓神龛的东西——一座巨大的金字塔形青铜架子，就像蚊帐架。看来只像个放得相当大的床架——不过如此罢了。可我知道这东西还不止尼亚加拉瀑布的一半高呢。在雄伟无比的穹顶笼罩下，反而显得不高了。四根巨大的方柱，或称柱子，等距离地排在教堂里，撑着屋顶，要我用什么对比法算出柱子的真正面积，我可办不到。我知道，每根柱子的面，大约有大房子的门面那么宽（五六十英尺左右），柱子的高度比普通的三层楼房还要高一倍，可看上去还是不大。我想尽种种办法去了解圣彼得堂究竟有多大，但总不大见效。有幅圣徒镶嵌像，用支六英尺长的笔在写字，看来却只有普通圣徒那么大。

　　过了片刻，我的注意力却给游人吸引去了。站在圣彼得堂的门口，朝教堂远端，隔开两个街口那么远的地方的游人看去，人就显得小了；他们四下全是巨幅绘画和大尊雕像，迷失在茫茫空间，看上去比站在露天、隔开两个街口的地方要小得多。有个人走过我身边，我就朝他

"打量"，目送他远远朝神龛那头经过，走过去了——目送他渐渐缩小，成了小不点儿的学生那么大，接着，在走过他身边的一堆默不作声的小矮子中不见了。最近，碰上纪念圣彼得的盛大典礼，教堂里装饰过了一次，这时正有人忙着从墙壁和柱子上拆下花饰和金纸。因为没有够得上那么高的梯子，工匠就从栏杆和大柱的柱头上用绳索吊着身子，悬空干活。穹顶里圈周围的高层回廊离教堂地面有二百四十英尺——在美国可没几座尖塔能造得这么高的。游客往往跑到那高处，俯瞰教堂，因为从那儿多少可以知道究竟有多高，有多远。我们正站在下面地上，只见一个工匠在一根长索头上从回廊上吊下来。我以前可没想到，一个人看上去竟会活像蜘蛛。这人小得可怜，那根绳子只不过像蛛网丝。看他只占那么一点地方，我才相信那个传说。据称有一次，一万个士兵开到圣彼得堂来望弥撒，过后指挥官来了，找来找去找不到他们，还以为他们没来呢。其实他们就在教堂里头——他们就在一边袖廊上。当时圣彼得堂底部可供——供好多人站着听道；究竟多少，我可不记得了。不过这无所谓——这样说也差不多行了。

Who Is Mark Twain?

☞　1835-1910.

☞　His real name was Samual Langhorne Clemens. He was famous for his pen name, Mark Twain.

☞　His family moved to Hannibal, a town of the Mississippi River much like the towns depicted in his two famous novels *The Adventures of Tom Sawyer* and *The Adventures of Huckleberry Finn.*

☞ He left school at an early age and worked in printing in Hannibal and in some other American cities, including New York and Philadelphia.

☞ In his early twenties, he worked on riverboats on the Mississippi.

☞ His articles, stories, memoirs, and novels are characterized by an irrepressible wit and a deft ear for language and dialect.

☞ His novel The Innocents Abroad was an instant bestseller, and *The Adventures of Tom Sawyer* cemented his position as a giant in American literary circles.

Chapter 10 St. Petersburg

The city of Peter remains a museum, open from 8:00 AM to 5:00 PM.
—Joseph Wechsberg

Quotes Featuring St. Petersburg

🖎 In Russian literature, Moscow is a calm city—but St. Petersburg is the place where all the bad things happen.
—Frank Miller

🖎 The duality of St. Petersburg and Leningrad remains. They are not even on speaking terms.
—Joseph Wechsberg

🖎 Old St. Petersburg remains a beautiful stage set but to the Russians it is not what Rome is to the Italians or Paris to the French. The decisions are made in the Kremlin.
—Joseph Wechsberg

Key Words

History, scenery, and Nevsky Prospect.

Questions

1. What do you know about the history of St. Petersburg? How did the city get its name?
2. In what ways is St. Petersburg a city of museum?
3. Nevsky Prospect is a famous street because of Nikolay Gogol's "Nevsky Prospect." Can you find other similar examples in which a city, a street, or any other places become famous because of literary works related to them?

St. Petersburg Today 今日圣彼得堡

St. Petersburg, a Russian city, may not be familiar to many Chinese. However, its history and literature have been written into the appearance of the city today.

St. Petersburg Today[①]

◎ Bradley Woodworth and Constance Richards

Short, dark winter days; long "white" summer nights—St. Petersburg's contradictions serve the soul of a winter well. The city along the wide Neva River is at once achingly beautiful and inconsolably dreary. Constructed on a swamp in Russia's cold North, the city boasts

---

① 选自 *Bloom's Literary Places—St. Petersburg*, by Bradley Woodworth and Constance Richards, with Introduction by Harold Bloom, Philadelphia: Chelsea House Publishers, 2005。

magnificent baroque[①] and rococo-style[②] structures in the pastel hues of Easter basket confections, as well as a network of canals and bridges that prompt its nickname of "Venice of the North." These grand concepts were imported by Peter the Great, inspired by the architectural flair of Venice or Versailles and other European metropoli, in his quest to create St. Petersburg as Russia's "Window on the West" at the dawn of the 18th century.

　　The capital of imperial Russia, an empire spanning Europe and Asia, St. Petersburg boasted architecture, administration, social life, and even language (the court's French) that were influenced by other cultures, so much so that it would be called Russia's most European city. But this, coupled with the city's very Russian winter and Russian inhabitants, many of them descendants of the workers Peter herded into the city to build it, makes for a place of uncommon contrast and mystery.

　　Palaces and ornate mansions line bridge-covered canals... A network of 500 bridges, from small foot bridges to multilaned thoroughfares, crisscrosses the waters of the magical city, linking museums like the grand Hermitage to the famed St. Petersburg Academy of Arts or the Peter and Paul Fortress to the rest of the city, not to mention connecting the quieter residential neighborhoods to bustling Nevsky Prospect.

　　Russia's "city of culture," spawned some of the country's greatest writers, composers, artists, and dancers. Today, over 50 museums lie within the city limits. The Kirov Ballet, now reverted to its pre-revolutionary name of Mariinsky, is known the world over. The Hermitage Museum rivals the Louvre.

　　Palaces and estates dot the countryside around the city, having served as prime real estate for Russian royalty. Yet tragedy would befall those grand places, not only when many buildings were indiscriminately pressed

---

① 巴洛克式，十七、十八世纪欧洲艺术过分装饰之形式，尤指建筑方面。
② 洛可可式，指家具、建筑等有很多精美漩涡形、菱形等装饰，如十八世纪末欧洲所用。

into service as military academies, factories, prisons, clinics, communal living quarters, and allowed to crumble into decay under the Soviet regime, but also when world war came to Russia and Nazi troops plundered the historical structures … forever losing the Catherine Palace's Amber Room, for example.

Decades of revolutionary fervor finally erupted in the early 1900s, bringing the Romanove dynasty to an end, and moving power back to Moscow under the new regime of the Soviets.

Though never invaded by hostile forces, St. Petersburg, then called Leningrad, endured the 900-day siege in World War Two. The city, with a great loss of many residents to cold and starvation, survived nearly three years of attacks. Even in over 70 years of the Socialist regime, St. Petersburg was able to keep its individuality with precious little imposing Soviet architecture dominating the city landscape—allowing the legacy of an imperial capital of 200 years to remain largely intact.

Today St. Petersburg is a city of beauty, elegance, and grandeur, that thrives on tourism and its reputation of intellectualism and culture. The White Nights in June see visitors from all over the world flocking to the city's classical music and performance festivals. But in its decline in the post-Soviet decade leading into the 21st century, St. Petersburg became a sad grande dame, whose crumbling facades and potholed[①] streets had seen better days … better centuries.

Fortunately, St. Petersburg enjoys glory days once again, albeit in fits and quivers—in part to the facelift it received celebrating its 300th birthday in 2003, its fame as birthplace of Russian President Vladimir Putin, and to investment by new industry.

While St. Petersburg has nowhere reached the proportions of the foreign and domestic investment of Moscow, which boasts construction at

---

① 到处是坑的。

near lightning speed, futuristic advertising billboards on every corner, and shopping excess on a grand scale, St. Petersburg is the genteel ballerina[①] to Moscow's brash chorus[②] girl—always classy and steeped in the culture of poetic history.

今日圣彼得堡[③]

◎ 布雷德利·伍德沃思　康士坦茨·理查兹

冬季的白天短暂又昏暗，夏季的夜晚反倒漫长又亮堂。在圣彼得堡，这样的现象不胜枚举。正是这些看似矛盾却又无比自然的事情可以滋养作家的灵魂和精神。坐落在宽阔的涅瓦河畔的圣彼得堡景致优美，无与伦比，但它的阴冷凄凉却也能穿透人的身体，冻结人的灵魂。未开发前的圣彼得堡原本是俄罗斯寒冷的北方一块泥泞荒芜的沼泽地。经过俄罗斯人几百年的努力，如今的圣彼得堡以宏伟的巴洛克和洛可可式建筑而著称，它们构思精美，犹如艺术大师的画作；它们色彩斑斓，又如复活节的各式甜点。河流交错、桥梁纵横的圣彼得堡还享有"北方威尼斯"的美誉。这些宏伟壮观的建筑充分体现了彼得大帝的建筑理念。他的灵感来自威尼斯、凡尔赛和其他欧洲都市的建筑风格。在十八世纪初，为了把圣彼得堡建造成俄罗斯"面向西方的窗户"，彼得大帝作出了不懈的努力，实行西化政策，引进西方的建筑理念。

---

① 芭蕾舞女演员。
② 合唱团。
③ 出自李巧慧、王志坚译：《圣彼得堡文学地图》，上海：上海交通大学出版社，2011年。

Neva River 涅瓦河

作为横跨欧亚两大洲的沙俄帝国的首都，当时圣彼得堡的建筑、行政、社会生活甚至语言（法语是宫廷用语）都受到其他国家文化的极大影响。正因为如此，有人认为它是俄罗斯欧化程度最高的城市。这带给圣彼得堡无比的荣耀和尊贵。但是，这里的作家具有地地道道的俄罗斯风格，这里的居民也保留了历史悠久的俄罗斯文化，他们中的大多数都是当初建造这座城市的工人的后代。为了变沼泽为城市，彼得大帝把成群的外地人赶到这个地方。外来影响和民族文化并行不悖，完全迥异的事物神奇地共存。这赋予圣彼得堡怪诞、神秘的独特城市氛围。

圣彼得堡运河交错，河上是千姿百态的桥梁，岸边是豪华的宫殿和大楼……圣彼得堡桥梁纵横，如网交织。这里共有五百座大小不等的桥，既有仅限单人独行的小桥，也有宽阔如马路般的多车道大桥。这些桥梁横跨不同的水域，通达各个名胜古迹，连接各大博物馆。冬宫和圣彼得堡戏剧艺术学院，彼得保罗要塞和城市的外围，安静的居住区和热闹的涅瓦大街之间，都有桥梁相接。

这座俄罗斯的文化之都哺育出一批批俄罗斯最伟大的作家、作曲家、艺术家和舞蹈家。如今，城区以内有多达五十个博物馆。马林斯基剧院饮誉海内外，它以前就叫马林斯基剧院，"十月革命"后改为基洛夫剧院，现在又恢复了原来的名字。冬宫可以和卢浮宫媲美，不相上下。

Mariinsky Ballet　马林斯基剧院

城区四周的乡间到处都是宫殿和庄园，因为这里曾是皇室的主要居住区。但是悲剧也会在这些一度富丽堂皇的地方上演。不仅如此，当二战爆发，德国侵入苏联时，法西斯军队烧杀抢掠，毁坏了许多历史建筑。就是在这样的灾难里，圣彼得堡永久地失去了叶卡捷琳娜宫的琥珀厅。

The Catherine Palace　叶卡捷琳娜宫

二十世纪初，孕育了数十年的革命热潮终于爆发，演变为一场前所未有的革命运动，颠覆了罗曼诺夫王朝的统治，建立了苏联新政府。随着政权的更替，首都也迁至莫斯科。

圣彼得堡，也就是当时的列宁格勒，在二战中被德军包围九百天，尽管这座城市没有被敌人的军队攻破，但饱受折磨和蹂躏。许多居民被冻死、饿死，但它坚持抗战将近三年，最终成功反击了德军的进攻。在苏联社会主义统治下的七十多年间，圣彼得堡依然保留了自己的文化特色和历史面貌。这个长达两百年的沙皇俄国的首都的各种遗产基本上完整无损。

如今，圣彼得堡的旅游业兴旺发达，学术中心和文化之都的美誉也经久不衰，这滋养了它美丽、优雅和高贵的气质。当六月的白夜来临时，来自世界各地的旅游者蜂拥而至，参加当地举行的音乐节和舞蹈节。但是在苏联解体之后甚至直到二十一世纪，圣彼得堡都处于下滑的趋势。断壁残垣的建筑和高低不平的街道都曾目睹了它辉煌的历史和灿烂的巅峰。这一切都让人觉得圣彼得堡是一位气度不凡但性情忧郁的贵妇。

幸运的是，圣彼得堡再度迎来了它的辉煌岁月。为了在 2003 年庆祝它的三百年华诞，整个城市装饰一新。作为俄罗斯前总统普京的故乡，圣彼得堡扬名世界。新兴产业也给它带来巨额的投资。

圣彼得堡根本无法赶上莫斯科的投资规模。莫斯科建筑业发展神速，城市的每个角落都矗立着前卫的广告牌，商场数量众多、规模宏大。如果说莫斯科是俏皮的时髦女郎，那么圣彼得堡就是端庄的上层贵妇。诗意的环境、悠久的历史和灿烂的文化滋养了她高贵脱俗的不凡气质。

St. Petersburg in Literature 文学圣彼得堡

Nevsky Prospect, an ordinary street in St. Petersburg, becomes extraordinary because of Nikolay Gogol's Nevsky Prospect, *in which the writer describes the hustle and bustle of life.*

Nevsky Prospect[①]

◎ Nikolay Gogol

There is nothing better than Nevsky Prospect, at least not in Petersburg; for there it is everything. What does this street—the beauty of our capital—not shine with! I know that not one of its pale and clerical inhabitants would trade Nevsky Prospect for anything in the world. Not only the one who is twenty-five years old, has an excellent mustache and a frock coat[②] of an amazing cut, but even the one who has white hair sprouting on his chin and a head as smooth as a silver dish, he, too, is enchanted with Nevsky Prospect. And the ladies! Oh, the ladies find Nevsky Prospect still more pleasing. And who does not find it pleasing? The moment you enter Nevsky Prospect, it already smells of nothing but festivity. Though you may have some sort of necessary, indispensable business, once you enter it, you are sure to forget all business. Here is the only place where people do not go out of necessity, where they are not driven by the need and mercantile[③] interest that envelop the whole of Petersburg. A man met on Nevsky Prospect seems less of an egoist than on Morskaya, Gorokhovaya, Liteiny, Meshchanskaya, and other streets, where greed, self-interest, and necessity show on those walking or flying by in carriages and droshkies[④]. Nevsky Prospect is the universal communication of Petersburg. Here the inhabitant of the Petersburg or Vyborg side who has not visited his friend in Peski or the Moscow Gate for several years can be absolutely certain of meeting him. No directory or inquiry office will provide such reliable information as Nevsky Prospect.

---

① 选自 *The Collected Tales of Nikolai Gogol*, translated by Richard Pevear and Larissa Volokhonsky, http://htmlgiant.com/tag/nevsky-prospect/.
② frock coat: 十九世纪男子所穿的一种方领角的长外衣。
③ 贸易的。
④ 四轮敞篷马车。

All-powerful Nevsky Prospect! The only entertainment for a poor man at the Petersburg feast! How clean-swept are its sidewalks, and, God, how many feet have left their traces on it! The clumsy, dirty boot of the retired soldier, under the weight of which the very granite seems to crack, and the miniature shoe, light as smoke, of a young lady, who turns her head to the glittering shop windows as a sunflower turns toward the sun, and the clanking[①] sword of a hope-filled sub-lieutenant that leaves a sharp scratch on it—everything wreaks[②] upon it the power of strength or the power of weakness. What a quick phantasmagoria[③] is performed on it in the course of a single day! How many changes it undergoes in the course of a single day and night!

涅瓦大街[④]

◎ 尼古拉·果戈尔

Nevsky Prospect 涅瓦大街

最好的地方莫过于涅瓦大街了，至少在彼得堡是如此；对于彼得堡来说，涅瓦大街就代表了一切。这条街道流光溢彩——真是咱们的首都

---

① 叮当作响的。
② 发泄。
③ 变幻不定的成群影像。
④ 出自 http://www.tianyabook.com/waiguo2005/g/guogeli/ggld/008.htm。

之花！我知道，住在彼得堡的平民百姓和达官贵人，无论是谁都是宁肯要涅瓦大街，而不稀罕人世上的金银财宝。不仅年方二十五岁、蓄有漂亮的唇髭和身着精心缝制的礼服的年轻人为它所倾倒，即便是满腮苍髯、脑袋光如银盘的老年人也对它情有独钟。而淑女们呢！啊，淑女们对涅瓦大街就更是青睐有加了。又有谁不钟爱这条大街呢？只要一踏上涅瓦大街，一种游乐气氛便扑面而来。即便是你有要紧的事情要办，然而，一踏上大街，准会把一切事情都忘得一干二净。这是唯一的清闲去处，人们到这里来并非为生活需求所迫，亦非为实惠和淹没彼得堡全城的买卖利欲所驱使。在涅瓦大街上遇到的人，似乎不像海洋街、豌豆街、铸铁街、平民街和其他别的街上的人那么自私自利，在那些地方，贪欲、自私、势利分明摆在那些步行的和坐在各式马车里疾驰如飞的人们的脸上。涅瓦大街是彼得堡的交通要冲。住在彼得堡区或者维堡区的人，如果好几年没有拜访过住在沙滩地或莫斯科关卡附近的朋友，那么他尽可以相信，一定会在涅瓦大街上彼此碰面的。无论是官员职名录，还是问讯处提供的信息，都不如涅瓦大街那样准确无误。涅瓦大街可真是无所不能！它是缺乏游乐的彼得堡的唯一消遣之地。人行道打扫得干干净净，天哪，那上面留下了多少脚迹啊！一个退伍的老兵，穿着又笨重又肮脏的皮靴，踩在花岗石的路面上仿佛要咔嚓欲裂；一位少妇足登小巧玲珑、轻捷如烟的女鞋，就像向日葵跟着太阳转似的，不停地转动着小脑袋去看那五光十色的商店的橱窗；一个满怀升迁希望的准尉挎着铿锵作响的军刀，在地面上划出一道深深的痕迹——他们都迁怒于这条大街，蹬着或重或轻的腿劲儿。一天之内，在这条街上发生着多少神速的光怪陆离的变幻！一昼夜之间，它又经历着多少世事的变迁！

Who Is Nikolay Gogol?

☞ 1809–1852.

☞ Ukrainian-born Russian dramatist, novelist and short story writer.

☞ He laid the foundations of 19th-century Russian realism.

☞ In his works, there is fundamentally romantic sensibility with strains of surrealism and the grotesque.

☞ Masterpiece works: novels *Dead Souls* and *Taras Bulba*, play *Marriage*, stories "The Nose," "The Overcoat," "Diary of a Madman" and "The Portrait."

☞ His early works were influenced by his Ukrainian upbringing, and later writing satirised political corruption in the Russian Empire, leading to his eventual exile.

☞ He died at the age of 42, perhaps of intentional starvation, on the verge of madness.

Bibliography

Andersen, Hans Christian. *Andersen's Fairy Tales Collection*.《安徒生童话全集》, 纪飞编译, 2006 年, 北京: 清华大学出版社。

Bal, Mieke. "Food, Form, and Visibility: *Glub* and the Aesthetics of Everyday Life" in *Postcolonial Studies*, Vol. 8, No. 1, 2005.

Dailey, Donna, and John Tomedi. *Bloom's Literary Place—London*, with Introduction by Harold Bloom, 2005, Philadelphia: Chelsea House Publishers.

《伦敦文学地图》, 张玉红、杨朝军译, 2011 年, 上海: 上海交通大学出版社。

Dickens, Charles. "The Street—Morning" in *London in Dickens' Time*, edited by Jacob Korg, 1960, Englewood Cliffs, N.J.: Prentice-Hall, Inc.

Doyle, Arthur Conan. "The Empty House" in *The Complete Sherlock Holmes*, 2009, Doubleday / Penguin Books.

《空屋》, http://ishare.iask.sina.com.cn/download/explain.php?fileid=6778596。

Edinburgh: Inspiring Capital, VIP%20Brochure%20PDF%20final.

Foster, Brett, and Hal Marcovitz. *Bloom's Literary Places—Rome*, with Introduction by Harold Bloom, 2005, Philadelphia: Chelsea House Publishers.

《罗马文学地图》, 郭尚兴、刘沛译, 2011 年, 上海: 上海交通大学出版社。

Frank, Anne. *The Diary of a Young Girl: The Definitive Edition*, edited by Otto H. Frank and Mirjam Pressler, translated by Susan Massotty, 1997, New York: Bantam Books.

Frommer, Arthur. *Surprising Amsterdam*, 1966, New York: The Frommer/ Pasmantier Publishing Corporation.

Gerrard, Mike. *Bloom's Literary Places—Paris*, with Introduction by Harold Bloom, 2005, Philadelphia: Chelsea House Publishers.

《巴黎文学地图》, 齐林涛、王淼译, 2011年, 上海: 上海交通大学出版社。

Gogol, Nikolay. "Nevsky Prospect" in *The Collected Tales of Nikolay Gogol*, translated by Richard Pevear and Larissa Volokhonsky. http://htmlgiant.com/tag/nevsky-prospect/.

《涅瓦大街》, http://www.tianyabook.com/waiguo2005/g/guogeli/ggld/008.htm。

Guillen, Nicolas. "From New York to Moscow, via Paris" in *Always Elsewhere*, edited by Alasdair Pettinger, 1998, London: Cassell.

Hugo, Victor. "A Bird's-Eye View of Paris" in *The Hunchback of Nortre-Dame*, Volume 3, Chapter 2, 2004, New York: Barnes & Noble Classics.

《巴黎鸟瞰》, http://www.woyouxian.com/b06/b060402/balishengmuyuan_cn33.html。

Joyce, James. "The Dead" in *Dubliners*, The Project Gutenberg Etext, 2001.

《死者》, http://blog.sina.com.cn/s/blog_5d7adaa60100gc6q.html。

Kafka, Franz. "The Great Wall of China" in *The Kafka Project* by Mauro Nervi, translated by Ian Johnston, Nov. 2003. http://www.kafka.org/index.php?aid=171.

《万里长城修建时》, http://bbs.dahe.cn/read-htm-tid-1474697.htm。

Muiri, Naoise O. "People Make Cities Great and Different." http://www.bjta.gov.cn/wngzzt/sjcslhkkms/xsfk_xsfk/352955.htm.

Neef, Sonja. "Killing Kool: The Graffiti Museum" in *Art History*, Vol. 30, Issue 3, June 2007.

Nkosi, Lewis. "Doing Paris with Breyten" in *Always Elsewhere*, edited by

Alasdair Pettinger, 1998, London: Cassell.

"Spotlight on Copenhagen." http://www.ebigear.com/news-124-30737.html.

"Surprising Amsterdam." http://www.tripadvisor.com/Travel-g188553-s 202/The-Netherlands:Culture.html.

Tomedi, John. *Bloom's Literary Place—Dublin*, with Introduction by Harold Bloom, 2005, Philadelphia: Chelsea House Publishers.

《都柏林文学地图》，白玉杰、豆红丽译，2011 年，上海：上海交通大学出版社。

Twain, Mark. *The Innocents Abroad*, Chapter 26, 1996, Oxford: Oxford University Press.

《傻子出国记》，陈良廷、徐汝椿译，1985 年，北京：人民文学出版社。

Wells, Ida B. "Memories of London" in *Always Elsewhere*, edited by Alasdair Pettinger, 1998, London: Cassell.

Woodworth, Bradley, and Constance Richards. *Bloom's Literary Places—St. Petersburg*, with Introduction by Harold Bloom, 2005, Philadelphia: Chelsea House Publishers.

《圣彼得堡文学地图》，李巧慧、王志坚译，2011 年，上海：上海交通大学出版社。